FINDING IVY

CLAIRE KINGSLEY

Always Have LLC

Edited by Elayne Morgan of Serenity Editing Services

Cover by Lori Jackson

Cover photography by Regina Wamba

ISBN: 9798540435949

Originally published as Remembering Ivy

www.clairekingsleybooks.com

❀ Created with Vellum

For David.
Because there's a little bit of you in every story.

ABOUT THIS BOOK

"He knew things about me that no one could. His explanation was impossible, but the alternatives were worse..."

After putting everything on hold to care for her dying father, Ivy Nichols feels lonely and disconnected. She's struggling to jump in and start again—especially when it comes to dating.

The mysterious William Cole walks into her life like a beacon of light in a fog. He's sensual and captivating—awakening Ivy in ways she's never experienced before.

But he knows things about her—deeply personal things. His story is unbelievable, but the truth might be worse. Her friends insist he's either a con artist, or he's crazy.

With her heart on the line, Ivy has to decide who—and what—she believes. The rational explanation from her trusted friends? Or the impossible story from the man without a past? The man who swears he will do anything to protect her.

One thing she is sure of—William doesn't just know facts about her life. He knows her, inside and out. He knows her as intimately as if he's spent every moment of his life loving her.

And according to him, he has.

Author's note: a steamy, stand-alone contemporary romance with a bit of suspense and a mysterious twist. It will make you question what you know about love, chance, and fate, and keep you turning the pages to find the answer to one question. Who is William Cole?

BLUE EYED STRANGER

❦

*B*oredom and loneliness were an unfortunate combination.

My oversized white German shepherd, Edgar, blinked at me, then huffed out a breath through his black nose. I'd taken him for a walk earlier, and these days he needed a nap to recover. His hips tended to bother him, and we'd had an active morning.

I looked down at my crossword puzzle, the book laid out flat on my small dining table. It was literary-themed, so it should have been a piece of cake. After all, I was a literature professor. I taught the classics in lecture halls filled with college students. But today, my mind wandered, the allure of puzzle-solving not enough to hold my attention.

Perhaps it was because I was facing yet another Saturday with no plans. There are certainly times when a long day free from outside obligations is a blessing. But other times, a girl needs a reason to go out. To put on something pretty. Wear those impractical shoes sitting untouched in the closet. Break out the red kiss-me-now lipstick. Maybe for someone who might kiss that lipstick right off.

It had been a long time since there had been someone to kiss the lipstick off these lips.

To be fair, I wasn't sure I owned red lipstick anymore. And the impractical shoes... I probably still had them... somewhere. If I'd had a reason to dig them out of the recesses of my closet, I'm sure I could have found them. But I didn't.

"*It is a great misfortune to be alone, my friends; and it must be believed that solitude can quickly destroy reason*," I said.

Edgar raised his head and blinked at me.

"Jules Verne," I said. "It means spending too much time alone can make you crazy. I think I'm proof of that, considering I'm quoting *The Mysterious Island* to my dog."

He put his head back on his front paws.

My phone beeped with a text. It was my best friend, Jessica.

Jessica: Busy today?

Me: So busy. This puzzle won't solve itself.

Jessica: Peter's ignoring me. Want to meet for coffee?

I smiled. Jessica and her husband were great together, but they were polar opposites—the passionate art history teacher and the nerdy math professor. Sometimes Jessica's social needs exceeded Peter's ability to keep up with them.

Me: Sure. Meet you at Café Lit?

Jessica: Yay!

"Well, buddy, it looks like Mama has a reason to put on real pants."

Edgar ignored me as I got up and went to change out of my favorite comfy gray sweats. I stopped in the bathroom to pull my long hair into a low ponytail. It was just coffee with Jess, so dressing up wasn't necessary. But I did put on a cute green sweater with my jeans, and slipped on a pair of black flats.

Café Lit was right across the street from Woodward

College, the small private university just north of Seattle where Jessica, Peter, and I all taught. The *Lit* in the name was supposed to be short for *literature.* Wood paneling and lots of brown leather gave it an old-fashioned library atmosphere, and there were shelves lined with books you could read while you were there. It was particularly popular with the college staff. Jessica and I met here often, usually in the morning before work. But sometimes we came in on a weekend, especially if she was restless and Peter was absorbed in a project.

Jessica was already at a table when I arrived, dunking a tea bag into a mug of steaming hot water. I'd known Jess for years. We'd met as wide-eyed college freshmen and been friends ever since. In some ways, she and I were as opposite as she and her husband. We looked it, at least. Jessica was dark-skinned and curvy, with a gorgeous mass of black curls. I was fair—she joked that I was so pale I was *clear*—with blue eyes and long blond hair.

I smiled and waved, then got in line to order. It was busy for a Saturday, although there was still open seating. The woman at the head of the line appeared to be placing an enormous to-go order. She held up a pad of paper and checked things off a list as she spoke to the barista. Glancing at Jess, I shrugged. I'd be in line for a while.

The man in front of me looked back over his shoulder. "I hope you're not in a hurry."

"Fortunately not," I said.

He shifted his feet, so he was partially facing me. "Me neither."

My stomach tingled with pings of anxiety. Was he about to flirt with me? Was he just making polite conversation because we were stuck in the same line? He was nice-looking, casually dressed, probably a bit older than me—mid-thirties, perhaps. No sign of a ring. Cute. Definitely cute.

"Well, you know... *There will be little rubs and disappoint-ments everywhere, and we are all apt to expect too much*," I said.

He raised his eyebrows.

"Jane Austen, *Mansfield Park.*" I cleared my throat. "Never mind."

"Do you go to school here?" he asked.

Being one of the youngest teachers at Woodward, I was accustomed to people mistaking me for a student. I tended to compensate by dressing in smart blouses and pencil skirts with practical black pumps. Pearls seemed to help. But today my casual clothes and careless hair probably made me look quite a bit younger than twenty-nine.

"No, I'm a teacher," I said.

"Really?" he asked. "What subject?"

"Literature."

"I guess that explains the Jane Austen reference," he said.

"Yeah," I said. "You know, what's interesting about Jane Austen is that she wrote such witty love stories, but her own love life never worked out. In fact, the first man she ever fell in love with would have lost his inheritance if he'd married her. She was too far down the social ladder. His aunt whisked him out of the country to get him away from her."

"Huh."

The woman with the large order finally finished and the line moved forward.

"It could have been a plot for one of her novels," I said. "Although if she'd written it, I think it would have had a different ending. It's not like he came back for her."

"Too bad," he said.

Nibbling on my bottom lip, I brushed a tendril of hair away from my face. I was so out of practice at this. Jessica caught my eye and gave me a thumbs-up. I winced and shrugged. What was I supposed to say now?

The cute guy got to the front of the line and put in his

order. He gave me a small closed-mouth smile as he walked over to the other side of the counter to wait for his coffee.

"What can I get you?" the barista asked.

"Sixteen-ounce latte," I said.

"A name for your order?"

"Ivy," I said. She paused, blinking at me, her Sharpie poised over the cup. People were forever asking me to repeat my name. "Ivy, like the plant."

She nodded and wrote it on the cup. I paid and glanced at the cute guy, but he was looking at his phone, so I went straight to Jessica's table.

"What was that about?" she asked.

I pulled out the chair and sat across from her. "What?"

"Why didn't you keep talking to him?" she asked. "He's cute."

"I don't know," I said. "As soon as I opened my mouth, he looked bored."

"Who did you quote?"

"What are you talking about? I didn't—" I sighed. "Jane Austen."

"Of course you did." She patted my hand. "Maybe next time don't lead with dead novelists."

I crossed my legs. "I'm terrible at this. I belong in a world with strict social norms where it's expected you'll settle for a husband based on your family's status."

"Except in that world, you're already an old maid," she said.

I scowled at her.

She started to speak, but paused, her eyes focused on something to my left. "Wow. Hello, gorgeous."

I glanced over my shoulder. A man stood a few steps inside the door. He was indeed gorgeous. Thick, dark hair. Exquisite bone structure, his strong jaw covered in stubble. He was dressed in a blue waffle-knit shirt and jeans—casual, but he wore it well. He was obviously lean and muscular—you could tell even through his clothes.

But his eyes. They swept across the room, like he was looking for someone, and for a second, they settled on me. Bright blue, they stood out in stark contrast to his dark hair and rough jaw. They looked... innocent, somehow. Almost strange in that face that was so rugged and masculine.

I blinked and tore my gaze away, hoping he hadn't seen me looking at him. Jessica gaped, her lips parted.

"Jess, you're married," I said. "Stop ogling him."

She startled, like she hadn't realized what she was doing. "What? Oh, come on, I'm just enjoying the view. I'm married, not dead. Besides, no one could possibly be immune to whatever magic that guy has."

I glanced at him again. He was probably the most beautiful man I'd ever seen in person. The kind of guy you see on billboards or in magazines—and you assume must be photoshopped in a hundred different ways, because no one actually looks that good.

This guy did.

Jessica started talking again and I watched the man from the corner of my eye. He took slow steps into the shop, looking carefully at everything. The way he moved reminded me of a detective in a movie—not the serious one with the gravelly voice and a drinking problem. The quirky one—the genius who no one really understands, but always seems to discover what no one else can see.

He stood back from the counter, studying the menu like he'd never seen one before. His brow furrowed, making a groove between his dark eyebrows. Two women came in and hesitated behind him. One said something, and he looked at her like he was confused that someone was speaking to him. But his expression quickly softened, and he smiled—a gesture that made him even more attractive—and waved them by.

"Ivy?" Jessica said.

I shook my head a tiny bit and turned to Jessica. "Sorry, I was… thinking about something else."

"Thinking about Mr. Amazing over there," she said.

"No."

"Go talk to him," she said.

I rolled my eyes. "No, thanks."

"Why not?"

"What am I supposed to say?"

She shrugged. "Hi, my name is Ivy. Would you like to have coffee with me?"

"That's so…"

"What? Direct? Honest? Effective?" she asked.

I shook my head. She might have been right, but I wasn't about to walk up to a man—especially a man who looked like *that*—and start a conversation.

"Ivy," the barista called.

I went to the counter to get my coffee and I could feel the man watching me. My back prickled and the hairs on my arms stood up like I had goosebumps. Why was he staring at me like that? Beautiful or not, he was starting to make me uncomfortable. I glanced away as I went back to my seat.

When I sat down, Jessica's smile was so sympathetic it bordered on pity. "I'm only bugging you about this because I want to see you happy. I know it's been tough since… well, you know."

"It's okay, you know we can talk about my dad without dancing around the subject."

After a grueling two-year battle with cancer, and a stroke near the end, my dad had passed away almost a year ago. Although I was coping with the grief of losing him, I was having a hard time restarting my life. When he was first diagnosed, I'd dropped everything to take care of him. Quit my job. Gave up my apartment. Moved home.

I had no regrets. I was grateful I'd had the time with him, even when it had been hard. But now I was ready to move forward with my life again. I just couldn't seem to figure out how. Thanks to recommendations from Jess and Peter, I'd landed a teaching position at Woodward, so at least I had that. And I loved my job. But to say my personal life was lackluster was a vast understatement.

"I'm glad you're doing better," she said. "You seem like you're adjusting. But I'd love to see you get out there more. You can't spend all your time with your dog, or doing word puzzles."

"I don't."

She arched an eyebrow.

"I hang out with you guys."

"And we love you, but wouldn't a date be nice?" she asked. "What about that guy you met who keeps hinting?"

Mr. Amazing had circled around us, and although I couldn't see him, I was sure he was behind me. It was like he was magnetic. The urge to turn and look was almost more than I could resist.

I was distracted again. I brought my attention back to Jessica. "Blake, the guy who works at Dorset Financial? I don't think he's been hinting anything."

"Sure he has," she said. "Based on what you told me, he's definitely interested. You just turned off your radar for too long, you don't recognize it."

"I don't know. Even if he was hinting, he's so… banker-ish."

"You mean so much like Julian," she said.

I sighed. I'd been dating Julian when my dad had gotten sick. Although I'd thought we were serious—maybe even forever serious—the strain of me moving ninety minutes away to care for my dad had taken its toll on our relation-ship. When Julian had gotten a job offer in Boston, he'd decided to take it. Which had meant leaving me behind.

"Yes, the fact that he works in finance reminds me of Julian," I said. "Although that's probably not fair to Blake. But I still don't think he's interested."

"When will you run into him again?" she asked.

"I have an appointment at Dorset on Tuesday, actually," I said.

Her lips turned up in a conspiratorial smile. "I bet if you give him the right signals, he'll ask you out."

"But—"

"Hear me out," she said. "If he strikes up a conversation, just relax. Make eye contact. Smile a little. And if he does ask you out, say yes. Oh, and save the lit references for at least the second date."

"I don't know…"

"It doesn't have to be a big deal," she said. "You need a dating ice-breaker. Something to get you past this block you've created."

Maybe she was right. I did want to get out of this rut. Maybe a dating ice-breaker would do the trick. I didn't have to commit to anything else. Just a date. *If* he asked.

I took a deep breath. "Okay. If he talks to me this time, I'll try not to bore him into oblivion. And if he asks me out, I'll agree. But I still don't think he will."

"I guess we'll see." She shrugged, looking a little smug, and took a sip of her tea.

Thankfully, Jess changed the subject, and we talked about work for a while. We both finished our drinks and I started wondering if they had any good muffins in the case up front.

Jessica's eyes narrowed and she looked over my shoulder for what seemed like the hundredth time.

"What do you keep looking at?" I asked.

"Don't look," she said, lowering her voice to a whisper. "Mr. Amazing has been sitting behind you this whole time and he keeps moving closer. He's leaning toward you like he's trying to listen in."

My back tightened, and prickles ran up my spine. "Really?"

She nodded. "He might be cute, but he's acting weird. Maybe we should go."

I nodded and picked up my bag. Jessica situated herself between me and Mr. Amazing, as if she was worried he was going to attack me, and we left.

Outside, Jess pointed across the street. "I parked over there. Do you want to go out to dinner with us tonight?"

I smiled, genuinely grateful for the invitation. But staying home with Edgar was preferable to being their third wheel yet again. "Thanks, but I'll pass. Another time."

"Are you sure?" she asked.

"Yeah," I said. "I'll talk to you later."

After saying goodbye to Jess, I walked to my car. My mind kept returning to the man in the café. Why had he been watching me? Had he really been listening? It was so odd.

I got home and took Edgar outside, but I couldn't stop thinking about him. Yes, he was attractive, but I'd never been one to get googly-eyed over a man, no matter what he looked like.

But those eyes. They were so blue. So searching. I could still see them, watching me, scrutinizing. There was something mysterious about him, like he was a puzzle. And I loved a good puzzle.

But I'd probably never see him again, which was kind of a shame. I'd have liked to know what he saw when he looked at me.

DOWNTOWN

⁂

*T*he building downtown was forty stories of dark blue glass, glinting in the sunlight. I didn't much like coming here—traffic was usually bad, parking was expensive, and it always seemed to take half a day. But since my dad's death, it had become a necessary evil. Dorset Financial was located here, and they handled the details of my inheritance.

My dad had known Arthur Horace, who worked at Dorset, for thirty years, and he'd entrusted the management of the financial portion of his estate to him. I'd kept Arthur on, hiring him to manage the accounts I now owned, mostly because of my dad's trust in him. Also because I had no idea what to do with the money I'd inherited.

I'd always known my dad had been financially secure. Growing up, we hadn't lived extravagantly, but we'd been comfortable. He hadn't seemed to worry about money. He'd paid for my college, all the way through my PhD program. I'd wondered how he could afford it, but he'd always assured me it was no problem. He'd been a practical man, so I'd assumed he'd simply been good at saving.

When he'd gotten sick, he'd given me access to his bank accounts so I could handle his bills and medical expenses. After his death, however, I'd discovered that there were accounts I hadn't known about. And those contained almost ten million dollars. Apparently, he'd made smart investments as a much younger man, including buying stock in some now-prominent software companies. And he'd never told me.

Since finding out about the money, I'd wondered many times why he'd kept it a secret. He'd had the money for decades. There was no explanation in his will. No letter he'd written that I'd been meant to read after he passed. I suspected it was because he'd felt the same way I did now— bewildered at the idea of being wealthy.

I went up to the twentieth floor. My meeting with Arthur was brief. He had some changes to go over, and as usual, I adhered to his advice. There were a few forms to sign, and he once again asked if I'd like to take a more substantial distribution. And again, I declined. He didn't seem surprised.

Waiting outside the elevator, I adjusted my handbag. It was a bit after three, but I didn't have any classes this afternoon. I wondered if I should go back to my office or head home for the day.

"Ivy. It's nice to see you again."

I turned at the voice. Blake Callahan stood next to me, dressed in a dark suit. He was handsome in a classic sort of way, with slicked-back hair and a chiseled jaw.

My mind immediately went to what Jessica had said, and I made eye contact. "Hi. Blake, right?"

He smiled. "I'm flattered you remember. You must have had a meeting with Arthur."

"I did." I thought about saying more, but I had a feeling if I kept talking, I'd somehow wind up quoting Tolstoy.

The elevator opened, and he gestured for me to get in. I did, and he followed me inside.

"Lobby or parking?" he asked.

"Parking, please," I said.

He pushed both the L and P buttons, then put his hands in his pockets. In the close confines of the elevator, I could smell his cologne. It was something classic, clean with a faint spiciness to it. It was nice.

But clearly, he wasn't interested. He'd only said hello to be polite.

"Forgive me if this is forward, but do you have plans this afternoon?" he asked out of the blue. "I was thinking of taking the rest of the day off. If you're free, maybe you'd like to join me?"

My brain scrambled to keep up. Was he asking me out? I was supposed to say yes if he did. I felt so flustered. "Oh, um… are you allowed to go out with a client?"

"Not if you were *my* client," he said. "But I'm in a different department."

Calm down, Ivy. Remember what Jessica said. Relax. Smile a little. "Then, yes, that sounds nice. Do you have something in mind?"

"I don't know—this is very spontaneous. What if we get some coffee and walk on the Bainbridge ferry? It's a beautiful day." The elevator reached the lobby and the doors opened. He gestured for me to go first. "Shall we?"

"Okay, sure," I said.

We walked side-by-side through the lobby, my heels clicking on the floor. Blake held the door and we stepped out onto the street.

"Do you mind walking?" he asked. "It's not far. But if you'd prefer, I can get my car."

The sun was warm, and the sky blue. "No, I don't mind walking."

I paused to get my sunglasses out of my bag. A short distance up the street, a man caught my eye. I did a double take, and sure enough, it was Mr. Amazing from Café Lit. He leaned against the building, like he might be waiting for someone. Those piercing blue eyes were fixed on me.

What was he doing here? Could it be a coincidence? But what were the chances of seeing him twice, in two completely different places?

I didn't have time to contemplate the odds. Blake slipped on a pair of sunglasses and gestured for me to walk next to him. I cast a quick glance over my shoulder, but Mr. Amazing stayed where he was. His arms were crossed, and although he didn't take his eyes off me, he didn't follow, either.

It was disconcerting, but at the same time, I didn't feel threatened. Something about his eyes were so disarming. It was strange to see him here—and stranger still that he'd been openly staring. But instead of being alarmed, I was intrigued all over again.

Blake hadn't seemed to notice him at all, so maybe he hadn't been looking at *me*. He could have been facing my direction and watching for someone else.

I was probably imagining things. I walked with Blake down toward the waterfront. We stopped for coffee and took our drinks to the ferry dock. The sun was shining, the light glinting off the water. It was a gorgeous day, and for the first time in too long, I was on a date. Jessica was going to be thrilled.

But I still looked over my shoulder more than once, wondering if Mr. Amazing was following me.

IMAGINING THINGS

*S*eeing Mr. Amazing downtown—I didn't know his name, so I had to call him *something*—had clearly messed with my head. In the week after my impromptu coffee date with Blake, it felt like I saw him *everywhere*.

I caught a glimpse of someone who might have been him at the grocery store. I thought I saw him again when I was taking Edgar for a walk. A man I could have sworn was him had been at the Thai place near my house when I stopped in to grab takeout. And I saw him—or someone I thought might be him—at least twice a day on campus.

Of course, I couldn't confirm any of those sightings. When I'd seen him downtown, he'd been standing in the open, right there on the sidewalk. Since then, I'd only seen him from behind, or from the corner of my eye. Glimpses of a man walking around a corner or ducking through a door. I couldn't be sure any of them had been him.

The problem was, it was all so unlikely. What were the chances that another person had suddenly adopted a routine and schedule that was almost identical to mine? It was possible he was new on staff at Woodward. I didn't know everyone who worked there, and people came and went all the time. Or maybe he was a student. Although I guessed he was roughly the same age as me, we had students of all ages.

That would explain seeing him around campus—even at Café Lit. But it didn't explain seeing him downtown, or any of the other places where I'd caught a glimpse of him.

I figured there were three potential explanations. One, I was imagining things, and other than running into him downtown, none of the other sightings had been him. Two, I *was* seeing him everywhere I went, but it was all an enormous coincidence. Or three, Mr. Amazing was stalking me.

Coincidence didn't seem likely. But the idea that he was stalking me was even less so. I needed to remember Occam's Razor: the simplest explanation was usually the correct one.

The problem with the stalking theory was the number of assumptions it required. The more assumptions one had to make for the explanation to be plausible, the less likely it was to be true.

To conclude that Mr. Amazing was my stalker, I had to assume he had a motive—a reason to stalk me. I had no idea what that could be. I wasn't famous, even on a small scale. I didn't use Instagram or other social media heavily enough that my face would be recognizable. My colleagues knew me, but outside the world of Woodward College, I wasn't a particularly important person.

There was the small possibility that it had to do with my inheritance. I could already hear Jessica musing over whether someone had discovered I had money. But how would a perfect stranger know? I could count on one hand the number of people who were aware of my recently upgraded financial status. Arthur, and some of the staff at Dorset Financial. And my friends Jessica and Peter. I hadn't told anyone else.

That made the explanation that Mr. Amazing had discovered I was wealthy, and determined that stalking me was the best course of action for—well, for what? Stealing my money? Worming his way into my life so he could marry me without a prenup, divorce me, and run off with my father's fortune? The number of assumptions grew, and the likelihood that I was being stalked diminished.

The simplest explanation was that I was imagining things. Simplest, and probably correct.

I told myself, rather sternly, that what I was experiencing was selective attention. It's like when you decide to buy a new car, and you settle on a red one. Suddenly, you see red cars everywhere, as if half the people in your city suddenly bought new red cars.

There aren't actually more red cars than there were before. Your brain is simply paying attention to them because your subconscious deems them important. I had seen Mr. Amazing at Café Lit, and again downtown, and he'd obviously made an impression on me. So now I was seeing men who resembled him, and jumping to the conclusion that they were all the same person. All Mr. Amazing. All watching me.

Parting the curtain on my front room window, I looked outside. The sky was just beginning to lighten, and the street lights still glowed. Once I'd thought I saw him on my street, but when I'd looked again, no one had been there. Still, I'd taken to keeping my curtains closed, just in case.

Edgar nuzzled my hand, flicking his tongue across the backs of my fingers. I smiled down at him and scratched behind his ears.

"Hey, buddy. Almost ready for your walk?"

The presence of my dog made it even less likely that I was being stalked. Edgar's white fur and black nose made him look like a cuddly polar bear. But he was not friendly. To me, he was the perfect pet—sweet and loyal, typically well-behaved. And he'd loved my dad. He tolerated Jessica, and treated Peter with a sort of canine indifference, as if he'd sniffed him out and found him uninteresting.

But he hated every other human on the planet.

He wasn't dangerous. But he eyed people with a great deal of suspicion, and he rarely let other people pet him. He'd move away when they tried and growl if they didn't take the hint. Plus, he barked when people came near the house. If someone was creeping around, watching me, Edgar would let me know.

I took him for his morning walk, let him do his business, and then headed to work. I parked in the lot near my building and walked across the street to Café Lit. Jessica had already texted to say she'd meet me there.

She and Peter were inside, standing near the back, both with to-go cups in their hands. Jessica was dressed in a purple paisley blouse, her mass of black curls pulled back. Peter pushed his dark-rimmed glasses up his nose. I noticed the corner of his shirt was partially untucked.

Jess smiled at me and there was something about her expression that made me pause. I took my place in line, but her eyes were wide, and she kept flicking them to one side. It was like she was trying to send me a signal—perhaps without Peter knowing—but I wasn't sure what she was getting at. Looking around, I didn't see anything unusual.

As I turned to meet them after ordering my coffee, I realized what she'd been trying to say. Mr. Amazing was here. My view of him had been obscured by someone sitting at another table, but there he was.

He sat at a table with two to-go cups in front of him. He had his hand wrapped around one, while the other sat across from him. I assumed it meant he was here with someone, and for reasons I couldn't explain, that bothered me. I glanced around the shop, but no one seemed to be heading toward his table. Whoever she was—did I have to assume it was a woman?—she could have been in the bathroom. Or perhaps she hadn't arrived yet, and he'd ordered for her.

I tried very hard to ignore the fact that he was watching me. Again.

Jessica grabbed my arm and yanked me closer as soon as I was within reach. "Girl, he is staring at you. Don't worry. Peter and I have this."

"We have what?" Peter asked.

"This," Jessica hissed. "Don't stress, honey. Peter, move over a little bit so you block his view."

Peter looked around as if just realizing there were other people present. "Whose view?"

"Shh," Jessica said. "I don't care how hot that man is, he's creepy. We'll get out of here as soon as your order comes up."

Peter shook his head and looked at something on his phone.

"I'm sure it's fine," I said. "It looks like he's waiting for someone, that's all."

"He looked like a dog on alert as soon as you opened the door," she said. "Sat up straight, eyes on you. If he had a tail, he'd have wagged it."

I laughed. "A dog analogy?"

Jessica shrugged. "It fits."

I shifted so I could take a quick peek at Mr. Amazing. I really needed to come up with another nickname for him. Or maybe see if I could sneak a look at his cup—the barista must have written his name on it. His eyes were still on me, as if we were the only two people here.

For a second, it felt like we were. A strange sensation overtook me—a tingling across my skin—and I was momentarily convinced that the cup of coffee sitting across from him was meant for me.

Just as I felt myself begin to move toward his table—as if

he were the moon and I was the tide being pulled by his gravity—the barista called my name.

I blinked and went to the counter to get my order. Jess and Peter moved toward the door, and I followed without looking back.

Jessica linked arms with me. Peter walked beside her, but as usual, he didn't seem to be paying attention to the world around him.

"I have to get to my office, so give me the quick version," she said.

"Quick version?" I asked. How did she know? I hadn't told her about seeing Mr. Amazing downtown, nor that I'd spent the last week thinking I saw him everywhere.

"Of your date," she said.

"Oh, my date." I blinked a few times, trying to get my head back on straight. What was wrong with me? I'd gone out with Blake again, this time for dinner. "Right. It was nice."

"Nice?" she asked. We crossed the street and she stopped. Peter kept walking until he realized we weren't beside him anymore, and paused. "That's it?"

A tendril of hair tickled the back of my neck, so I adjusted a bobby pin. "What do you want to know? We went to dinner and talked."

"And?"

"And, nothing," I said. "I met him there, so I drove myself home."

"You're so boring," she said, rolling her eyes.

"I'm sorry my fledgling love life isn't entertaining enough for you," I said. "I'll try to make the next date more exciting."

"So there will be a next date?"

I shrugged. "I guess so."

"You're not very enthusiastic," she said.

"I'm just not sure," I said. "On paper, he seems great. He's good-looking, well-dressed, successful. I did learn he's never been married, and he calls his mother every week."

"All good things," she said. "But?"

"But I don't know if I'm attracted to him," I said. "I didn't feel much of anything. I think you were right about needing a dating ice-breaker, but I'm not sure if this is going anywhere."

"Well, that's fair," she said with a little shrug. "If there's no attraction, you can't really force it. Do you think you've given it enough of a chance?"

"I don't know," I said. "Maybe not? I'll probably go out with him again."

She gave me a subtle smile. "How many times did you quote Jane Austen?"

"What? None."

"Who did you quote, then?" she asked.

"I don't know… Fine, I think Melville and maybe Tolstoy. I can't help it."

"If you found someone who is not a lit teacher who will ask you out again after dealing with an evening of your literary references, you need to at least give him a few dates," she said.

"Fair enough."

"If he does word puzzles, you might have to marry him," she said.

I rolled my eyes and started walking toward my building. "I'll see you later, Jess. Bye, Peter."

Peter glanced up and nodded. Jessica caught up with him and he slipped his arm around her waist, then leaned down to kiss her forehead. They were so cute.

My back prickled, and I glanced over my shoulder. Mr. Amazing was watching me. He stood outside the coffee shop across the street, leaning against the building like he had been when I'd seen him downtown. As if he didn't have a care in the world, and staring at a perfect stranger was a completely normal thing to do. He had both cups of coffee in his hands, and I wondered again if he'd ordered that second one for me.

Which was proof of how crazy I was being. Of course he hadn't bought me coffee. That was just silly.

RUNAWAY

*T*he dog park was mostly empty—just an older man with a yellow lab who was much more interested in chasing a tennis ball than in anything Edgar was doing. Low clouds hung in the sky, threatening rain. I hoped it wouldn't pour on us before Edgar had a chance to run his energy out. Sometimes he was happy to nap all day, but today he was antsy. He'd been driving me crazy at home, so we'd walked to the dog park where he could run free in a much larger space than my backyard.

I threw a ball and he brought it back, covered in dog slobber. But I was used to it. In between tosses, my phone buzzed. It was Jessica, inviting me over for a movie tonight. A likely excuse. She just wanted to hear about my date with Blake.

I'd gone out with Blake again the night before. Dinner at a nice Mediterranean bistro. It had been… okay. We'd chatted through dinner, and nothing about the evening had been *bad*. But I'd still felt the lack of chemistry. I couldn't figure out why I was having no physical reaction to this man. He was always dressed in a well-tailored suit, for god's sake. That was to women what lingerie was to men.

Like I'd told Jessica, he checked all the right boxes. He was intelligent and successful. Attractive. He had an air of confidence: a man who knew what he wanted, and wasn't afraid to go after it. I had no doubt he melted the panties off half the women he met.

Mine, however, had remained firmly intact.

I wondered what was holding me back. Was it simply that he and I weren't hitting it off? He'd seemed to enjoy my company, and I knew he was going to ask me out again. In fact, I'd gotten the distinct impression that if I'd been willing, our date wouldn't have ended with dinner.

Maybe I was simply too out of touch with my sexuality. I'd put everything on hold to be my dad's caregiver, and it hadn't helped that my ex had left me in the midst of it. Was there a switch I could flip to turn it back on?

I tossed the ball again for Edgar, wondering what my dad would have thought of Blake. It was hard to say. My dad had been a quiet man who kept his cards close. I hadn't been sure what he'd thought of Julian until after our relationship had ended. Only then had he told me he hadn't thought much of him, and he'd been relieved I hadn't married him.

It had been a bit surprising, because Julian was a lot like my dad. Studious and rather stoic. Dedicated to his work. Blake was much more outgoing. I could imagine him engaging my dad in conversation, feeling him out to see what he was interested in. Settling in on a topic they could both engage with. Blake had that sort of social acumen my dad had lacked, but appreciated in others.

Edgar dropped the ball at my feet.

"We're done, buddy," I said. "It's time to go home."

He bent his legs, like he was ready to spring, and nudged the ball with his nose.

"Nope, let's go." I put the ball back in the bin and took Edgar through the gate. I was just about to clip on his leash when his ears swiveled. He barked once, then took off running.

"Edgar!"

A squirrel raced down a tree and darted across the road, Edgar close behind. I called for him, but he ignored me, running after the squirrel. Despite getting older, he was still fast. In no time, he disappeared around a corner.

My stomach dropped. He hadn't run away from me like this since he was a puppy. I hurried up the street, still calling for him, expecting him to come back any second. I turned the corner, but saw no sign of him.

"Edgar!"

I kept going, but didn't see or hear him. At the next cross-roads, I paused, looking around. He could have gone anywhere. Up one street, down another, in someone's yard. I had no idea which way to go.

Picking a direction, I jogged for a while, calling his name. When I didn't see him, I doubled back and tried another street. The longer I went without finding him, the more I started to panic. Where had he gone? What if I couldn't find him?

The streets around my house were all quiet, but if he went too far in any direction, he'd encounter traffic. What if he ran out in front of a car? What had gotten into him?

I decided to circle back to the park to see if he was there. Still no sign of him—just the man with his yellow lab.

"Oh my god, Edgar," I muttered. I pulled out my phone to text Jessica. If she and Peter came to help, we could spread out and cover more area. I typed while I walked, heading toward my house in case he'd found his way home.

Just as I was about to hit send, a man came around the

street corner, carrying Edgar. *Carrying* my one-hundred-pound dog.

I ran toward them, but stopped in my tracks when I realized who the man was. The guy from Café Lit. Mr. Amazing. My maybe-stalker.

His face was so… calming. It was difficult to be alarmed by those dreamy blue eyes. He had the look of a man who hid nothing—who wore his soul on the outside, rather than tucked away in some deep, dark place that required a lot of digging to find.

But if he was carrying Edgar—

"Oh my god, is he okay?" I asked, running the rest of the way toward them. Edgar would never let a stranger pick him up like that. "What happened? Is he hurt? Did he get hit by a car?"

"No," the man said, the corners of his mouth turning up in a smile. "No, he's okay. He took me on quite the chase, though. He was limping a little, so I picked him up. I think he's just worn out."

"He's… you chased him?" I scratched the sides of Edgar's face. "Edgar, what got into you? You silly old man, you can't go running off like that."

The man lowered Edgar to the ground and he promptly flopped to his side. I crouched next to him and stroked his fur. His tongue lolled out of his mouth, but other than needing some water—and maybe a nap—he seemed fine. His hips were probably sore from all the running.

"Don't do that to me again," I said.

Edgar just leaned forward and sniffed my face.

I glanced up at the man. He was watching me with a little half-smile, his hands in his pockets. His cheeks were flushed and there was a light sheen of sweat on his forehead. I felt like I should have been wary—my creeper-guy alarms going off. But they weren't.

"How did you find him?" I asked.

"I saw him run off," he said. "So I ran after him."

I stood slowly, wondering whether my intuition was failing me, and I was about to get kidnapped. But I couldn't convince myself to be scared of this guy. "You just happened to be nearby?"

He shrugged.

"Do you live around here?"

"No," he said.

I paused. "Have you been following me?"

His eyes twitched, just a hint of emotion passing across his features. Too quickly for me to tell what it meant. "Yes."

I'd been poised to argue, assuming he'd deny it, so his reply caught me completely off guard. "Wait, did you just say yes?"

There was that half-smile again, just the corner of his mouth twitching upward. "Yes, I have been following you."

"Why?"

"Because you're Ivy." His tone was completely serious—not a hint of sarcasm—as if that should explain everything.

"I… I don't know what to say to that."

He stepped closer and held out his hand. Edgar glanced up at him, but didn't so much as growl.

"I'm William," he said. "William Cole."

I slipped my hand into his. My skin tingled at his touch. "Ivy Nichols."

He nodded and squeezed my hand, more of a caress than a proper handshake. "It's *so* good to finally meet you, Ivy."

"Finally? I… What?"

William crouched down and rubbed Edgar's belly. His back leg twitched. "You gave your mama quite a scare, buddy. Don't do that again."

I was so bewildered, I had no idea what to say. This man —William; at least I knew his name now—had just appeared out of nowhere, carrying my dog. He admitted to following me, and was now giving Edgar—who hated people—a belly rub.

A few drops of rain fell, splattering against the pavement. One landed on my cheek, a little shock of cold on my skin. I blinked and glanced up at the sky. It was definitely going to rain.

Edgar stood, as if he didn't want to get soaked any more than I did. William straightened and gave me a warm smile.

"You should probably get inside," he said. "I'll see you later."

As William turned and started walking away, the rain got heavier. Large drops pattered against the ground and Edgar shook his head. I wanted to say something else, but it was like I'd forgotten how to speak. I watched, dumbfounded, while William walked down the street, pulling his hood up against the rain.

Edgar nudged my leg with his nose.

"What just happened?" I asked. He looked up at me as if to say, *why are we standing here getting wet*? "Good question, buddy. Let's go."

With one more glance at the retreating figure of William, I turned toward home. Edgar stayed by my side—no more chasing squirrels, thankfully. The rain got heavier, and by the time we got to my house, my coat was dripping wet. Edgar shook himself before we went inside, but I still had to towel him off. He went to the kitchen, drank down half a bowl of water, and promptly fell into his dog bed, exhausted.

"Oh sure, you scare the crap out of me and then you get a nap."

He ignored me.

I glanced out my front window. The sky was dark with clouds and the rain came down hard.

Who was William Cole? Why had he been following me?

It occurred to me then that he'd known my name. When I'd asked him why he'd been following me, he'd said *because you're Ivy*. What did that mean? How did he know who I was?

Once again, I had to acknowledge that everything about this should be alarming—but wasn't. He'd admitted to following me, and that should have thrown up red flags all over the place. But I wasn't concerned. I was intrigued. More than intrigued, I was fascinated. Who *was* this man?

I didn't know the answer. But I was sure about one thing. That wasn't going to be the last time I ran into William Cole.

BECAUSE YOU'RE IVY

*t didn't surprise me to see William standing outside Café Lit Monday morning. The sky was cloudy, but it was dry, and he wore a black coat. He smiled at me as I approached and held out one of the two coffee cups he held.

"Good morning," he said.

I hesitated, but reached out to take the coffee. "Morning."

"Sixteen-ounce latte?"

"How did you know?" I asked, curling my hands around the warm cup.

"I asked the barista," he said.

At least that made sense. Some of the baristas here remembered my usual drink. "Okay… thanks."

"Can I walk you to work?" he asked.

I glanced through the window into the coffee shop.

"She's not here," he said.

"Who?"

"Your friend," he said. "Jessica."

"She's… oh." I pulled out my phone and sure enough, I

had a text from Jess, saying she was running late this morning. "Wait, how do you know her name?"

"The barista."

"You asked the barista for her name?"

"No, the barista calls out names with orders." He shrugged. "I just pay attention."

I eyed him for a second. That must have been how he knew my name. "Well, okay then."

He smiled again, and it gave me funny tingly feelings in my tummy. He fell in step next to me and we crossed the street.

"Thanks again for getting Edgar for me the other day," I said. "I can't remember the last time he ran off like that."

"You're welcome."

"So… you were just walking by and happened to see Edgar bolt?"

"I was in the neighborhood, yes."

"Because you've been following me."

"Yes."

God, this was so strange. "Do you know where I live?"

"Yes."

"So, what have you been doing? Trying to peek in my windows?"

He glanced at me with his brow furrowed, like he was confused. "Why would I try to peek in your windows?"

"Well… I don't know," I said. "Isn't that why a man would follow a woman around? Trying to get a peek at something he shouldn't?"

He stopped and put his hand gently on my arm, turning me to face him. He looked so concerned. "Has someone been peeking in your windows?"

"What? No." His touch was so distracting, even through my coat. "That's not what I meant. You're the one who's been stalking me, so if you're not peeking in my windows, then I guess no one is."

"Good," he said, sounding relieved. "But if someone ever does, let me know."

I gaped at him for a second. He gave my arm a gentle squeeze and started walking. As if propelled by a force beyond my control, I walked with him, staying by his side. I noticed he knew exactly where to go; he obviously knew which building was mine.

"Listen, you need to tell me what's going on," I said. "You can't just admit to following someone without offering an explanation."

"It's hard to explain."

"Try."

"I've just been looking out for you," he said.

"Why?"

He paused again and met my eyes. "Because you're Ivy."

"You said that on Saturday," I said. "And it still doesn't make sense."

He smiled and there was that funny feeling in my insides again. We resumed walking.

"That's it?" I asked. "Just because my name is Ivy?"

"No, not because of your name," he said. "Because that's who you are."

"Still not making sense, William."

"I said it was hard to explain."

"Why do you think I need someone to look out for me?" I glanced around and didn't bother to keep the hint of sarcasm out of my voice. "Am I in danger?"

He hesitated, as if he was giving my question a lot of thought. "I don't know."

That sent a chill down my spine. "You don't know if I'm in danger?"

"I don't think you are now," he said. "But you might be someday. I'm not sure."

This conversation was making less sense the longer it went on. "I really don't understand."

"You don't need to worry about it," he said. "That's why I'm here."

"Who are you?" It probably wasn't the right question, but it was all I could think to ask.

We'd reached my building and he stepped back, that cryptic almost-smile on his face. "I told you, my name is William Cole." He gestured to my building with his coffee. "And I think you have to go to work."

"Well, yes, I do."

"I'll see you later, Ivy," he said.

I stood there, staring at him as he walked away. My sense of equilibrium was gone, like the ground and sky had switched places.

"Bye, William," I muttered.

"Are you okay, Dr. Nichols?"

I gasped at the voice. One of my students was looking at me with her head tilted to the side.

"Sorry, I didn't mean to scare you," she said.

"No, it's fine," I said. "I was… distracted. I'll see you in class?"

She nodded. "Yeah."

I smoothed my hair back from my forehead and went in to my office.

My heart was still jumpy when I sat down at my desk and opened my laptop. *Focus, Ivy.* I had work to do.

But all I could think about was William. Those eyes. That smile. He was so disconcerting, yet irresistibly intriguing. What kind of man would follow me around, and then introduce himself as if he hadn't been doing anything strange?

And his explanation was that he was looking out for me? Because I was Ivy? What did that mean?

I Googled his name, wondering if I'd find anything. There were lots of results for William Cole, but none of them were him. I had a feeling this wasn't going to get me anywhere.

"Hey."

I gasped and clutched my chest, my heart suddenly racing. Jessica stood in my doorway. "God, people keep doing that to me today. You startled me."

"I stood here for a solid minute and you didn't notice me," she said with a laugh. "What's going on?"

I debated for a second whether I should tell her about William. How could I explain him? But I knew she'd hound me until I did. She could read me like a book. I motioned for her to come in and she took the seat across my desk.

"Do you remember that guy we saw at Café Lit a couple of times?" I asked. "The one you called Mr. Amazing?"

"You mean the creepy one who was eavesdropping on our conversation?" she asked. "The one who was staring at you the next time we saw him?"

"Well, yes, if you want to emphasize that," I said.

"What about him?"

I tapped a finger against my desk. "He was… kind of stalking me."

"What?" she asked, raising her voice.

"Shh," I said. "You don't have to yell. I think he's harmless. But it was so strange. I kept thinking I saw him everywhere. Then on Saturday, Edgar ran off when we were leaving the dog park. William brought him back. He introduced himself, and when I asked him if he'd been following me around, he said yes."

"He just admitted it?" Jessica asked.

"Yeah, he didn't even try to lie about it or anything," I said. "Looked right at me and said yes."

"That's very odd," she said.

"I know, but in a way, it wasn't," I said. "I don't know how to explain it. He's… kind of mesmerizing."

Jessica arched her eyebrow. "Mesmerizing? Ivy, if he's stalking you, that's not sexy. It could be criminal."

"He didn't do anything criminal," I said. "Besides, if he hadn't been there, Edgar could have gotten hurt or lost."

"You have some interesting logic there," she said. "It's a good thing someone was stalking you because he was around to find your dog?"

"I realize how that sounds," I said. "That's part of what I can't figure out. I kept telling myself I should be concerned, but I wasn't. He's… well, he's really nice."

She nodded. "Oh good, I'm glad your stalker is nice. That's a relief."

I rolled my eyes. "Well it's better than him being scary. He said he's just been looking out for me."

"Why would he do that?" she asked.

"I don't know," I said. "Anyway, I saw him again this morning. He bought me coffee."

"And now you're dating your stalker," she said, her voice laced with sarcasm. "Have you lost your mind?"

"It wasn't a date. He was outside when I got there, and he'd already bought coffee." I rubbed my temples. "God, Jess, what am I doing?"

"I have absolutely no idea," she said.

"I know it's crazy, but I kind of like him," I said. "He's very…"

"Very not the man you're actually dating?"

I scowled at her. "That's not fair. I've been out with Blake a few times. It's not like we're exclusive. And it doesn't matter, because I didn't *go out* with William. That's not what this is."

"Well it's something," Jessica said. "You have a guy

stalking you and now you're having coffee with him and telling your best friend that he's *nice*. Did you hit your head over the weekend?"

"Thanks, that's very helpful."

She tilted her head and gave me a very maternal smile. "Honey, I'm just concerned. You can't have some guy following you around."

"I know. I'll deal with it."

"Okay," she said, her eyebrow arching again, like she wasn't sure if she believed me. "So, I came over here because I had an idea. What if we double date?"

I opened my mouth to say I hadn't had a real date with William, so it was way too soon to double. But I realized she meant Blake. "Oh. Um… yeah, that might be fun."

"Might be?" she asked. "Come on, I need to meet this guy. I know you're not sure if you'll keep seeing him. But if you are, he has to pass the Jessica-test."

I laughed. "Okay. I'll submit Blake for Jessica-testing. He said he'd call to make plans, so I'll bring it up and see if he's interested."

"Great," she said. "We're free this weekend, so let me know."

"Does Peter know about this?"

She waved her hand. "Peter will be fine. I'll make it worth his while."

"A little oral bribery?"

"It's not bribery, it's knowing his currency," she said with a wink. "I should get going, but text me about this weekend. And make sure you get Mr. Creepy to stop stalking you."

"His name is William, you don't have to call him Mr. anything now."

"Stop defending your stalker." She got up and adjusted her sweater. "You're already halfway to Stockholm syndrome."

37

CLAIRE KINGSLEY

"I am not," I said. "That requires kidnapping or a hostage situation."

"Well, if he kidnaps you, you're going to be very susceptible," she said. "Just warning you."

"Bye, Jess."

"See you," she said with a smile, and walked out the door.

I picked up my coffee looked at it, as if it would explain the mystery that was William. Sadly, it didn't.

STALKER

William wasn't at Café Lit the next morning, but he was outside my building when I left for lunch. The next day, I saw him later in the afternoon. He walked me from my last class back to my office. Same thing on Thursday. Friday, he was once again waiting for me before work, coffee in hand.

He walked me to my office and asked a few questions about my classes and my weekend plans. I found myself omitting the fact that I had a date tonight. It was silly to keep that from him. Blake and I weren't *together*—we were only seeing each other casually. And the time I'd spent with William couldn't be considered *dating* him. Not by anyone's definition. He appeared out of nowhere—with no warning—and either walked me somewhere or had lunch with me. But not because we'd made plans, or because he'd *asked* me to join him. He was simply… there.

But I still didn't say anything about Blake. I had the strange feeling that it would bother William. And in the back of my mind, I knew that meant something. A man who was nothing but a casual acquaintance—and who had no intention of becoming more—wouldn't mind that I had a date with someone else. If William did mind, I'd have to wrestle with what that meant, and I wasn't ready for that.

His reasons for appearing in my life were still a mystery to me. I tried asking questions, but got mostly the same answers. He was just looking out for me. I didn't need to worry. It was because I was Ivy. None of it made sense, but he always managed to redirect the conversation, or give me another non-answer right when I needed to get back to work and couldn't ask more questions.

We got to my building and he stopped in front of the door.

"Bye, Ivy. I'll see you later."

God, that smile. I had to admit, my lady parts *noticed* William. Being near him made me feel warm and tingly. His voice was deep and calming, his eyes mesmerizing. I got a whiff of his scent and it made me want to pull him close and bury my face in his neck.

My face flushed hot and I wondered if he could guess what I was thinking. "Bye, William."

As I watched him go, I had a crazy thought. A *very* crazy thought. What if I followed *him*?

That was clearly a terrible idea. I couldn't follow him around. Who would do something like that? Certainly not the practical and pragmatic Dr. Ivy Nichols.

Although, he had followed *me*. He'd found out where I lived, where I worked, even what coffee I ordered. He'd followed me downtown, hung around my neighborhood. Would it be any different if I trailed him for a little while? Just to see where he went. It wouldn't be like I was stalking him—not really. Didn't stalking imply it happened over a length of time? It would only be just this once.

He was a puzzle—a riddle I had to solve. Puzzles were like crack to me, and he was the purest, strongest drug I'd ever encountered. It was why I hadn't protested when he'd started appearing every day. I wanted to see him. I wanted to figure him out.

Before I could give good sense a chance to have its way with me, I followed William across campus. Luckily, he went to the same lot I always parked in—which didn't surprise me, when I thought about it. I was sure he knew what I drove.

He got into a black Jeep Wrangler. I waited, hoping he didn't see me lingering near the adjacent building, then rushed to my car when he pulled out onto the road.

I sent Lisa, my grad student assistant, a voice message, letting her know I had personal business to attend to and I'd need her to cover my class today. I only had one on Fridays, and she taught it as often as I did, so I didn't feel too guilty about springing it on her.

William drove away from campus and got on the freeway heading south. I stayed back where I could see him, but he wasn't likely to see me. At least, I hoped not. I'd never done anything like this before, so I wasn't sure what I was doing.

When we got into Seattle, he exited. It was harder to follow without getting too close, and I worried I'd lose him among the hills and crowded streets. He drove to a tall building and pulled into the underground parking garage.

It looked like apartments, so I supposed this was where he lived. I circled the block and found a place to park where I could see the entrance.

After a few minutes, I started to feel ridiculous. What was I going to do, sit out in front of his building all day? He might not come out for hours. I wasn't sure what he did for a living, but he might work from home, or have Fridays off. Maybe that was why he'd met me this morning, instead of later in the day. Maybe he worked nights, or had shifts that varied, so he was going home to sleep.

What was I doing out here?

The front door opened, and William walked out. Ridiculous or not, I was here, and he was walking down the sidewalk. I was doing this.

I got out and paid for my parking spot, then hurried down the street. It was easier to follow him on foot, although heels weren't ideal for walking up and down hills. And Seattle was nothing if not hilly.

Two blocks from his building, he went into a grocery store. I lingered outside, trying not to look suspicious. Although there wasn't anything unusual about a woman in a skirt and trench coat, waiting on the sidewalk. Was there? Maybe I should have had a newspaper. Wasn't that what people did in the movies when they were following someone? Stood out of the way and pretended to read something?

I didn't have time to contemplate whether I needed props to be a stalker. William came out just then with two grocery bags. I panicked for a second, thinking he was about to walk back in my direction. Why hadn't I thought about the fact that he was probably shopping and would go home afterward? But he didn't go back toward his building. Instead, he continued down the road in the other direction.

He turned at the next block and I hurried to catch up. When I got close, I peeked around the corner. He stood in front of an older man who was sitting on the sidewalk, his legs crossed. The man was scruffy with scraggly hair and a rough beard, his clothes worn and dirty. He looked like he was probably homeless. I was just close enough that I could hear them talking.

"Did you bring me roast beef again?" the man asked. "You know I don't eat no roast beef."

"I know," William said, holding out something wrapped in brown paper. "No roast beef. This is turkey and swiss."

The man took it and opened one side. He looked it over,

like he was giving it a thorough inspection. "All right. As long as you know. I don't do roast beef."

"No, you don't," William said. "I remember now."

"What you been off doing?" the man asked. "Haven't seen you around in a while."

"I've been busy," William said.

"Oh, all mysterious still, huh?" he said. "Fine, keep your secrets. See if I give two shits."

"Let me know when you give three, and maybe I'll tell you," William said.

The man burst out laughing. "Kid, you never make sense. You crazier than me. Thanks for the sandwich."

"No problem," William said. "See you later."

He continued down the same street, then turned at the next block. I passed the homeless man, but he was occupied with inspecting his sandwich. Maybe he was searching for an errant piece of roast beef.

After walking another block, William stopped at an apartment building and knocked on one of the doors. An elderly woman answered, her face lighting up with a smile when she saw him. He gave her the grocery bags and she patted his cheek. He didn't stay long, and I wasn't close enough to hear what they said. But after a moment or two he left, and she went back inside, closing the door behind her.

Seriously, who was this guy?

I got the distinct impression that this was something he did regularly. These people obviously knew him, and didn't seem surprised when he brought them things.

His pace slowed, so I hesitated behind him. He wandered down the street with his hands in his pockets, pausing to glance into restaurant or store windows. I kept my distance, and it didn't seem like he'd noticed me.

My phone rang, making my heart jump into my throat. I pulled it out of my bag and quickly ignored the call, then turned the sound off. It was Jessica, but I'd have to call her back.

And of course, it wasn't like he'd heard it. He was too far away, and there were people everywhere. One cell phone ring wouldn't stand out.

I slipped my phone back in my bag in time to see William disappear down a set of stairs. It took me a minute to catch up. The stairs went down to the basement level of the building and there was a door at the bottom. A sign near the top said *Bookstore Underground—This Way*.

I debated whether to go down. I'd been to this bookstore before. It was big, sprawling across the basement level of the building. Unless he was still right inside the entrance, I could probably go in and stay out of his sight, as long as I was careful.

And it was a *bookstore*. I really wanted to know what he was doing in there.

I crept down the stairs and peeked through the door before going in. I didn't see him, so I went inside and looked around.

It took me a minute to find him—long enough that I started rehearsing excuses for being there because I was sure he'd come up behind me. I spotted him across the store, looking carefully at a row of books. His head tilted, and he took slow steps sideways, like he was scrutinizing every title.

"Can I help you find something?"

I gasped and turned toward the voice. A young guy with a thick beard and knit hat smiled at me.

"Oh, no, I'm just looking."

His eyes flicked over to William, then back to me. "Okay, cool. Sorry if I startled you."

"It's fine."

"Let me know if you need anything," he said.

"Thanks."

I picked up a book so I didn't look like a stalker. William stayed in the same section, and from here, I couldn't tell what he was looking at. He picked up a book and read the back cover, but replaced it. I continued pretending to browse while he looked at several more.

The guy in the hat eyed me like he could tell exactly what I was doing. I put down the book in my hand—I hadn't even looked at it—and moved deeper into the store. It put a large shelf between me and the nosy bookstore guy, but I couldn't see William very well either.

He stayed in the same general area, wandering up and down. Taking a book off the shelf, reading the back, replacing it. I wondered what he was looking for. Whatever it was, he didn't seem to be finding it. He crouched down to take a book off a low shelf, but put that one back too.

I peeked around the corner to check on bookstore guy. He stood behind the front counter flipping through a magazine. I moved down the aisle to get a better look at William, but he seemed to have found what he wanted. He paged through a book, then closed it again and took it to the counter.

He paid cash for the book, pulling a wad of money out of his coat pocket. The bookstore guy chatted with him for two or three minutes—much longer than it took to make his purchase. It gave the impression that he knew William, or at least that William was a regular customer.

Finally, William smiled and picked up his book off the counter. Tucking it under his arm, he walked out of the store. The door clicked shut behind him.

I bit my lip, wondering if I should follow. Although *should* was probably not the correct word choice. I shouldn't have followed him in the first place, so what I *should* do was stop and go back to work.

But I really wanted to know what book he'd bought. It

had taken him nearly fifteen minutes to decide, and he'd been browsing in the same section the entire time. What had he been looking for? What did a man like William read?

Trying to appear casual—which I was realizing was not a skill I possessed—I wandered to the section where William had been looking. The bookstore guy caught sight of me and narrowed his eyes a little. He was so onto me. It would be a very long time before I'd be brave enough to come back to this store again.

I stopped where William had been standing. It was the religion section. That was interesting. It was impossible to tell what religion he might have been looking at. He'd picked up books from all over the shelves, and there were numerous religions represented. I looked closer. Most of the titles seemed to be historical, or books *about* various religions, rather than spiritual books or religious texts such as Bibles.

I couldn't tell what book he'd bought. I hadn't been able to see him well enough.

Deciding I ought to buy a book as cover, I grabbed one at random on my way up to the front counter.

"This all for you?" the bookstore guy asked. He scanned the book and his brow furrowed as he looked at the cover.

"Yeah." My face flushed hot as I realized I was buying a book titled *How to Please Your Woman in Ten Easy Steps*. "Um, it's a gift for someone."

"Mm hmm," he said.

I handed over my credit card without really hearing what it cost. God, this was embarrassing. Couldn't I have grabbed something a little less ridiculous?

He gave me my credit card and receipt.

I took a deep breath. I'd humiliated myself this much, I might as well make it complete. "Would you mind telling me what the man who just left bought?"

His eyebrows drew together again, and he crossed his arms. "Why?"

"Oh, I…" *That's a very good question. Why should he tell you?* "I was just wondering."

"I don't remember the title."

I could tell by his tone and the way he glared at me that he remembered *exactly* what it was, but he was certainly not going to tell *me*. I gave a little nod before grabbing my book and hurrying out of the store.

"Well, Ivy, you have officially lost your mind."

I went up the stairs to street level and didn't see any sign of William. Which was just as well. I didn't know what I'd been thinking. What a ridiculous thing to do. Being stuck with a copy of *How to Please Your Woman in Ten Easy Steps* served me right.

Hoping I wouldn't accidentally bump into William on the way, I walked back to my car. I wondered where he'd gone. Home? Or did he have more stops to make? Far from helping me solve the puzzle that was William Cole, my little morning excursion had only made him more of an enigma.

When I got to my car, I checked my messages. I wasn't surprised to have a voicemail and a text from Jessica, asking if everything was all right. I sent her a quick message, saying I had something to take care of downtown. It wasn't exactly a lie, but I cringed a little nonetheless. But what else could I say? *Hey Jess, I decided to stalk the guy who's been stalking me. Heading back now. TTYL.*

I'd see her tonight, but it would be on a double date. With Blake.

"That's right, Ivy," I said to myself in the rear-view mirror. "Blake, the perfectly normal man who you've been out with enough times that after tonight, you'll have to admit you're *dating*."

I didn't particularly like the way that sounded. But

another date was fair. And I didn't want to cancel when Jessica had been so excited.

I still found myself imagining William picking me up tonight. That gave me a little flutter in my tummy. I turned on the car, but paused and looked up at his building, wondering when I'd see him again.

DOUBLE DATE

*M*y favorite thing about art galleries was always the lighting. I did enjoy looking at the art, and attending exhibitions with Jessica had increased my appreciation for it. But there was something about the lighting. Soft, casting subtle shadows. Illuminating the pieces to show off their best features. It created a mood, like music does for a movie. Without the right lighting, an art gallery was just a room with paintings.

Blake had suggested the gallery exhibition when I'd mentioned Jessica's idea to go on a double date. He knew the gallery owners, and had offered to get us tickets to the event. It had definitely earned him a few extra Jessica-points. She'd still subjected him to the third degree during dinner. He'd taken it in stride. Her patented eyebrow arch hadn't done anything to shake his confident demeanor.

It was me who was uncomfortable.

From the moment Blake had picked me up at my house, I'd sensed something was different. On our first few dates, he'd been friendly and courteous. Tonight, he was bordering on aggressive.

Nothing he'd done so far had been inappropriate, really. A lot of touching. A hand on my back or my arm. He'd moved my hair over my shoulder once or twice. And there was an intensity in his eyes. It all said that he was ready to take this to the next level. That tonight, he didn't expect the date to end at the art gallery.

If it had been another man, I might have found it all very arousing. Jessica had clearly noticed and gave me knowing smiles from across the table. But I wasn't getting pleasant tingles of anticipation. It was making me jumpy and nervous.

And I couldn't stop thinking about William.

I wondered if he knew where I was tonight. What book he'd bought earlier. What he did other days of the week. Did he always bring the homeless man a sandwich on Fridays? And what did he do for a living? His apartment was in a nice building, so it couldn't be cheap.

Blake's gentle hand on my elbow steered me to the next painting and I blinked, coming back to reality. Jessica and Peter had wandered off together, but I could see them across the gallery. I took small sips of champagne from a fluted glass as we moved, taking our time to admire each piece. Soft classical music played in the background and people spoke in low voices, like in a library. It was all very smart and sophisticated, and I felt guilty for not paying better attention to my surroundings.

"What do you think of this one?" Blake gestured with his champagne glass toward a painting of a cliff with ocean waves breaking against it.

"It's beautiful." I took a quick sip of champagne and tried to think of something else to say. Something that would bring my mind to the present. To my *date*. "There's such a sense of movement in the water."

"Powerful. It's almost violent, don't you think?" His fingers lingered on my elbow, giving me a light caress.

I thought about pulling away, but he dropped his hand. "Yes. Very powerful."

"Callahan."

We both turned at the voice behind us. A man in a dark suit stood with a glass of red wine perched in his hand. He was attractive and businesslike, with a smooth jaw and hair that looked like he'd just had it cut.

He looked a lot like Blake.

"Darrington," Blake said, shaking his hand. "Ivy, this is Samuel Darrington. He used to be one of my colleagues at Dorset, until he got too full of himself and went elsewhere."

I offered my hand and he took it. For a second, I thought he might bring it to his lips, but his eyes flicked to Blake and he simply shook it gently.

"Ivy Nichols," I said. "It's nice to meet you."

"The pleasure is all mine," Samuel said.

Blake cleared his throat. "Dr. Ivy Nichols. She's being modest."

"Oh?" Samuel asked.

"I'm a literature professor," I said. "I teach at Woodward College."

"Impressive," Samuel said, but I wasn't sure if he meant he was impressed with me, or impressed that Blake was with me. He turned to Blake. "So are you in for next week?"

"Now isn't the time," Blake said.

Samuel took a sip of his wine. "Just wondering if you want to keep playing with the big boys."

Blake's eyes narrowed and there was an edge to his voice. "I'll be there."

"Good," Samuel said. His tone was relaxed, but there was a tightness around his eyes that didn't match his casual response. "Did you get my invitation?"

"I did," Blake said.

"And you'll come?" he asked, then looked at me again. "I'm

throwing a little housewarming party in my new place. You should see the view. It's incredible."

"I'm sure it is," Blake said before I could respond. "We'll be there."

"Great." Samuel leaned closer to Blake and said something in a low voice. Blake's face was a hard mask. Samuel stepped back and both men's expressions smoothed over, like the interaction hadn't happened. Samuel took my hand, and this time he did place a light kiss on the backs of my fingers. "Ivy, it was an absolute pleasure. You two enjoy your evening."

Samuel walked away, and I got the sense there was some sort of rivalry between them. I didn't like feeling as if I were a piece on a game board that Samuel had just attempted to steal. And why had Blake said *we* would be at this housewarming party? We weren't a couple who automatically did things together.

"Keep playing with the big boys?" I asked. "What was that about?"

Blake ran a hand down my arm. "Sorry about that. He was talking about our monthly poker night; he takes it way too seriously. Samuel is… interesting. But he's harmless."

I didn't believe that for one second. Samuel seemed about as harmless as a hungry shark. "Why did you tell him we'd be at his housewarming party?"

"Well, if we're both free, it would be good to make an appearance," he said. "We won't have to stay long."

That wasn't the answer I was looking for. Everything about this evening was making me uncomfortable. I set my champagne glass down on a little table. "Excuse me for a moment. I need to go to the ladies' room."

Blake licked his lips and looked at me like I was on his own personal dessert menu. "Sure. Hurry back."

My stomach felt uneasy as I walked away. I found Jessica and hooked my arm with hers.

"Restroom?"

She startled a little but nodded. "Okay. Peter, I'll be right back."

The restroom was single occupant, but I dragged her inside with me anyway.

"What's going on?" she asked once I'd closed and locked the door.

"I don't know," I said. "Blake just had a strange conversation with someone he knows. Then he said we'd be at some housewarming party without even asking me. And he's looking at me like…"

"Like he's thinking about taking that little black dress off your cute little body?" Jessica asked.

"Yes, exactly."

Jessica sighed. "And what's wrong with that? Don't you want the man you're dating to look at you like he wants you?"

"I'm not *dating* Blake," I said. "That's not what this is. This is just…"

"Just what?" Jessica asked.

"Just *a date*," I said. "There's a difference."

"Okay," Jessica said. "Does *he* realize that?"

I crossed my arms. "I don't know, and that's the problem. I'm not sure if I like where this is going."

"What do you need, honey?" she asked. "You want me to sneak you out? I can have Peter distract him."

"No," I said. "I'll handle it. I just want you to tell me I'm not crazy."

"You're not crazy," she said. "But are you sure you're not balking because he obviously likes you, and you're scared of what that means?"

I sighed out a long breath. It was a fair question. "Maybe? I don't know."

"What's going on with you?" she asked. "You've been distracted all night."

"You're right, I have been," I said. "I just have some other things on my mind."

"Well, if you're distracted, maybe that's why the date feels a little off to you." She gave me her signature maternal smile. "He's not Julian. It's okay to let someone get close to you again. Not every guy is going to bail at the first sign of trouble."

"I know."

"Blake obviously likes you," she said. "If you're not ready for things to heat up, just tell him. But don't make this about Julian, or your dad, or anything else."

I took a deep breath. Talking to Jess was calming me down. Yes, his conversation with Samuel had been a little odd, but maybe the undercurrent of antagonism I sensed was just typical male banter. And maybe Blake had accepted the invitation for both of us because he expected we were going to keep seeing each other. After all, he didn't know I was having doubts.

"I'm sorry, I just got a funny feeling and kind of panicked."

"You're doing fine," she said. "But if you're really uncomfortable, Peter and I can take you home."

"No, I think I'm okay."

"Then get out of here or I'm going to pee in front of you," she said.

I laughed and went back out to find Blake.

GOODNIGHT, IVY

*he rest of the date went smoothly, but the pings of anxiety returned on the drive home. I knew exactly what was coming, and I wasn't sure how I felt about it. He was going to kiss me goodnight, and ask if he could come in. The latter was a definite no. I'd already decided that. I felt far too conflicted to sleep with him. But a goodnight kiss? Would that be so terrible?

I sat in the passenger seat of his car, calm and collected on the outside. On the inside, I was a mess. Distracted and confused. I shouldn't have followed William today. All the unanswered questions rolling through my mind were making it hard to sort out how I felt about Blake. William's constant presence in my thoughts was like a recurring interruption.

We got to my house and parked. Blake walked me up to my front door, his hand on the small of my back. We stopped, facing each other. His eyebrow lifted, just a centimeter, and the corner of his mouth hooked. He stepped closer and placed his hand on my waist. Leaned down and—

"Ivy."

Startled by the voice, I moved back. William was walking up the path toward my door. His hands were in his pockets—his posture completely non-threatening—but I had the strangest feeling that if Blake so much as flinched in my direction, William would lay him out with one punch.

"William?" I glanced between the two men. Blake's eyebrows were drawn in as he watched William approach. God, how was I going to explain this?

"Ivy, I, um…" Apparently William didn't know what to say, either.

"What are you doing here?" I asked.

"I'm sorry, who's this?" Blake asked.

Well, William was kind of stalking me. And then I decided to stalk him back earlier today. You know, no big deal.

"Oh, this is William. He's…" I fumbled. "He's my neighbor. Was Edgar barking again? I'm really sorry about that."

William blinked at me.

Please go along with it.

"Yeah, he…" William paused. "It's okay."

"Thanks for letting me know." I widened my eyes and gave William a tiny nod, gesturing for him to leave, then turned to Blake. "I do need to take Edgar outside. He can't wait as long as he used to."

Right on cue, Edgar barked.

"See?" I said with a little shrug.

William was heading toward the street, half turned so he could still watch me and Blake. But at least he was leaving.

"No problem," Blake said, his expression smoothing over as if the interruption hadn't occurred. Before I could think about what was happening, he leaned in and placed his lips against mine.

I didn't close my eyes—not all the way. And I didn't quite

kiss him back—not really. I *almost* looked to the side to see if William was watching. But I didn't have to. I knew he was. And I knew I felt bad about it.

Blake's kiss had an edge of assertiveness that told me if I gave him any encouragement, I'd have a tongue in my mouth in half a second. I gently pulled away, keeping it lips-only.

"I had a nice time," I said. "Thanks again."

"I did too." Blake tucked a piece of hair behind my ear and ran his finger down my cheek.

I could see the unspoken question in his eyes. Could he come in?

"Goodnight, Blake." I kept my voice firm and stepped back to put space between us.

A flash of frustration—maybe even anger—crossed his features. It was gone almost before I noticed, but I'd seen it. He was not happy with how this date was ending. The question was, would he take no for an answer?

I took out my keys and unlocked the door, watching Blake from the corner of my eye. He seemed on the verge of stepping into my personal space again. My back tightened, and I held my breath.

"Goodnight, Ivy," he said. "I'll call you."

The air whooshed from my lungs as I opened the door. Blake walked back to his car as I slipped inside and shut the it behind me.

Edgar was waiting, his body tense, his ears perked up.

"Hey, buddy," I said. My stomach felt a little sick. He licked my fingers and I scratched behind his ears. "Do you need to go outside?"

He hesitated, his focus still on the front door. For a second, I wondered if Blake had come back—or maybe William had. But the flash of headlights through the front window and the noise of Blake's engine told me he was leaving. Once the sound of his car faded down the street, Edgar relaxed and headed toward the back door.

I put my purse and keys down and took him out back. The porch light winked on and Edgar went to his spot to do his business.

Although Edgar wasn't acting like a stranger was around, I had a feeling William hadn't gone far. "Are you out here somewhere?"

A slight pause, then William's voice came from the other side of the fence. "Yes."

I shook my head. This was getting out of control. I went to the side gate and opened it.

William appeared from around the corner of the fence. His hands were still in his pockets, and at least he had the grace to look guilty.

"What was that about?" I asked.

"I'm not your neighbor," he said.

"I realize you're not my neighbor, but I had to tell him something. Would you have preferred I introduce you as my stalker?"

"No."

Edgar came up and sniffed William's pants. William absently took his hand out of his pocket and scratched Edgar's head.

"How do you do that?" I asked.

"Do what?"

I looked down at my dog. I'd never seen him take to another person this quickly before. His dislike of all humans besides his chosen few had started early. "Edgar doesn't usually let people pet him."

The corner of William's mouth turned up and he glanced at Edgar, scratching behind his ears. "You should close the gate. He'd be hard to chase in the dark if he got out."

"But… he's…" God, I was so flustered. I was still trying to process everything. My date. Blake's kiss. William barging in on us.

William stepped into my yard and closed the gate behind him.

My mouth hung open. "I didn't invite you in."

"I'm just making sure Edgar doesn't run away."

Edgar sat between us, his tail swishing through the grass.

"Edgar's not the point," I said. "What are you doing here?"

"I told you, I'm just looking out for you."

"I don't need anyone to look out for me."

"That's obviously not true," he said, crossing his arms.

I put my hands on my hips. "And what is that supposed to mean?"

"He kissed you."

The accusation in his tone made me angry. And feel guilty —which made me angrier. "So? He took me on a date. There's nothing wrong with a goodnight kiss after a date."

"You didn't want to kiss him," he said.

"How would you know?" I asked.

"Because I know you."

I sighed, shaking my head. "No, you don't."

"Yes, I do."

"You know where I have coffee, and you know where I work. You know my address. But you don't know *me*."

"Yes, I do," he said again, his voice softening. If Edgar hadn't been taking up the space between us, I think he might have moved in closer. "I know a lot about you, Ivy."

"How?" I asked. "Have you been researching me, too? What did you find?"

"No, it's nothing like that," he said.

"Then why do you think you know me?" I asked.

"It's not something I can explain."

"Come on, Edgar," I said, tapping my thigh. "William, you can't keep following me around. I should have told you to stop already. This is ridiculous."

"I'm sorry, I didn't mean to upset you," he said.

"This isn't normal," I said. "People don't pick strangers at random and decide they need to look out for them."

"No, this isn't random," William said. "You're…"

"I'm what?"

He pressed his lips together and his eyes were so intense. But he didn't answer.

"I'm Ivy, is that it?" I said, finally. "I'm going inside. Close the gate behind you."

I tapped my leg again and Edgar followed me to the back door.

"You shouldn't be with him," William said.

With my hand on the door, I paused, letting out a sigh. *Don't ask him, Ivy. Don't encourage him.* "Why?"

"Because you don't want love that comes into your life with pomp and blare," he said. "That guy is all pomp and blare."

Pomp and blare? "What?"

"*Perhaps, after all, romance did not come into one's life with pomp and blare, like a gay knight riding down; perhaps it crept to one's side like an old friend through quiet ways.*"

"Did you just quote *Anne of Avonlea* at me?" I asked.

"Yes."

I stared at him. *Anne of Avonlea* was one of my favorite books. And he just quoted one of my favorite passages. "William… I just… you make me so flustered. Look, I've only been out with Blake a few times. I'm not *with* him. But it's not your business, either. And how many times have you read *Anne of Avonlea* that you can quote it?"

"I've never read it."

"Then how do you know that passage?" I asked.

He shrugged. "I just do."

"You make less and less sense every time we talk," I said.

"Have coffee with me tomorrow," he said. "I'll try to explain. I don't know if I can, but I'll try."

"Explain why you're following me?" I asked. "And why you think you know me?"

"Yes."

Logical Ivy knew I should say no. I'd been encouraging this insanity by spending time with him, and I needed to stop. But apparently logical Ivy wasn't in charge tonight. "Okay. I'll have coffee with you."

"Good, thank you. Can I..." He trailed off and looked down, like he was suddenly nervous. It was so endearing, it made me want to drag him inside and snuggle with him on the couch. How did he do that to me? "Can I have your number?"

"My number? I'm surprised you don't have it already."

"No." He sounded surprised, almost offended, like he was shocked I would suggest such a thing. "I've never asked for your number. How would I have it?"

"You found out where I live," I said.

"That's not the same," he said. "You have to ask a woman for her number."

I started to say it was exactly the same, but I didn't want to argue with him. And I had what was more than a small twinge of guilt for knowing where *he* lived without him being aware of it. I just wanted this conversation—this entire day—to be over.

"Okay," I said. He pulled out his phone and I gave him my number.

"Thank you," he said. "I have a few things to do tomorrow, so I'll call you when I'm done. Then we can get together?"

"Sure," I said. "I guess I'll talk to you then."

He smiled and went to the gate. "Don't forget to lock your doors."

"I won't."

"Goodnight, Ivy." With one more glance at me, his eyes gleaming even in the darkness, he left.

STRANGER THAN FICTION

William was standing outside the café when I arrived. The way he stood—hands in his pockets, watching me approach as if no one else existed— gave me a sudden case of butterflies. He had a quality that made it seem as if he didn't belong in the world. I half-expected him to tell me he'd been raised by monks in an isolated mountain monastery. Or by animals in a jungle somewhere.

His smile was subtle, his mouth only turning up slightly. But his eyes gleamed. It made me feel like he wouldn't be happier to see anyone but me.

"Good afternoon, Ivy."

"Hi, William." I brushed my hair back from my face and tucked it behind my ear. I'd worn it down, which I didn't often do.

He opened the door for me and once we found a table, he pulled out my chair. "Can I order for you, or would you like to?"

I had to give it to him, aside from the whole stalking

thing, his manners were impeccable. "Oh, you can, thank you. But I didn't expect you to pay."

"I'd like to."

He went to the counter and ordered our coffees, then came back and sat across from me.

"Your hair looks pretty today," he said.

My cheeks warmed, and I fidgeted in my seat. "Thank you. Um… how was your morning?"

"It was fine," he said.

"Did you have to work?" I asked. "You've never really told me what you do for a living."

"No, I didn't have to work. But here," he said, pulling out his phone. He tapped the screen a few times, then passed it to me. "This is what I do."

I stared at his phone. It was a picture of him, but it was more than a photo. It was an ad for what looked like expensive cologne, although the text was in Italian.

"You're a model?"

"Kind of, yeah," he said. "There's more if you swipe. James sent them to me."

I flicked through more ads, all for the same brand. All of them featured close-ups of William's face. Those mesmerizing blue eyes. "Is this a billboard? Where is this?"

"Italy," he said. "I don't think they use my pictures over here."

It probably shouldn't have surprised me that William was a model. He certainly looked like one. "Wow, this is impressive."

"Thanks." He took back his phone, but I got the feeling he didn't think his profession was anything remarkable.

"Do you model in fashion shows, too?" I asked.

His brow furrowed a little. "No. I just do photo shoots with James."

"Can I ask who James is?"

"Yes," he said. "He's my friend. And he's a photographer."

"Okay," I said. Why did it feel like he was willing to tell me anything, and yet it was like playing twenty questions to get real answers? "So, you work as a model, but just with James?"

"Yes."

"Do you have an agent or a manager?"

"No, just James."

"Then how did you start working with James?" I asked. "Did you just bump into him and he said you'd make a good model?"

"Yes."

It occurred to me that I needed to ask him open-ended questions if I wanted more than yes or no answers. "How did you meet him?"

"It was like you said, although I didn't actually *bump* into him. I was at a park. He walked by and asked if he could take my picture. I said yes. I ran into him again a few days later and he asked if I'd pose for more pictures for him. So I did."

"And that's how you became a full-time model?" I asked. "It was that simple?"

He shrugged. "I guess so. James sold the pictures to a designer in Italy. And they always want more."

I wondered if this James guy was a decent person, or if he was taking advantage of William. "And James is your friend now?"

"Yes," he said. "I hope you'll get to meet him sometime."

The barista called William's name before I had a chance to answer. He got up to get our coffees, then came back and took his seat.

"You said last night that you'd tell me why you've been following me," I said.

He wrapped his fingers around his mug and nodded

slowly. "Like I told you, it's hard to explain. This is going to sound strange at first."

"Okay."

"I was sent to save you."

I waited for him to say more, but he didn't. "That's… okay. That does sound strange. Do you mean save me from harm, or save me in the spiritual sense?"

"From harm," he said, his voice completely serious.

I had so many questions, I didn't know where to begin. I took a sip of coffee to give myself a second. "Okay… Who sent you?"

"I don't know."

"What are you supposed to save me from?"

"I'm not sure."

I sighed. "Could you at least come up with a story that sounds plausible?"

"I knew you wouldn't believe me at first," he said. "That's all right."

"Well, you're not giving me very much," I said. "Why do you think you were sent to save me?"

He met my eyes and held them captive. His irises were like crystals of blue ice sparkling in sunlight. He leaned closer, resting his forearms on the table. I couldn't have broken his gaze if I'd tried.

"Because everything inside of me knows this is true," he said, his voice soft. "I've always known. Your voice is the music that plays constantly in my mind. Your name is the first thing I think of every morning, and the last thing I think of every night. There isn't much that I'm sure of in this world, but I'm sure of this. *You* are why I'm here."

I stared at him, my lips parted. He'd struck me completely speechless.

"I'm sorry for following you," he said. "I didn't mean to

make you uncomfortable. But I had to find out if it was really you. I couldn't believe I'd finally found you."

"What do you mean, found me?"

"I didn't know who you were at first," he said. "I had to put the clues together. But they led me to you, just like I knew they would. I had a feeling it was you that day, when I saw you for the first time. And then I heard your name."

"So, you didn't know who I was, but you knew my name?"

"Yes," he said. "I knew your name, and I knew enough to find you."

"Is that why you keep saying it's *because I'm Ivy*?" I asked.

"Yes. I've had your name on my lips for a long time. But it wasn't just your name. If I'd met someone else named Ivy, I would have known she wasn't you."

"How?"

"I know your voice."

I stared into my coffee cup for a moment. What he was telling me didn't make an ounce of sense. He couldn't have been sent to save me. Things like that didn't happen in the real world. Besides, what made me so special?

But a part of me wanted to believe him, although I didn't understand why.

"I don't know what to say. You realize this is all impossible?"

"Why?" he asked.

"Because people aren't sent to save other people by mysterious unknown forces for reasons they don't understand," I said.

"How do you know that?"

"I... well, because I do. Everyone knows that. Some things are real, and some things aren't. That's the way the world is."

"No one understands all the mysteries of the world," he said. "Humans have been trying to make sense of reality for as long as we've had brains large enough to tackle those big questions. But there are still things we don't comprehend."

"Yes, but we're not talking about the nature of the time-space continuum. Obviously there are scientific realities that are beyond our understanding. But this is more like magic, or some strange spiritual phenomenon. Those don't exist."

"How do you know?" he asked again.

"Because some things are demonstrably not real," I said. "I can objectively say that magic does not exist."

"Maybe not," he said. "I never said anything about magic."

I let out a sigh. "No, but I don't know how you expect me to believe you."

"I have proof."

"What proof?"

His eyes went all intense again, with that sparkle that drew me in so deep I couldn't get free. "You grew up with more adults for friends than kids. You spent afternoons in your dad's office with grad students and stacks of books. He took you to the library to keep you busy while he worked."

A chill ran down my spine and I stared at him.

"The house you grew up in had a big tree in the backyard. Your father built a swing that hung from one of the branches. When you moved, that tree was what you missed the most."

I gave him a feeble nod.

"You love teaching literature because you believe in the power of language," he said. "And you're afraid there are too many adults in the world who don't appreciate how beautiful words can be."

"How are you doing this?" I asked, my voice barely a whisper.

"I know you," he said. "My mind is full of you. Not just your name and your voice, but who you are. I know that you love the sound of rain. That you read *The Great Gatsby* at least once a year. That it wasn't your idea to get Edgar, but you loved him as soon as you brought him home. That you once thought you might marry someone named Julian, but when he was gone, you didn't miss him. And I know the thing you fear most is being left alone in the world."

Tears stung my eyes. Everything he said was completely true. How could he possibly know?

"William, you're scaring me," I said. "How do you know these things?"

"Please don't be afraid of me." He placed his hand gently over mine. I didn't pull away. "I'm sorry, I know this is overwhelming. I swear to you, Ivy, I'm not here to hurt you. Quite the opposite."

"I really don't know what to do with this," I said. "I don't understand how you know things about me. Personal things. How did you find out? How did you know about the tree... and Julian... and my childhood?"

His expression was so understanding. So open and vulnerable. I searched his face for the lie. For the trace of manipulation. But I couldn't find it.

"I think some of them were things I needed to know to find you," he said. "The rest... I don't know. I wish I had better answers for you, I really do. I've been trying to make sense of it all, too. Until I met you, I wondered if I was ever going to figure it out. But then, there you were. And the parts that didn't make sense didn't matter as much anymore. Because I know they will someday."

"But *how* do you know these things?" I asked. "You can't just know something. It has to come from somewhere."

"Everything I know about you, it's just here." He touched his temple. His other hand was still resting on mine, and I still didn't pull away. Strange as it was, his touch felt like the only thing grounding me to reality. "Think of it like this: How do you know what to call the color red, or that a doorknob turns to open, or how to count to ten?"

"I suppose my dad taught me those things when I was little," I said.

"But do you remember that?" he asked. "Do you remember being taught? Or does it feel like you might as well have always known?"

"I guess… no, I don't remember being taught."

"That's what this feels like to me," he said. "All these things about you, they're just here. Like someone taught me and I don't remember the teaching part anymore, just the knowledge."

"But… you can't have been taught things about me so long ago that you don't remember it."

"No, that's true," he said. "I don't mean it as a literal comparison. But that's the best way I can think to explain it, because that's what it feels like."

"And you know other things?"

He nodded and opened his mouth to say something.

"Wait, I don't think I can hear more right now," I said.

He squeezed my hand. God, why did that feel so good? Why was it making me feel better?

I sat for a few minutes, staring at the table, trying to figure this out.

"Do you want me to leave?" he asked. The hope in his voice nearly brought tears to my eyes. I could feel how much he wanted me to say no.

"No," I said. We were basically holding hands at this point, and I didn't know what to do with that either. But it felt too right to let go. "No, I just need to think."

I didn't believe in the paranormal. I hadn't even believed in things like Santa Claus when I was a kid. William might as well have just told me he'd traveled through time, or come from a different planet.

But how did he know those things?

"Stranger than fiction," I said, more to myself than to him.

Mark Twain had said that. A literary genius. And a man who'd believed in the unexplainable. "Oh my god, the metal coffin."

"What?" William asked.

"Mark Twain," I said. "When he was a young man working on a steamboat, he had a terrible dream. He saw a metal coffin supported by two chairs. His brother, Henry, was inside the coffin with roses laid on his chest—white, with a single red one. It was so vivid, when he woke up, he was convinced it was real. But his sister told him it couldn't be, because only rich people were buried in metal coffins, and they weren't rich. Not long after, his brother was in a steamboat accident and he died of his injuries. When Twain went to see him, he was in a metal coffin supported by two chairs. One of the nurses who'd cared for him brought roses and laid on them on his chest—white, and one red."

"That's spooky," he said.

"It is. Of course, there are people who dispute the accuracy of the story. But…" I trailed off, but William didn't fill the silence. He stroked his thumb across the back of my wrist, a slow gentle movement that seemed to keep my heart from beating too fast. Mark Twain's supposed prophetic dream wasn't proof that William had been sent to save me. But I did have to admit that some things were outside the realm of the explainable.

Maybe there was an explanation for all this. I didn't think it was some form of divine intervention in my life. William was a man, not an angel. But the things he'd said had been right. And there would have been no simple way of finding those things out. I didn't think even Jessica knew about the tree in my backyard. I'd never had a reason to talk about it.

"What is it you want?" I asked.

"Well…" He paused, meeting my eyes. "I guess right now I just want to be your friend. I want to be in your life."

There was heat in his gaze that hinted at something else—made my core tingle in a way that had a blush creeping up my neck and across my cheeks.

I swallowed hard, still feeling the warmth of his hand on mine, the soft caress of his thumb against my wrist. "Friends?"

He nodded.

"Okay," I said. "We can be friends."

That smile again. It warmed me from the inside and I found myself smiling back.

And a part of me knew that it was going to be very hard to remain *just friends* with William Cole.

BREAKFAST

❧

*E*dgar barked before the car's engine had shut off. Someone was here, and he wasn't happy about it.

"What's going on out there, buddy?" I asked. "Who's here?"

It was still morning, and I hadn't opened the curtains yet, so I couldn't see outside. Edgar's ears swiveled, and he stood up from his dog bed, a growl rumbling deep in his chest.

"Edgar, stop."

He barked again at the knock on the door. I got up and peeked through the gap in the curtain, half expecting to see William's Jeep outside. Then again, Edgar probably wouldn't have barked at William. But it was Blake. That was strange. I wasn't expecting him. Had I missed a message?

"Just a second," I called through the door. Edgar barked again. "Buddy, you're going outside if you can't behave. Sit."

He sat, and I opened the door.

Blake smiled. "Morning. I thought I'd surprise you with breakfast." He held up two brown to-go bags.

"Oh, wow. This is unexpected."

"Can I come in? The food's getting cold." He stepped inside—I had to move out of his way—before I could answer.

Edgar growled.

"Edgar, go lie down," I said. He went over to his dog bed, but he didn't take his eyes off Blake. "Good boy."

"So, this is Edgar," Blake said. Edgar growled again, and Blake took a step back. "Interesting name for a dog."

"I was going to name him Poe, but Edgar seemed to suit him better," I said, watching with confusion as Blake went to the dining table. He took off his coat and hung it on the back of a chair. I shut the door.

"Get us plates, would you?" He started pulling things out of the bags and setting them on the table.

I hesitated for a second, then went into the kitchen to get plates. "Did you text me and I missed it?"

"No," he said.

"So, you're just here at nine in the morning on a Sunday?" I handed him the plates.

He smiled and started to lean in like he meant to kiss me. I turned and grabbed one of the bags and pulled out another container.

"Well, I'd hoped we would have had breakfast together yesterday." He paused, raising an eyebrow, as if to emphasize the innuendo. "Since we were interrupted, I thought we could have breakfast together today."

"It would have been nice if you'd have called first," I said.

He slipped a hand around my waist and drew me closer. "I'm sorry. I thought you'd like this."

I pushed against him and stepped back. "We've been on a few dates. I don't think we're quite to showing-up-unannounced territory."

"Ivy, I never go out with a woman more than once if I don't see the potential for something more," he said.

It irked me the way he said that, as if I should be flattered.

"That's good to know, but I'm not sure I understand your point."

"My point is," he said, moving close and putting his hands around my waist again, "that I really like you. And I know you like me, too. I haven't stopped thinking about you since Friday night. That mouth. That body. All I want to do is spend the rest of the day fucking you."

The kiss happened so suddenly, I didn't have a chance to decide whether I wanted it or not. Which I decidedly did not. But his lips were against mine, hard and aggressive—and not in a way I found appealing in the slightest. I didn't kiss him back, but put my hands on his chest and pushed him away.

"Blake, stop."

Edgar stood and growled again. This time, I didn't tell him to sit.

Blake's brow furrowed. "What's wrong?"

"Everything," I said. "You show up here unannounced, saying you want to have breakfast, but really you're just trying to get my clothes off."

"Well, in all fairness, mine are coming off too," he said. "I like to keep things equal."

"Do you think I'm joking?"

"No, I think you're overreacting." He straightened the cuffs of his sleeves. "Why don't we sit down and eat. Then we can let whatever happens, happen."

There was no way I was sitting down with him after he'd just told me he wanted to spend the rest of his day fucking me. "I'm not overreacting."

He looked me up and down. "I didn't expect this, but I like it. You want me to be the boss, is that it? Order you around?"

"What the hell, Blake? I'm not sleeping with you. I'm not trying to get you to talk me into it, or pretending so you'll be aggressive about it. I'm saying no. You need to leave."

He blinked in surprise. "What?"

"You heard me."

"Ivy, listen, if I came on too strong, it's only because of the signals you're sending," he said.

"Oh, no, you aren't turning this around on me," I said. "I'm not sending any signals. If this is what you thought I wanted, you had the wrong idea."

He narrowed his eyes. "I think I know exactly what you want. You're just afraid to admit it."

"Oh my god, stop," I said. "Get out. Now."

In an instant, his body language changed. He stood tall and stiff, the lines of his face all hard edges. "You're making a huge mistake. I am not a forgiving man."

"Then my biggest mistake was saying yes to you the first time."

His eyes were cold steel, sending a shiver down my spine. He plucked his coat from the chair and draped it over his arm. With a hard glare at me—one that had Edgar's low growl rumbling again—he walked out the door.

Edgar followed and stood at the door, guarding the entrance to his domain until the sound of Blake's car faded.

"What an ass." I left the food where it was and sat down on the couch. Edgar jumped up and put his head in my lap. I ran my hand down the back of his head. "Was he serious?"

I was sure he'd been quite serious. He'd come over thinking he could push me into sleeping with him. That was a hard no. I hoped he'd take his bruised ego and go elsewhere. I was done with him.

I rubbed Edgar's head and scratched behind his ears. What would I have done if it had been William at my door with a surprise breakfast? He'd been showing up unannounced, and I'd never been angry about it. Not once.

Of course, William never made me feel like he was barging into my life. And I couldn't imagine him pushing like that. It was more like he'd been tip-toeing around the outskirts of my world, looking for a way in. Even when he'd been following me, I hadn't felt violated. He'd still kept a certain distance.

And whether or not I believed his story—which of course I didn't, because how could I?—I didn't sense any malice. I'd seen hints that Blake might push too hard. But not William. It was almost as if William saw something I couldn't yet see, and he was simply waiting for me to catch up.

I wondered what I'd find when I got there.

PUZZLES

I looked up at the knock on my office door. It was already half open, and a young woman with a bright smile looked in.

"Happy Monday," she said, her voice full of enthusiasm. "I have a delivery for Ivy Nichols."

"That's me," I said, a little bewildered. My surprise grew when she revealed a bouquet of flowers in a delicate vase.

She brought them in and set them on my desk. "Have a wonderful day."

"Wait, who sent these?" I asked.

"There's a card," she said with a shrug. "I just deliver them."

I pulled the card from the plastic fork that held it in place, and opened the envelope.

YOU LOVE PUZZLES, *especially of language.*
  ~William

. . .

WILLIAM? Why was he sending me flowers? And that message. I did love word puzzles, but why would he put that on a card? Was it to remind me that he inexplicably knew things about me?

The flowers were an odd mix. I wasn't even sure what they all were. No roses or carnations or baby's breath—things you might see in a typical bouquet. I recognized purple pansies, and a lighter purple flower with four distinct petals. Mixed among them were little blue blossoms that might have been periwinkle, and clusters of flowers with deep magenta petals and white centers. Woven through it all were sprigs of delicate green ivy.

"Hi, Dr. Nichols." Lisa, my grad student assistant, looked in from the hallway. "Wow, pretty. They look like wild-flowers."

"Yeah, they do," I said.

"Who are they from?" she asked.

"Yes, who are they from?" Jessica moved past Lisa and parked herself in the chair on the other side of my desk. "Did Blake send flowers? They're pretty, but he seems like more of a roses kind of guy. This is an interesting choice."

"Blake?" Lisa asked. "Who's Blake?"

"The man she's dating," Jessica said, lowering her voice like she was sharing some juicy gossip.

"No, the man I'm *not* dating," I said.

"What?" Jessica asked, eyebrow arch on full display.

I widened my eyes at her.

Lisa let out a soft chuckle. "I get the hint. Do you need me to teach on Friday again, Dr. Nichols?"

"No, I don't think so," I said. "Thanks."

"Sure," she said. Her eyes swept over the flowers, like she could tell they had something to do with why I'd skipped out last Friday. She gave me a knowing smile and shut the door.

"Talk," Jessica said, pointing a manicured fingernail at me.

"I'm not seeing Blake again," I said.

"Why?" she asked. "You guys seemed to be getting along so well on Friday."

"Yeah, well, he puts on a good show."

"What happened?" she asked. "Did he get pushy when he dropped you off?"

I opened my mouth to answer, but paused. He had been a little pushy, but William had interrupted. "Kind of, but that's not what did it. He showed up at my house yesterday morning with breakfast."

"That's sweet," she said, but I gave her my own eyebrow arch. "It wasn't sweet?"

"Not at all," I said. "He didn't tell me he was coming, but I could have overlooked that. It was when he started in on how much he wanted to spend the day fucking me that I got uncomfortable."

She winced. "Too soon, Blake. Way too soon."

"It got worse from there, but I'll spare you the specifics," I said. "He wasn't interested in taking no for an answer. And when I told him to leave, he said I was making a huge mistake and that he's not a forgiving man."

"Oh, hell no," Jessica said. "Not a forgiving man? I'll show him unforgiving."

"Exactly," I said.

"So, what are these?" she asked, gesturing to the flowers. "His attempt at an apology?"

"No," I said, drawing out the word and looking at the flowers like they might suddenly bite me. "They're not from Blake."

Eyebrow arch. "And who, may I ask, are they from?"

I sat back in my chair, like I needed to keep my distance from Jessica. "They're from William."

"William, the stalker?"

"He's not stalking me anymore," I said.

She rotated a finger, gesturing for me to keep talking.

"Well, not really," I said. "Stalking is the wrong word anyway. It sounds too dramatic. He's… he's my friend."

"Your friend?" she asked. "First of all, what? And second of all, why is your *friend* sending you flowers?"

I decided to ignore her first question. "I actually have no idea. Maybe he thought I'd like them."

"Maybe he's apologizing for stalking you," she said, her tone dry. "But male *friends* don't send flowers. And these are… they're pretty, but they don't look like something a guy would send. Unless he's a florist or a gardener or something."

"No, he's a model."

"Well… okay, I can see that." She clicked her tongue. "But Ivy, you see that this is weird, right?"

God, she had no idea how weird it was. But I wasn't about to bring up the things he'd told me on Saturday. "Yeah, I know. It's… unconventional. He's like that, though. He's different. I think you need to meet him to understand. He's… I don't know, he's William."

"That makes me feel so much better," she said.

"Edgar likes him," I said.

Her eyebrows lifted. "Edgar, the most anti-social dog in all of existence? He doesn't like anyone except you."

"He likes you fine," I said.

"He allows me in your presence," she said. "He doesn't *like* me."

She had a point. "Well, he likes William. He even lets William pet him."

"How do you know William doesn't keep dog treats in his pockets?"

I rolled my eyes. "You can't bribe Edgar that easily, even

with treats. Edgar is really friendly with him. I think that's a good sign."

"Hmm, maybe," she said, by which she meant *I'm not convinced but I'll drop it for now.*

There was another knock at my door.

"Come on in," I said.

The door opened and a guy peeked in. "Hey, sorry to bother you, but I'm looking for Ivy Nichols?"

"That's me."

He pushed open the door and came in carrying an enormous bouquet of red roses. "Where would you like them?"

I stared at him, open-mouthed.

Jessica looked back and forth between me and the guy with the flowers. She pointed to a bookshelf. "How about there."

He set them down. "Cool. You ladies have a nice day."

Jessica got up and shut the door behind him, then plucked the card from the plastic holder. "Do you want to read it, or shall I?"

I couldn't seem to remember how to speak. Or close my mouth.

"Okay, I will." She slid the card out of the envelope. "Dear Ivy, please accept my apology. I'm an idiot, and I'm so sorry for how I acted yesterday. I hope you'll give me another chance. Blake."

"He's trying to apologize?" I asked.

"Looks like it." She tossed the card onto the shelf next to the huge mass of red.

"This is so weird," I said.

She shrugged. "Maybe he's just really into you, and he thought you felt the same. You caught him off guard when you weren't."

"He was an ass," I said. "He tried to say if he was coming on too strong, it was my fault for sending the wrong signals."

She shook her head and rolled her eyes. "Yeah, definitely an ass. But… at least you have pretty flowers? They smell good."

"I don't want them," I said.

"I'll get rid of them if you want," she said.

"Please do."

"What about those?" she asked, pointing at the flowers William had sent.

"Oh, no, these are fine."

She arched an eyebrow, but picked up the vase of roses. It was so big, she had to balance it on her hip. "All right honey, I have a class in fifteen. Sorry Blake turned out to be a jerk. But be careful with that William guy, okay?"

"I know, I will. And thank you for taking those."

Jessica left, and I breathed out a sigh of relief. The scent of roses hung heavy in the air. I got up and opened the window. Normally I found the smell of roses pleasant, but those had been stifling. I waved my hand around, trying to get rid of the scent.

The open window was helping, so I sat at my desk and picked up William's card. *You love puzzles, especially of language.* What had he meant?

I studied the flowers, wondering why he'd sent such a mix of colors. Purple, blue, magenta and white. It didn't look like a ready-made bouquet. It was pretty, and well put-together, but it didn't have the polished look of something a florist had designed. Had William chosen them?

The purple ones were pansies, but I wasn't sure about the rest. I Googled and found pictures that matched. The little blue ones were periwinkle, like I'd thought. The other purple blooms were called *Honesty*. That was interesting.

Were the flowers a message? Was he trying to tell me he was being honest? But what about the others?

You love puzzles, especially of language. In Victorian England, there had been something called *the language of flowers*. At the time, the social norms had been so strict, it limited what people could say to one another. They'd often used flowers to convey messages. Could he know about that?

I looked it up and found a chart of flowers and their meanings. Periwinkles meant early friendship. I supposed that fit. The purple Honesty flowers indeed stood for truthfulness, a message of *I'm being honest with you*. The purple pansies said *You occupy my thoughts*.

And the magenta flowers… oh my god, they were called Sweet William. And there was ivy.

William and Ivy… Early friendship… You occupy my thoughts… I'm being honest with you.

I stared at the flowers and couldn't help the silly smile that crept across my face. I was proud of myself for figuring it out, basking in the hit of dopamine I got from solving a puzzle.

He'd known. He'd known I'd be compelled to figure it out. That I'd make the connections. That I'd understand his message, and enjoy the little mystery he'd sent.

Who was this man and where had he come from?

I did a little more digging online and texted him a picture of a deep pink rose. That meant *thank you*, or even *thank you for being in my life*. A few minutes later, he replied with a picture of a pineapple plant. Already suspecting what it meant, I looked it up. *You are welcome.*

Biting my lip, I smiled at his text. He really did know me. Despite the strange way this had all started, I liked William. I liked him a lot, in fact. And it wasn't because he was gorgeous. That was nice, but there was more to it than his face, his body, his smile—even his eyes, mesmerizing as they were. He drew me in, as if something in him beckoned to

85

something deep inside me. I'd never experienced this feeling before, and I wasn't sure what it meant.

The little pings and sparks, the flutters and shivers he made me feel were quickly becoming addictive. Maybe Jessica was right, and I did need to be careful. But I wasn't sure if I could.

VIEW FROM THE LEDGE

❦

*W*illiam didn't keep appearing unannounced. But he did keep appearing. The difference was, he started texting me first.

Monday evening, he texted to say he was sorry he hadn't seen me since Saturday, but he'd been busy. He asked if we could meet for lunch the next day. At lunch on Tuesday, he said he would come by campus the next day in the afternoon. And so it went for the next couple of weeks. William came to see me most days, but always asked first.

Thursday, he met me after my afternoon class. He brought muffins and we took advantage of the nice weather, walking around campus while we chatted and ate. We passed Lisa outside the English building and she watched him with wide eyes. I wondered if she'd say anything about it later, but she didn't bring it up when I saw her during my open office hours. She just gave me a knowing smile.

Friday morning, I expected to meet him for coffee before work, but he texted to say he couldn't make it. I went to my office and worked on grading essays.

"Morning." Jessica appeared in my doorway dressed in a

colorful tunic. She smiled and came in to stand in front of my desk. "Rough week?"

I pushed my laptop over a few inches. I was trying—and apparently failing—to hide my disappointment at not seeing William. "No, I've had a great week, actually."

"You look upset," she said. "And I've hardly seen you. What's got you so busy lately?"

As if on cue, William appeared in my doorway. "Hi. I'm sorry I'm late."

I blinked in surprise. "I didn't think you were coming this morning."

"Of course I was," he said. His eyes moved to Jessica, who was staring at him with her mouth wide open. "You must be Jessica. It's so nice to finally meet you. I'm William Cole."

"Jessica Olson," she said, sounding bewildered. "It's nice to meet you too."

He smiled at her—a full smile, his cheeks puckering with dimples beneath his rough stubble. He was like a magician wielding a spell with that thing. Jessica was powerless against it. Her expression softened, and she smiled back.

"I'm sorry if I'm interrupting," he said. "I got caught up doing something this morning. But I thought you might have a little time before your first class."

"No, you're fine," Jessica said, glancing between the two of us. "I actually have to go. I was just stopping by for a minute. It's nice to meet you, William."

"You too," he said.

Jessica left, tossing me a raised-eyebrow glance over her shoulder on her way out.

"You didn't have to come all the way out here," I said. "I have to teach a class in ten minutes."

"I know," he said. "That's okay. I'll walk you."

"You drove up here just to walk me to my class?" I asked.

He shrugged. "Yeah."

It seemed like such a silly thing for him to do, but I was so glad he had. He had me feeling all kinds of swishy, swoony things—things I'd never felt before with anyone.

I was in trouble with this guy.

He waited while I gathered my things for my class, that little almost-smile on his face. We walked outside together, taking our time, and followed the brick path toward the lecture hall. Neither of us said much—just strolled side-by-side. I found myself thinking about holding his hand—which led to other thoughts. His arms around me. His lips against mine. Our bodies tangled beneath the sheets.

My cheeks flushed, and I knew I must be blushing bright red. It was not the first time I'd thought of him that way. My mind wandered with little fantasies about him all the time.

We got to the building and stopped. Students passed us on their way in, so we stepped to the side.

"Ivy, I was wondering…" He trailed off, putting his hands in his pockets and glancing down. Was he nervous? He was so cute, I almost giggled. "I was wondering if we could get together and do something tomorrow."

I'd been seeing him all the time—almost every day. But I could tell he was asking for something different.

"Do you mean… like a date?"

He stopped fidgeting and met my eyes. "Yes, a date."

"Sure, I'd love to," I said.

His smile seemed relieved and I wondered if he'd actually thought I'd say no. Then again, we hadn't talked about Blake. He might think I was still seeing him.

"Great," he said. "I thought about asking you with flowers, but at a certain point that gets a little ridiculous."

I laughed. "Yeah, that's true."

"Can I pick you up at nine?" he asked. "Or is that too early?"

"No, nine is good."

His eyes drifted to my mouth and little tingles of anticipation filled my chest. All the feelings I'd been missing with Blake were hitting me hard with William.

"I should let you get to work," he said. "But I'll see you in the morning."

I tucked a loose tendril of hair behind my ear. "Sounds great. I'll see you then."

* * *

I was up early, anticipation for my date with William making it hard to sleep. I showered and dressed, took Edgar for a walk, and had some breakfast, all before eight. The next hour was spent fidgeting, waiting for William to pick me up.

Edgar alerted me to his arrival. He padded over to the door, but he didn't bark. His body language was relaxed, but alert. His tail even wagged. A moment later, William knocked.

I opened the door and he smiled. His clothes were simple—a jacket over his jeans and t-shirt. But my god, he looked good.

"You look beautiful this morning," he said. The hint of awe in his voice as much as his words made my cheeks warm.

"Thanks." I looked down at my clothes. I was dressed similarly—jeans and a casual shirt. I'd texted him to ask what we were doing so I'd know what to wear. He'd replied with *don't dress up*.

Edgar sat in front of William, his tail swishing. William scratched his head. "Are we ready?"

"Sure, let me just get Edgar his new Nylabone. It's his consolation prize for being left alone."

"Edgar can come," William said.

"Really?"

"Of course," he said.

"Wow, thank you." I'd never been out with someone who wanted to bring Edgar along. "You hear that, buddy? You get to come too. But where are we going? Am I dressed okay?"

William glanced up at the sky. It was gray, but dry. "You could bring a jacket, but it looks like we got lucky with the weather. Oh, but put on comfortable shoes. We're going to do some walking."

"Okay," I said, narrowing my eyes at him. "Is that all you're telling me?"

He winked. "Come on, Edgar. Wanna go for a ride in the car?"

At the word *car*, Edgar dashed outside. William followed and led him to his Jeep.

"Over here, buddy," he said, opening the door. Edgar jumped in and William looked at me. "Coming?"

"Yeah, just a second." I changed into tennis shoes and grabbed my small backpack. I kept a few things for Edgar in it—portable food and water dishes, a container of dog food, a few treats. I took my jacket off a hook by the door and went out to William's Jeep.

We both got in and he pulled out onto the street. Edgar sat in the backseat, watching out the window.

"So, where are we going that we can bring Edgar?" I asked.

He glanced at me, the corner of his mouth hooking in a little grin. "Do you trust me?

"Yes," I said, without hesitating. And the amazing thing was, I really did.

"Good."

We drove out of town and got on the freeway heading south, then east. Edgar happily watched the scenery roll by; he loved car rides.

I chewed on the inside of my bottom lip. I needed to tell

William about the day I'd followed him. I'd been thinking about it a lot, but I hadn't brought it up. Keeping it from him felt wrong.

"William, I have a confession."

He glanced at me with those beautiful blue eyes and my heart fluttered. "Yeah?"

"I followed you once," I said. "You met me before work, and when you left, I didn't go to my office. I trailed you to your car, and then I followed you into the city."

I peeked at him from the corner of my eye. But he didn't seem angry or annoyed. His lips turned up in the barest hint of a smile.

"What did I do?"

"Well… you went home," I said. "At least, I think the building was where you live. It looked like apartments. I was going to leave at that point, but then I saw you come out. You went to a grocery store, and then you took a sandwich to a guy sitting out on the street."

"Bruce," he said. "I bring him lunch on Fridays sometimes. He hates roast beef."

"Yeah," I said. "Then you brought groceries to an elderly woman. After that, you walked around for a while, and I followed you down to the Bookstore Underground."

"Did you go in?" he asked.

I nodded. "I did, and the guy who was working was totally suspicious. I saw you buy a book. I left after that."

He laughed. "That was well done. I never saw you."

"You aren't mad?"

"I'd be a hypocrite if I was," he said. "I followed you around a lot more than once."

"Yeah, that's what I told myself when I was doing it," I said. "I still felt weird about it, though. I wasn't trying to violate your privacy. I just wanted to figure out who you were."

"I know exactly what you mean," he said.

"Why did you start bringing a sandwich to Bruce on Fridays? Did you just see him out there all the time?"

"Not exactly," he said. "I almost hit him with my car."

"What?"

"It sounds worse than it is," he said. "He walked right out in front of me. I had a green light, he just wasn't paying attention. But I pulled over and let him yell at me for a few minutes. Then I offered to buy him lunch."

"You have an interesting way of making friends," I said.

He laughed. "I liked him. He has moxie. I'd seen him around, so I knew where he usually hung out. Figured he could use a decent meal once in a while, so I started bringing him a sandwich."

"As long as it's not roast beef," I said.

"I forgot *one* time," he said. "And he's never let me live it down."

"What about the lady with the groceries?" I asked.

He looked at me with a grin, his dimples puckering. "Guess what her name is."

"I have no idea."

"Mrs. Ivy."

My eyes widened. "You're kidding."

"No," he said. "Not long after I moved into my apartment, I was behind her in line at the market. The cashier knew her —called her Mrs. Ivy. I knew she wasn't the one I was looking for; I could tell by her voice. But it seemed like a funny coincidence, so I struck up a conversation with her. Turns out her name is Carolyn Ivy. Her husband passed away a few years ago, and she has trouble making ends meet. I bring her groceries sometimes, just to help out."

"You really are amazing, you know that?"

He shrugged. "Not really. I have more than I need, so I can afford it."

After a forty-five-minute drive, we turned off the freeway near North Bend, in the foothills of the mountains. We drove down a curving road to Rattlesnake Lake Park. William pulled into a parking spot and I stared at him.

"Are we hiking up to Rattlesnake Ledge?" I asked.

"Yes."

I swallowed back the lump in my throat. "Do you know about this, too?"

He took my hand and stroked the back of it with his thumb, just like he'd done in the coffee shop. "Yes."

"Tell me."

"Your dad used to bring you here every summer, and you'd hike up to the ledge together to look at the view. When you were older, he told you he did it so you'd never forget that there are beautiful things in the world, and to keep your eyes open for them."

"That's exactly what he said." I didn't ask how he knew.

"I thought maybe you'd want to see the view again," he said. "And I've never been here."

"You haven't?" I asked, and he shook his head. "Well, let's get going."

With Edgar on his leash, we headed out. It was about a two-mile hike to the top, up a switch-back trail that was well-maintained. It was a popular hiking spot, but the over-cast sky seemed to have kept a lot of people at home. It wasn't crowded, just a handful of other hikers braving the threat of rain.

The trail wasn't long, but it got steep, and I was breathing hard by the time we got to the top. Even without a clear sky, the view was amazing. Miles of deep green forest, the blue lake at the bottom of the valley, mountains rising in the background.

We found a place to sit and I got out Edgar's water.

"Beautiful, isn't it?" I asked.

"Very." He paused for a moment. "Can I ask you a question?"

"Sure."

"What happened to your dad?"

I glanced at him. "You don't know?"

He shook his head.

I looked out over the valley below and took a deep breath. "He had cancer. And then a stroke. He died about a year ago."

"I'm sorry." He took my hand and twined our fingers together.

"Thank you."

We sat in silence for long moments, our hands clasped. I was grateful he didn't say anything else. So often people tried to say things they meant to be helpful, but weren't. William's silence and the warmth of his hand were comforting in a way nothing else had been since my dad's death.

Edgar finished his water and laid down next to me, putting his head in my lap. I absently stroked his fur. Although it was bittersweet to be here—in a place that had so many memories of my dad—it felt good, too. It felt right. Like I'd needed to come here and see it again, although I hadn't realized how much.

"I miss him," I said after a while. "But the last two years of his life were so hard. I'm glad he's not in pain anymore. It's just difficult to feel so disconnected. He was the only family I had."

"I understand what it's like to feel disconnected," he said.

"Do you have family nearby?" I asked.

"No, I don't have any family."

"As in, not at all?" I asked.

He shook his head.

"Neither do I," I said. "People are always so surprised to hear that, like it's impossible. But I never knew my grandparents on either side. My mom died when I was two. My

95

parents didn't have siblings, so I never had aunts and uncles or cousins. It was just me and my dad. We had other people in our lives over the years, but it's not really the same."

"People are surprised when I say it too—that I don't have family. You're the only person I've ever met who isn't."

"Are you lonely?" I asked.

He didn't answer right away, but when he did, his voice was soft. "Sometimes."

"Me too."

"But not now," he said, squeezing my hand.

"No, not now." I looked over at him and he met my eyes with that little smile. "I'm not seeing Blake anymore," I said, blurting it out before I'd thought about what I was saying. "I just… I don't know why I said that. I guess I wanted to make sure you knew."

"I know."

"Of course you do," I said with a laugh. "You know all about me."

"I don't know everything," he said. "But you need to be careful of him."

"Be careful of Blake?" I asked. "Why? I'm not going out with him again."

"I still think you need to be careful," he said. "He's hiding something."

"What do you mean? Hiding what?"

"I'm not sure," he said. "But you don't need to worry. I won't let him hurt you."

I didn't understand what he was talking about. "Okay, well, if I see him I'll be careful."

"Good. And you know you can always call me if anything happens. Or if you need me."

"Right, because you're here to save me," I said.

He looked over. "Are you making fun of me?"

I laughed. "Only a little."

He shifted so he was turned toward me. "Can I ask you something else?"

"Sure."

"Can I kiss you?"

I smiled and bit my bottom lip. "Yes."

He brushed my hair back, his dazzling blue eyes locked with mine—hypnotic. With his hand still against my face, he leaned in and touched his mouth to mine. He kissed my lips gently—once, twice. Again, still soft. But he didn't feel hesitant, like he wasn't sure of himself. It was more like he was taking his time—exploring. He kissed the corner of my mouth, then slid along my lower lip to the other side. Kissed the corner again.

I enjoyed his closeness, his skin brushing mine. His stubble rough against my face. He kissed me harder, the tension in his body rising. My heart started to race, the butterflies in my tummy turning into a warm whirlpool of sensation. He sucked my lower lip into his mouth and caressed it softly with his tongue. Had my eyes not already been closed, they would have rolled back. My god, he was good at this.

His lips parted, and I followed. Our tongues slid against each other as we deepened the kiss. Faces tilted. Mouths tangled. He kissed me long and slow—unhurried, like we had all the time in the world to enjoy the feel of our sensitive lips and deliciously wet mouths.

Someone cleared their throat behind us and I remembered we weren't alone.

William slowly pulled away, showing no urgency to stop. He gave me another soft kiss on my lips before he leaned back, a little grin on his face.

I was so dazed, all I could do was blink.

"That was even better than I imagined," he said.

And it was. It was the best kiss I'd ever had.

HARD STARE

❦

I had to admit to Jessica that I was now dating my stalker. Of course, he wasn't *really* a stalker, and he wasn't following me in secret anymore. She was still skeptical, although meeting William a few more times seemed to help. He had an interesting effect on people that was hard to put into words. It was impossible not to like him, and very hard not to trust him. Even Jessica agreed with me there. There was something about him.

The fact that he treated me like spun gold also made a difference. It wasn't just that he had good manners—which he did. He always seemed so happy to see me. He texted me randomly throughout the day. Called me at night, often saying he just wanted to hear my voice. We could sit and talk for hours. Even when I talked about books, or my favorite authors, he'd insist he could listen to me forever.

And the way he made me feel… His kisses were like magic. I would have been flitting through each day on a puffy cloud of happy hormones, if not for Blake.

Shortly after William took me hiking, Blake sent me a text, asking if I'd be willing to meet him for lunch or coffee. I politely declined, and hoped that would be the end of it. He tried again, apologizing for the way he'd acted. Asking for the chance to make it up to me. Once again, I said no. When he called the next day, I let it go to voicemail. His message, delivered in that maddeningly soothing voice, implied I was playing hard to get—and he enjoyed the game.

I was *not* playing a game. I fired back with an angry text— I didn't want to talk to him—telling him to stop trying to contact me. I was seeing someone else, and he needed to stop. He didn't reply.

I knew there was a good chance I'd run into him at Dorset Financial. I usually did. So when William insisted he come along to my appointment with Arthur a week later, I didn't hesitate to say yes. Knowing William would be with me took away the worst of my anxiety over whether I'd see Blake.

My appointment was in the morning, so I met William for breakfast beforehand. We chatted for a while over omelets and toast.

When we were almost finished, he put down his fork and wiped his hands on a napkin. "Can I ask you a question?"

"Sure."

"What's your appointment for?" he asked.

I brushed my lips with my napkin. "Well, when my dad died, he left me a considerable amount of money. Arthur at Dorset Financial manages my investments for me."

He nodded. "I was just curious."

"It's fine, you can ask me anything," I said. "It's strange because I never knew my dad had a lot of money. He never told me."

William regarded me with that piercing gaze of his. "It makes you uncomfortable, doesn't it? Not that he didn't tell you. I think you understand that part. But the money itself."

"Yes, you're right," I said. "Is this something you already knew about me?"

"No," he said.

"And yet, you understand me so well."

He shrugged with a little smile.

"I feel like having all this money should change me, somehow. Or that it will, and I don't want it to. It's silly, because there are so many people in the world who don't have enough. And here I am, worrying about what I'm going to do with too much."

"It won't change you," he said.

"I hope not. I'm trying to do good with it," I said. "Arthur helped me set up contributions to organizations I believe in, that sort of thing. But as far as the rest of it… I don't know. Jess kept telling me I should take a vacation. But I didn't want to go alone."

He met my eyes and smiled again. An unspoken thought passed between us—that I wouldn't be alone if he was with me.

I glanced at the time. "We should get going. I don't want to be late."

The building was just up the street, so we walked and took the elevator up. My heart beat faster the closer we got to Arthur's office. Would Blake be here today? Would he try to talk to me? What would William do if he did?

My body thrummed with nervousness as we got out of the elevator. We stopped just outside the doors. Dorset's floor was in chaos.

Employees stood around in small knots, some talking in hushed voices, others looking around in confusion. A police officer stood in front of the receptionist's desk, and several others spoke to people nearby. The air was thick with tension. William kept a hand on my arm and stepped slightly in front of me, like he was going to put himself between me and whatever was going on here.

A police officer approached us. "Are you here for an appointment?"

"Yes, I'm here to see Arthur Horace," I said. "Is everything okay?"

"There was a break-in," he said. "I'm afraid I can't let you in."

"Ivy." Arthur came up behind the police officer. Perspiration gleamed on his bald head and his cheeks were flushed. "I'm so sorry. I should have called to reschedule."

"That's okay," I said. "What happened?"

"Someone broke into the office last night," he said.

"Oh my god. Was anyone hurt?"

"No," he said. "And there's no need to be concerned. Your information is secure."

"Do you know what they were after?" I asked.

"I'm not sure," he said. "As far as we can tell, nothing is missing. IT is going through our system now to see if there's been a breach. I've been here for over thirty years, and we've never had something like this happen."

"This is awful," I said.

"We'll get it sorted," Arthur said. "And I'll be in touch to reschedule. I'm sorry you came all the way down here."

"No, don't apologize, it's not your fault," I said.

William stiffened, and I glanced at him. His usually pleasant expression had been replaced by a hard stare—his blue eyes narrowed, his jaw clenched. I followed his gaze and saw Blake watching us. His eyes were locked with William's and his upper lip twitched.

The tension in William's body made him seem like a predator ready to strike. I'd never found him frightening, but this side of him scared me. Not for myself, but for whoever dared to cross him when he looked like that. Blake's face was full of challenge, but William was a stone wall. Unyielding, impervious, and utterly confident.

Arthur looked between me and William, blinking a few times, and the police officer eyed us as well. I decided we needed to get out of here before Blake tried to get into a testosterone-induced pissing contest with William.

I slipped my arm around his and tugged. "We should go."

For a second, I thought William might not move, but he turned to me and nodded.

"I'll be in touch soon," Arthur said.

"Thanks," I said. Blake was still watching us. I pulled on William's arm again. "Come on. I think they have enough to deal with. Arthur doesn't need his coworker and his client's boyfriend having it out in the lobby."

William raised his eyebrows, like he was surprised, but he didn't say anything. Just steered me back to the elevator and pressed the button. I caught the look he gave Blake as we got in—one side of his mouth hooking in a smile. The last thing I saw as the elevator doors closed was Blake's face, growing redder by the second.

We started going down and without a word, William pushed me up against the wall. He pinned my arms, his hands on my wrists. I gasped as he kissed me—hard and deep. His mouth was firm, his kiss so overwhelming, I completely forgot where we were. He didn't stop until the elevator dinged, and the doors opened to another floor.

He pulled away and let go of my arms.

A man and woman got in, speaking in low voices, their conversation continuing as the doors closed. My back was still to the wall and William stood in front of me, staring, his eyes intense. He was so close, he almost pressed against me. We were both breathing hard and I was vaguely aware of the sudden silence. The man and woman had stopped talking. Their discomfort was palpable, but it barely registered. All I could see was William, looking at me like he wanted to rip my clothes off right here.

The elevator dinged again, and the doors opened. The man and woman hurried out, and I glanced at the floor number. Ten. The doors closed, leaving us alone.

William brushed my hair back from my face. The fierceness was gone from his expression, his eyes once again sparkling blue. He touched my chin and kissed my lips, soft this time. "I liked hearing you say *boyfriend*."

My heart was still pounding when we reached the building lobby. William took my hand, twining our fingers together, and we walked out.

We were halfway to where we'd parked before either of us said a word.

"Are you okay?" he asked.

"Yeah," I said, although my lips were still sensitive and swollen from that mind-numbing kiss. "I just feel bad for Arthur."

"How do you know him?"

"My dad knew him for a long time," I said. "Arthur handled Dad's investments from the beginning, as far as I know. That was close to thirty years ago."

William pulled me to the side so people could get by and stopped, turning to look at me. "Ivy, how much money did your dad leave you?"

"It's a lot," I said. "Just over ten million dollars."

"Who else knows about it?"

"Only Jessica and Peter," I said. "Why? What are you worried about?"

"Nothing," he said, squeezing my arm. "I just wondered who knew."

He took my hand again and we kept walking.

"Well, at least I probably don't have to worry about Blake calling again."

William stiffened. "He called you?"

"Yeah, last week," I said.

He tightened his grip on my hand. "Not since then?"

"No."

We got to his Jeep and paused next to the passenger's side door.

"Tell me if he does again," he said.

I pulled my hand away. "William, there's nothing going on between me and Blake."

His expression softened, and he kissed my forehead. "I know. That's not what I'm worried about. I just don't trust him."

"He's nothing but a guy with a sore ego," I said. "I wounded his pride. I'm sure he won't have any trouble finding someone to help him get over it."

"Still. Let me know if he keeps calling. I'll take care of it."

I laughed. "Take care of it?"

"You don't need to worry." He kissed my forehead again. "But if he touches you, I'll end him."

The smile left my face and a chill ran down my spine. He opened the door for me and I got in. He'd said that so matter-of-factly, I could have almost believed he was kidding. Or exaggerating.

He got in the driver's side and took my hand, bringing it to his lips for a kiss. And I knew he wasn't kidding. Not in the slightest.

BROKEN GLASS

*he weather was gorgeous, the sun shining as we
walked around the booths. William had picked me
and Edgar up and brought us to the Seattle Food and Wine
Tasting Festival. It was an outdoors event, a bit like a farm-
ers' market. Restaurants, wineries, and breweries had booths
offering samples of their food and drink.

We wandered around, sampling things. William held my
hand or kept a light touch on my back. It was a bit more
crowded than Edgar liked, but people tended to give him
space. He'd been a good dog—no growling at anyone—and
the proprietors at many of the booths had dog treats on
hand. Those seemed to make up for the abundance of strange
humans.

William pointed to another booth displaying little tarts
filled with fruit. "Dessert?"

"I'm so full, I don't think I have room," I said.

"Me neither." He paused and tucked my hair behind my
ear. His eyes were so captivating. He gave me his little half-
smile, one side of his mouth turning up.

He grabbed my hand and led me through the crowd,

veering toward a break in the booths. I had to quicken my pace to keep up. I was just about to ask where we were going when he pulled me around the corner of a building and stopped.

His hands slipped around my waist and his mouth came to mine. I wrapped my arms around his neck and he drew me against him. His kiss was deep and hungry, his tongue tasting faintly of wine. I ran my fingers through his hair and he held me close.

Kissing him felt so good, I didn't care if anyone walked by. He slid one hand down and squeezed my ass. My body pressed tighter against his and I felt the hard bulge of his erection. God, that was such a turn-on. He groaned into my mouth as I rubbed against him again. I loved making him do that. He was usually so relaxed, it was exhilarating to feel the urgency in his touch, the need in his kiss.

Edgar's leash went slack, but I could hear his tail thumping against the ground. William kept kissing me, finally getting bold with his hands. He lifted one side of my skirt and squeezed my ass again. I gasped, and he backed me up against the side of the building. His hand moved lower, lifting my leg, and his fingertips brushed the crease of my thigh.

I was on fire for him. My inhibitions burned away by the rising tension between us, I reached down and stroked his cock through his pants. He groaned again and moved his hand around to my front, sliding it between my legs. His fingers slipped beneath my soaked panties, pushing them to the side. Touched my desperately sensitive skin. I squeezed him again and he carefully dipped his fingertips into my pussy.

I shuddered with pleasure. He stroked me gently, his mouth never leaving mine. I wanted more. I wanted his fingers deep inside. I wanted friction and pressure. I rubbed his cock and moved my hips. He grunted, grazing his teeth across my lower lip.

Edgar's wet nose nudging my leg startled me back to reality. He barked, a short, quiet sound, and William pulled back. Took his hand out from between my legs. His cheeks were flushed, and he was breathing hard. He stared at me, his eyes full of lust.

A second later, footsteps and voices. I realized I still had my hand on William's erection. I gasped and let go to quickly smooth down my skirt. A small group of people walked by, heading away from the festival. Edgar stood guard, watching them pass with his ears at full attention.

William blinked slowly, like he was coming to after being unconscious. Desire still flowed hot through my veins, but the interruption had cooled me off enough to clear my head.

"Maybe we should get going," he said, his voice rough.

I nodded, still feeling dizzy. "Yeah."

In a daze, I followed William to his Jeep. Edgar got in the back and I opened the window, hoping the wind would cool me down. William held my hand as he drove, glancing at me out of the corner of his eye every so often, his mouth hooking in that enigmatic smile.

By the time we reached my house, I was rational again. I could still feel the tantalizing sensation of his fingers stroking me, but I was glad we'd been interrupted—even more so that Edgar had warned us first. I wanted William—I was so ready for this—but outside against a building was probably not the best place.

Although it *had* been thrilling. I'd never done anything like that before.

Edgar barked when we pulled into my driveway. I let him out of the car, but instead of running for the front door like usual, he stayed back and barked again.

"What's up, buddy?" I looked around, but didn't see

anything. There was no one else parked on the street nearby, no dogs or animals that might agitate him. I reached down and clipped on his leash, just in case he decided to bolt. "Do you see something?"

William looked down at Edgar. Their eyes met, and I could have sworn they shared a look of understanding. Edgar barked again.

We walked down the driveway to the front door. I unlocked it, but Edgar growled, and William stepped in front of me to go inside.

At first, nothing seemed amiss, and I was about to tell Edgar to hush. He kept growling. I looked through to the back of the house and realized the back door was broken—the glass smashed.

I gasped, and a surge of adrenaline made my hands and feet tingle. I clutched Edgar's leash and backed up toward the front door.

"Stay there," William said, his voice hard. He checked the back, then made a quick circuit of all the rooms. I heard doors opening and shutting. He was inspecting everything—rooms, bathrooms, closets. He went out to the garage and came back a moment later.

"Whoever it was, they're gone," he said.

I moved to where I could get a closer look at the back door. Jagged shards of glass lay everywhere, sparkling in the light. I held Edgar's leash tight, so he wouldn't step on any and cut his paws. I was hoping to see something that would explain the break—something other than an intruder. A tree limb, perhaps. But I knew that wasn't likely. The trees in my backyard weren't large, or close enough to have caused this.

William put his hand on the back of my neck and squeezed gently. "We should call the police."

I nodded, but I wanted to see what else was out of place. Had they stolen anything? Why had someone done this?

"Does it look like they stole anything?" I asked.

"Probably," he said. "They went through your bedroom, and your office."

"Oh my god." I handed Edgar's leash to him and went to check the other rooms.

He was right. My bedroom was torn apart. Drawers opened, their contents strewn all over the floor. Clothes and containers ripped out of the closet. My office was the same. Desk drawers emptied—pens, pencils, papers, and files everywhere.

"Was your laptop here?" William asked.

"No," I said. "I left it at work; I usually do on the weekends."

"That's good," he said. "Your TV is gone."

"I didn't even notice when we walked in," I said. "They probably took other stuff. It'll be hard to tell until I can get this all cleaned up."

A sick feeling spread through my stomach. I felt so violated. Someone had done this—been inside my home and gone through my things. I pulled out my phone and called the police. After I explained that the perpetrator was gone, they said they'd send someone out.

While I spoke to the police, William got Edgar some food and water. He put it by the front door, so Edgar wouldn't walk near the broken glass.

"Thank you," I said.

He slipped his arms around me and drew me close. Kissed the top of my head. "I'm so sorry this happened."

I leaned against his chest, letting the warmth of his body seep into me. I felt better—safer—in his arms.

"I should call Jessica and let her know what's going on," I said.

He kissed my head again and let go of me, but he stayed close. I brought up Jessica's number and called.

"Hey, Ivy," she said.

"Hey, listen, I'm okay, but someone broke into my house while I was out today."

"Oh my god," she said. "Do you need me to come over?"

"No, it's okay," I said. "I called the police and they're on their way."

"I'm coming," she said. "You shouldn't be alone."

"Really, you don't have to," I said. "I'm not alone. William is here."

"Oh," she said. "Was he with you when it happened?"

"Yeah," I said. "We were out with Edgar."

"Did they steal anything?" she asked.

"My TV," I said. "I'm not sure what else. I don't have much here that's worth stealing, but they certainly looked everywhere. It's a mess."

I heard the muffled sound of her talking to Peter.

"You should come over after you talk to the police," she said. "Stay with us tonight."

I met William's eyes and moved the phone away from my mouth. "She wants me to come stay with them tonight."

He shook his head. "No, you're coming home with me."

A wave of heat swirled in my core at the thought of spending the night with William. I shouldn't have been thinking that way. I'd just been robbed. But my cheeks flushed, and I took a deep breath, trying to ignore the very distracting rush of tingles between my legs.

I put the phone back to my ear. "Thanks, Jess, but I'll stay with William tonight."

"Are you sure that's a good idea?" she asked.

"Yes, I'm sure."

"Ivy…"

"Don't use your mom-voice on me," I said. "You don't even have kids."

"I don't have a mom-voice." She sounded offended.

"You absolutely do," I said. "I'm fine. Promise. I'll talk to the police and go to William's. Then I'll figure out what to do about the mess here."

"Okay," she said. "And don't come to work tomorrow. Take at least a couple of days off, okay?"

"Yeah, that's a good idea," I said.

"Call me if you need anything. And let me know what the police say."

"I will. Thanks, Jess."

A police officer arrived just after I ended the call. He inspected the house and took a report. He said it looked like a typical home invasion. The thief had probably been watching the house and waited until he saw us leave. My backyard was fenced, but the gate didn't lock, so it wouldn't have been difficult to get in and break the glass door. He'd gone through my things looking for valuables, and likely made off with anything he thought he could sell to make some quick cash.

After the officer left, I sent a message to my boss, and to Lisa, letting them know what had happened and that I needed a couple of days off to deal with it. Then William helped me clean up the glass. We found some plywood in the garage and boarded up the hole. I'd have to get someone out here to replace the door.

But for now, I was exhausted. I packed a bag with some extra clothes and a few essentials. William had already put Edgar's dog bed in his Jeep, along with his food and a bag of toys.

"Are you sure you don't mind?" I asked. "Edgar's a big dog. Can you have pets in your building?"

William shrugged. "I don't know. But I have space. It's fine."

I was too tired to worry about him getting in trouble with his landlord. The three of us got in his Jeep and left.

PAINTINGS

❧

William parked in the below-ground garage and grabbed my things to carry them upstairs. Edgar hopped out, alert to the newness of his surroundings. We followed William to the elevator and up to his floor.

I felt jittery, my hands trembling. Was it because of the break-in? Or because I was about to be inside William's apartment for the first time? Probably a combination of both.

He paused in front of his door and rubbed the back of his neck.

"Is everything okay?" I asked.

"Yeah." He got his keys out, but didn't unlock the door. "Sorry, I wasn't expecting to bring you here tonight, and I hadn't thought about…"

"If you're not comfortable letting us stay here, it's fine," I said. "I can always stay with Jessica and Peter."

"No," he said, "that's not it at all. I want you here. I just… wasn't quite ready."

"For me to see your apartment?" I asked. "If it's messy, don't worry, I won't judge you."

"No, it's clean. I just don't have people over very often." He finally unlocked the door. "It will be fine."

I wasn't sure if he was reassuring himself, or me. He let me in and Edgar paused to sniff things. I waited near the door while Edgar got used to the unfamiliar scents, and William flicked on a few lights.

His apartment was spacious, and sparsely furnished. He was right, it was clean. He had a couch facing a TV. A big window with closed blinds. A bookshelf stuffed full of books, and rows of movies in a cupboard below the TV. Another corner had a punching bag hanging from the ceiling.

Edgar tugged on the leash, so I walked deeper into the apartment. William stood near the couch, his hands stuffed in his pockets. His eyes were on me, his expression worried. I didn't understand what had him so nervous. Was it just me being in his apartment? It didn't seem like he had anything to be embarrassed about.

Then my eyes drifted to the walls. They were covered with paintings on stretched canvas. No frames, and the edges were a bit messy, with brush strokes of paint on the sides. Near the window he had an easel and a shelf of paint supplies.

"Do you paint?" I asked. "You painted all these?"

"Yes."

I looked more closely at the picture nearest to me. It was an ocean beach, beautifully done. It was so realistic, it seemed familiar. "They're gorgeous. Were you shy about letting me see them?"

William nodded, and the concern hadn't left his eyes.

"Why? They're amazing." I walked slowly through his apartment, still holding Edgar's leash. He was happy to sniff his way around. "I had no idea you were so talented."

I stopped in front of another, realizing it was the view

from Rattlesnake Ledge. "Is this new? Did you paint it after our hike?"

"No," he said.

"Oh," I said. "I thought you hadn't been there before."

He didn't answer, just kept watching me. I looked at the painting next to it. This one depicted a large tree with branches that sprawled over a creek. A swing hung down from a thick limb. He'd painted the ephemeral shape of a little girl sitting on the swing with an open book in her lap. It looked remarkably like the swing my dad had built in the backyard of my childhood home.

I looked at the other paintings. There was a familiarity to all of them. A birthday cake made to look like a castle, only parts of it were tilted—just like the cake my dad had tried to make for my ninth birthday. A room with a cluttered desk, the surface covered with haphazard piles of papers and stacks of books—so much like my dad's old office. A window with a white puppy peeking out. It reminded me of Edgar the first time I'd seen him.

It was uncanny, like walking into the gallery of my mind.

"William, what are these?" I asked.

"My paintings," he said, but he winced, like he knew that wasn't what I'd asked.

"Why did you paint these things?" I asked.

"They're things I see."

I looked at the tree again. It looked almost exactly like the tree in my memory. William had mentioned the tree as part of his proof—one of the things he knew about me.

"What do you mean, things you see? How do you see them?"

"They're my visions."

I realized then how many paintings he had. Dozens. Some were displayed on the walls. But he also had stacks of painted canvases leaning against each other near his easel.

"What do you mean by visions?" I asked.

"I see these things," he said. "Just like I paint them. They're in my mind like memories. But I know they're not mine."

"These look like things I know," I said. "That looks like Edgar when he was a puppy. And that tree… it looks like the one that was in my backyard."

He nodded.

"Are these about me?" I asked.

"Yes."

"All of them?"

He nodded again, his brow furrowed with worry.

My heart raced as I stared at his paintings. How was this possible? It was like he could see into my past—like he'd reached into my memories and pulled out the meaningful moments. Painted them.

"Is this how you know things about me?" I asked. "You have visions?"

"Some of it, yes," he said.

"Why did you paint them?" I asked.

"Because sometimes it feels like too much," he said. "I can't think straight. I can't remember things because all I can see are these visions. I painted them to see if it would help."

"Did it help?" I asked.

"Yes."

I took a few more slow steps, Edgar tugging on his leash. "How long have you been having visions about me?"

"As long as I can remember."

"What?" I asked. Edgar's ears twitched.

"That's not as long as you might think," he said.

"What do you mean?" I gripped Edgar's leash like I needed something to tether me to the ground. "You need to stop making me ask questions and explain what this is, William."

"Okay. About ten months ago, maybe a little more, I

found myself in a park in Seattle. This," he said, sweeping his hand to gesture at the paintings, "was all I knew. I knew my name was William Cole. And I knew I was supposed to find Ivy. I could see these things, these places. And others. Like a trail of breadcrumbs that would lead me to you. A puzzle I had to figure out."

I stared at him, horror-stricken. "You don't remember anything before that?"

"It's not that I don't remember," he said. "There isn't anything before that."

"What do you mean? There has to be something. You didn't just appear out of thin air."

"I don't know how I got to that park," he said. "But I wasted too much time worrying about it already. It's not important."

"What's more important than that?" I asked. "What happened to you? Were you in an accident? Are you telling me you lost your memory?"

"No, that's not what I'm telling you." He came closer. "I know who I am. I'm William Cole. And what's more important than that is you."

"William, this is insanity," I said.

"Is it really that hard to accept?" he asked. "I already told you, I know you. I know so many things about you. I just painted some of them."

It felt like the air had been sucked from my lungs. He *had* told me, but hearing it and seeing it were two very different things.

"William, this is overwhelming," I said.

"I know," he said. "I was worried it would scare you to see these. But Ivy, you don't have to be afraid."

"How can this be real?" I asked. "How can you have no past? How can you have *my* memories in your head? I don't understand."

"I don't understand it either. Not all of it, at least. But I don't think we're meant to." He came closer and took my hand. "This is what I do know: These visions led me to you. They were right, and they were true. And I think they're going to tell me what I need to know to keep you safe. And that's all I care about."

"Why?" I asked, my voice small in the space between us. "Why do you care about me so much?"

His face softened, the concern in his eyes melting away, and he squeezed my hand. "Because I know who you are on the inside. I know the woman who lives behind those eyes. And I will do anything to protect you."

He pulled me to him and I surrendered, collapsing against his chest. His arms around me felt so safe. He kissed the top of my head and rubbed slow circles across my back.

We stood there for a while, silent. I peeked out at the paintings, confused. Conflicted.

"It's getting late," he said, finally. "Do you want to get some sleep?"

I nodded. I was exhausted.

"You can have my bed. I'll sleep on the couch."

"You don't have to do that," I said. "I can sleep on the couch."

He touched my chin and kissed my lips. "No."

I smiled and put a hand on his chest. "Thank you."

William offered to take Edgar outside while I got ready for bed. I washed my face and brushed my teeth, then changed into the pajamas I'd brought—pink plaid shorts and a t-shirt with a moon on it.

When they got back, Edgar settled down on his dog bed in the corner of the bedroom. I felt a little twinge of apprehension at getting into William's bed. And the truth was, even with Edgar here, I was agitated and jumpy.

William stood in the doorway, leaning against the frame. "Do you need anything?"

I sank down onto the edge of the bed and swallowed hard, trying to stop the sudden flood of tears. I didn't want to cry. But everything came crashing in, overwhelming me. I put my hand over my mouth and took a shuddering breath.

He was by my side in an instant. As soon as his arms wrapped around me, I lost the ability to hold myself together. All the stress of the day came pouring out, tears spilling down my cheeks.

"I'm sorry," I said into his shoulder. "I don't mean to cry all over you."

He caressed my hair and kissed my head again. Without a word, he got up and turned off the light, then stripped down to a t-shirt and boxer briefs. He pulled back the covers and we both got in his bed. I settled in his arms, my head resting against his chest.

How could he be the source of so much confusion, and yet feel so *good*? After a few more trembling breaths, my tears stopped. I melted against the warmth of his body, basked in the feel of his muscular arms and strong chest. Regardless of everything that had happened, this was where I wanted to be. With William. In his bed, wrapped in his arms.

NEIGHBORLY FAVORS

*L*ight streaming in through the window woke me. I blinked and glanced at the bedside clock. It was almost nine. I couldn't remember the last time I'd slept so late. Edgar usually needed to go outside before seven, but he wasn't in the room. Neither was William. He must have been up early, and taken Edgar outside for me.

I'd slept better than I had in years. William's bed was comfortable, but it was him that had made the difference. He'd held me for most of the night, first with my head against his chest and his arms around me. Later I'd woken up and found myself on my side with him curled up behind me, his arm draped over my waist. His breathing had been rhythmic and slow against my back, lulling me to sleep again.

I got up and used his bathroom, wondering if he was home. It was so quiet. He might have gone for a run, or to the gym. I slipped on a long cardigan and went out to find him.

He was standing behind his easel, shirtless and barefoot in a pair of paint-splattered gray sweats. God, his body was phenomenal. He was lean and muscular, but more than that, he looked strong. Like his muscles were for more than just looks—like he knew how to use them.

His dark hair was carelessly messy, and he had a spot of green paint on his cheek, just above his stubble. He didn't look up when I approached, his eyes intent on his painting. He tilted his head to the side, then applied a few strokes with a paint brush.

Edgar lay nearby. His ears twitched, and he blinked his eyes open to look at me. Then he huffed out a breath and went back to sleep.

"Good morning." I kept a little distance, not sure if he wanted me to see what he was working on.

His smile lit up his face. "Hi, beautiful."

I nibbled on my bottom lip and tucked my hair behind my ear. Hearing him say that gave me a tingly feeling in my tummy. "Hi."

"How did you sleep?"

"Really good," I said. "Thanks for taking care of Edgar this morning."

"Sure," he said. "I was awake, so I figured I'd let you sleep in."

"That was nice. I think I needed it." I stepped closer. "Can I see what you're working on?"

He looked at his canvas, then back at me. "Sure. It's close to being finished."

I went around to where I could see it. He'd painted a red brick building, the façade covered in thick green ivy. The landscape around it was hazy and indistinct, but many of his paintings were like that. It was as if certain things stood out in his mind while the rest were fuzzy.

"What is it?" I asked.

"I don't know," he said. "I thought maybe you could tell me."

"This is from one of your visions?" I asked.

"Yes," he said. "One of the most vivid. I see this building all the time. You don't recognize it?"

I moved around him, so I could look at it from another angle. It was a beautiful building. But it didn't seem even vaguely familiar.

"No," I said. "I don't think I've ever seen it before."

"Are you sure?"

"Positive," I said. "I'd remember a place like this. It's beautiful. But I don't think I've ever seen it."

He put his palette and paint brush down. "Can I show you more of them? I don't want to freak you out, but I thought you'd recognize all of them. I want to see if there are more that are unfamiliar. That might be important."

"Sure," I said with a shrug. I didn't know if I'd ever be able to explain how he could see these things, but at this point it wasn't doing me any good to dwell on the impossibility of it all. He *had* painted them, and other than this one, they were things I knew. Figuring out *how* would have to wait.

He pulled out the canvases that were leaning against the wall. Flipping through them, he showed me each one. I was able to easily identify them all. A park with a twisty slide I remembered from childhood. I'd been afraid to go down it and my dad had bought me an ice cream cone after I'd finally conquered my fear. A girl in the backseat of a car, surrounded by teddy bears and books—just like the time Dad and I had taken a road trip to California. Marshmallows over a campfire. My dad had engineered what he believed was the perfect roasting stick.

There were more, and in every case, I knew exactly what, or where, they were. All except the brick building.

William put his hands on his hips and stared at the painting. "Something must be wrong with it. Maybe I don't have it right."

"Or maybe it's something else," I said. "Maybe it's one of *your* memories."

"No, I've never seen this building," he said.

"Well, what if there are things you can't remember?"

He met my eyes. "That isn't what this is. I'm sure of it."

Before I could respond there was a knock at his door.

"I'll be right back." He leaned in for a quick kiss, then went to answer it.

"Hi, William." An unreasonably attractive woman in a blouse and skirt stood just outside his door. She had a little boy perched on her hip. He was probably about three, with brown hair and bright blue eyes. "Oliver's babysitter is sick. I have to go into the office and I'm already late. Is there any way you could watch him again?"

I stared at her while she talked to William, my blood running hot with jealousy at the way William smiled at her.

He turned to me. "Do you mind?"

"No, not at all," I said, struggling to keep my voice even.

William opened the door wider, inviting them in. I lingered near the back of his apartment, feeling awkward in my pajamas and cardigan, with no makeup and messy hair. Especially because her hair was shiny and perfect, and her clothes looked like they'd been custom tailored for her body —and what a body it was. Her eyes took in William's exquisite torso and I wanted to launch myself across the room.

"Ivy, this is Stella and Oliver," he said. "They live next door."

"Hi," I said.

"Oh my god, I'm so sorry," she said, adjusting her son on her hip. "I didn't realize you had a guest. I can figure out something else."

"No, it's okay," William said in that matter-of-fact tone of

126

his. "Oliver can stay. You get to work. I know how busy you are."

"You are the best," she said, beaming at William again. She put Oliver down. "I owe you for this."

Owe him what, exactly? I hated how jealous I felt, but this woman was gorgeous. Knowing she was William's neighbor —and they obviously knew each other fairly well—made me envious beyond reason.

"Before I forget," William said, "you left something last time you were here. Let me go get it."

He disappeared into his bedroom and my jealousy reached rage-inducing levels. What had she left here that would be in his *bedroom*?

"William is so amazing," Stella said. "He's such a sweetheart. And Oliver just loves him."

"Yeah," I said, trying desperately to keep the burning envy out of my voice. "William is great."

He returned with a book and handed it to her. "Here."

"Thanks, I totally forgot you had this. And thank you again for watching Oliver." She stepped in and wrapped her arms around him. He hugged her back and I dug my fingernails into my palms. "I'll see you later."

She crouched down to talk to her son, reminding him to be good for Mr. William. After kissing him goodbye, she gave William one last stupidly beautiful smile, and left.

William closed the door behind her and ruffled Oliver's hair. "Did you have breakfast?"

The kid nodded.

"Do you want to watch cartoons?" he asked.

Oliver nodded again, then ran over and climbed onto the couch.

Edgar sniffed in Oliver's direction while William turned on the TV. He seemed to deem him unimportant for the time being, and went back to his nap.

William came over and tucked my hair behind my ear again. Beautiful neighbor or no, it was hard to feel anything but a little wave of giddiness when he did that.

"Thanks," he said. "He probably won't be here all day. He usually isn't. Can I get you breakfast?"

"It's fine," I said. Oliver *was* a cute kid. He looked a little bit like William. I coughed and started walking to the kitchen to cover the renewed wave of jealousy that hit me at that thought. "I'll just have some coffee for now, if you have any."

"I'll make you some," he said.

"That's okay, I can do it."

He smiled and followed me into the kitchen, casting a glance at Oliver, who sat happily watching cartoons.

We moved around the kitchen together, William pulling things out of cupboards and handing them to me. I realized I was being silly by insisting I make the coffee. He was the one who knew where everything was. But I needed to *do* something. The combination of jealousy and being in close quarters with a shirtless William was making my head spin.

"So, how long have you known Stella?" I asked when the coffee was brewing.

"She lived here before I did," he said.

"Do you know a lot of your neighbors?"

"Not really."

That wasn't the answer I'd wanted. What was so special about her? I focused my gaze on the coffee pot, trying to ignore William's broad chest and the lines of his abs. I knew I was being ridiculous. He'd told me he'd liked it when I used the term *boyfriend*. We hadn't talked about it outright, but we were exclusive. Weren't we? He couldn't have something casual on the side with one of his neighbors. Could he?

I wasn't giving William enough credit. That didn't seem like him. Plus, I already knew William was the type of man who liked to help people. I'd seen him bring groceries to an elderly woman, and a sandwich to a homeless man. Why wouldn't he be willing to help out a single mother? That was a good thing.

And it wasn't as if he had Stella's memories decorating his walls. Points to Ivy for that one.

I managed to keep my foolish jealousy to a low simmer all morning. William was good with Oliver. But then William was good with people in general, so it wasn't surprising. He didn't talk to him like a little kid—just spoke as if he was a regular, grown person. Always with that relaxed, calm tone he used with everyone.

After Oliver's show was over, we took Edgar for a walk. Oliver wanted to play with him, but Edgar made it clear he was not interested in the small human. He didn't growl, just turned his head away like the snob he was. William distracted Oliver by giving him a shoulder ride while I held Edgar's leash.

I realized as we walked that we probably looked like a little family—two parents with their son and their dog. Indulging in the fantasy made me blush, but it was definitely enjoyable. William glanced at me a few times, that half-smile playing on his lips, and I wondered what he was thinking.

When we got back, William made lunch for Oliver—a peanut butter and jelly sandwich cut into triangles. I felt a little pouty, wondering why he kept peanut butter and jelly on hand. Did he eat that himself, or were they for when Stella and Oliver came over?

Rather than sit at the table pondering the nature of William's relationship—past or present—with Stella, I excused myself and went to his bedroom. I still needed to call my insurance company about the break-in. And I was making myself crazy. Getting jealous because he had peanut butter and jelly?

I was feeling fiercely territorial. But I knew my jealousy

wasn't fueled by antagonism toward Stella. It was a sign of how deep my feelings for William ran. Despite all the strangeness surrounding him and his entrance into my life—the way he'd stalked me, how he knew things he shouldn't, his visions now on canvas all over his apartment—I was falling for him. Hard.

FIRST

❧

I called my insurance company, then checked in with my boss. She was glad to hear from me, and said it was fine if I took a few days off to deal with everything. That was a relief. I still had to clean up the disaster that was my house, figure out what else had been stolen, and get the back door fixed.

My stomach still felt a little sick at the thought of someone being in my home. Would they have tried to break in if I'd been there? Would Edgar have been enough of a deterrent? I couldn't be sure, but I resolved to look into home security systems.

When I came out, Oliver was finishing up his sandwich. William sat next to him at the table, flipping through a book. I wandered over to his bookshelf and scanned the titles. He had an interesting mix. Books about myths and legends, religions—both modern and ancient—and several about other forms of spirituality. A number of them were about angels.

Picking one up, I thumbed through the pages. Was he simply interested in topics of religion and spirituality? Or was he looking for answers in these books? I suspected he was searching for meaning. For evidence that his own story was true. I wondered if he'd found anything.

There was a knock at his door and I put the book back on the shelf while William got up to answer it.

Oliver jumped down from the table. "Daddy!"

A tall man in a button-down shirt and slacks crouched down while Oliver ran to him. If I'd thought Oliver bore a resemblance to William, I didn't anymore. This man was like a grown-up clone. He had to be Oliver's father.

"Hey, kiddo." He picked up Oliver and smiled at William. "Thanks again, man. Stella won't be home until later tonight, so I got off early."

"No problem," William said.

"We owe you," he said. "Ollie, can you thank Mr. William?"

"Thank you," Oliver said.

"Sure." William ruffled his hair again.

Oliver's dad seemed to notice me for the first time. His eyebrows lifted, and he grinned at William, giving him an approving nod.

William glanced over at me, then grinned back at him, like they'd just shared a virtual bro-fist. "See you guys later."

I gaped at them as they left, and William shut the door.

"That was Oliver's dad?" I asked.

"Yeah."

"Stella's husband?"

"Of course."

I smoothed down my hair and tried to act casual. But inside I was kicking myself for being so ridiculous. Stella wasn't even single, and I'd had my panties in a bunch over her for half the day. "They seem nice."

"Yeah, they are." He narrowed his eyes at me, his mouth turning up in that subtle smile. "You were jealous, weren't you?"

"What? No." I crossed my arms and walked toward his bedroom. I wasn't sure why, exactly, except I wanted to hide my suddenly flaming hot cheeks.

William's footsteps followed behind me. "Yes, you were." His voice was amused.

I stopped next to the bed. "No, why would I be jealous?"

He moved in close behind me, putting his hands on my arms. I froze. When he spoke, his mouth was next to my ear, his voice low. "You don't need to be. But I like it."

"You do?"

"Ivy, I'm jealous of everyone who's ever been near you." He gathered my hair in his hand and pulled it to the side, keeping it tight in his fist. "Everyone who's touched you or held you. Who thought, even for a moment, that they could call you theirs. Because you weren't. You were always meant to be mine."

He leaned in and pressed his lips to my neck. That simple kiss lit up my entire body, awakening the desire slumbering in my core. I tilted my head and he kissed the sensitive skin at the base of my neck, working his way up to the soft hollow behind my ear.

One arm slid around my waist, drawing me into him. I arched my back, pressing my ass against his groin. He groaned, pulling on my hair to bare more of my neck to him. He kissed me harder, his warm tongue sliding against my sensitive skin.

He spun me around and pushed me down onto his bed. Crawled on top of me, hiking my skirt up around my hips. His mouth caressed mine, languid strokes of his lips. Flicks of his tongue. I slipped my hands beneath his shirt and ran them up his back, feeling the hard planes of muscle, his warm skin.

Shifting, he pressed his groin between my legs. I moaned as his erection rubbed against me. Our clothes were thin—

just his sweats and my panties between us. I could feel his hard length, solid and needy. He started to move, thrusting his hips, grinding into me.

Soft kisses became frantic. He growled low in the back of his throat with every thrust. I pulled his shirt up, yanking it over his head. I needed more of him. More skin, more contact. He took my shirt off and tossed it to the side. His eyes moved over me as I lay beneath him in my lace bra.

"You're so beautiful." He touched my face, tracing down my cheek to my neck. Moved his hand along my shoulder and slid my bra strap down my arm. His finger slipped beneath the top of the lace cup and he gently pushed it down, revealing my hard nipple.

Cupping my breast, he slid his tongue over the hard peak and I shuddered. He pressed his cock between my legs while he sucked on my nipple.

"Oh my god, William," I breathed. "I want you inside me. I want you now."

He paused, breathing hard, and looked into my eyes. "Do we need protection? I don't have anything."

I practically whimpered in disappointment. "Are you sure?"

The corner of his mouth twitched, and a look of nervousness passed across his features. "I'm sure. I wasn't prepared to have you here. And… I've never done this before."

"What do you mean? You've never…"

"No," he said, his voice so serious. "I've never wanted anyone else. I told you, I've had you in my mind for as long as I can remember. It's always been you, Ivy. Only you."

I grabbed the back of his head and brought his mouth to mine. In the back of my mind I knew this probably wasn't his first time. That there had to be something before last year—a past he couldn't remember. But it didn't matter. He was like a clean slate, untainted and unspoiled. And the idea of being his first—the first for the man he was now—was intensely erotic.

"Do it anyway," I said into his ear. "Just a little bit. You can pull out, but I want to feel you inside me."

"Are you sure?"

"Yes," I said. "Please. I need you."

He nodded, and we pulled off the rest of our clothes. We paused for a moment, staring at each other. His body was gorgeous, a perfect mixture of hard lines and soft skin. He looked athletic and lean, with his broad chest, ripped arms, and deliciously defined abs. He slid his underwear off and my heart fluttered, the heat between my legs sparking. His cock was as beautiful as the rest of him. Long and thick, it stood straight up, the tip framed by the muscular Adonis belt cutting between his hips.

Settling between my legs, he kept the tip of his cock right at my opening. His skin was hot on mine, his weight on my hips tantalizing. He met my gaze, his intense blue eyes locked with mine. I put my hands against the sides of his face.

He pushed his cock in, slowly. Tenderly. His eyes rolled back, and he groaned, the sound coming from deep in his chest. He stretched me open, his thickness filling me. I was so wet the only resistance was the tightness of my pussy around his cock.

"Oh fuck, Ivy," he said, his voice strained. He pushed in farther, as deep as he could go, and held there. "You feel so good."

All I could do was nod. Even without rhythm or friction, just the pressure of his cock had me speechless. It had been a long time for me—long enough that this all felt deliciously new. He touched his forehead to mine and I held him tight, reveling in the intensity of this moment. Nothing I'd experienced had ever felt this perfect. This real.

"I need to fuck you," he said, his lips brushing against mine. "I'll stop before I come, but I need to."

"Yes." My pussy was hot with desire. I needed him to fuck me or I was going to go crazy.

He slid out and plunged back in. Slow and deep, taking his time. Whether he had experience or not, his body knew exactly what to do. He thrust his hips, flexed his glutes. Drove into me with a steadily increasing rhythm.

I closed my eyes and let him have me. Massaged my fingers into his muscular back. Heat spread through my core, my pussy tightening around him. I moved my hips to take him deeper and he groaned, his pace increasing.

Grabbing his tight ass, I let my legs fall open wider and pushed against him, grinding him into me with each thrust. He fucked me harder. Deeper. He moved faster, the intensity increasing. The heat in my pussy built, my wetness making us both slick.

The pressure grew, my clit and pussy pulsing with the need to climax. He sucked on my neck, still thrusting hard. I whimpered and moaned, my mouth near his ear. I clutched at him, swept away by the heat of his body melding with mine, the feel of his thick cock inside me.

Suddenly, he stopped, his cock buried deep. His chest moved fast, pressed against mine. "Baby, I have to stop, or I'll come."

I grabbed his ass and held him inside me. "No, don't stop," I whispered. "Just a little more."

He groaned again, a low throaty sound that made my blood run hot with lust. I pressed against his ass so he couldn't pull out and bucked my hips against him. Begging him for more.

Then he unleashed.

His hips drove hard, thrusting his cock deep inside. Over and over while he grunted into my neck. I knew what I was doing, knew he would come, and I didn't care. I wanted it. I wanted him to lose himself inside me, pour every bit of himself into me.

One more hard thrust and I came undone. I burst apart beneath him, waves of pleasure rolling through my body. I called out, uninhibited, my body moving with his.

Just when I thought it was over—that I'd peaked—he stiffened, and his cock throbbed. He drove into me, groaning, and one orgasm rolled right into another. I rode the high as he came inside me, his muscles flexing, his voice low in my ear.

He paused, still deep inside me, as we both caught our breath. I ran my fingers gently up and down his back, caressing his warm skin. He kissed my neck, then my cheeks. Kissed me over and over until I giggled beneath him.

"That was amazing," he whispered in my ear.

"For me too."

He brushed my hair back from my face and those captivating blue eyes held mine. I thought he might say something, but he just stared, then kissed me again.

I got up to use the bathroom, then came back to bed. He gathered me in his arms and held me close.

"This feels good," he said.

"*Love comforteth like sunshine after rain.*" I clicked my mouth closed. Never mind that I was once again vomiting out literature quotes—Shakespeare this time—I'd said *love*. About us. Were we ready for that?

"What's wrong?" he asked.

"Nothing, just me babbling again. Sorry."

He rolled me onto my back and leaned over me, his eyes fierce. "Why are you apologizing?"

"I don't know," I said. "Someone told me once that using other people's words too often makes it sound like I can't think of anything original to say."

"And what do you think?"

"I think… some things have been said with such beautiful words, why not borrow them and revisit their beauty and meaning?"

A slow smile crossed his face, deepening his dimples. "I love you."

"You do?" I blinked, knowing that wasn't the right thing to say. But he kissed my forehead before I could backtrack.

"Ivy, I loved you before I ever laid eyes on you," he said. "And when I did see you? When I saw how beautiful you are? God, I wanted to lie down at your feet and worship you. I wanted to tell you everything. How you consume every piece of me. How I feel like my soul isn't mine, it's simply a part of yours, and I'll never be complete without you. But you had no idea who I was. I knew so much about you, but I was a stranger. And every day since, I've been waiting for the moment when I could finally tell you how I feel."

I stared at him, feeling the depth of his words. Knowing their truth. I put my hand alongside his face. "I love you, too."

Smiling again, he took a deep breath. Then kissed me, soft and slow. We settled back into the softness of his bed and basked in the glow of happiness. Of feelings shared, and the relief of knowing we were exactly where we were meant to be.

MUTUAL SUSPICION

We spent the afternoon in bed, our bodies tangled together. He held me in his arms, tracing circles on my skin with his thumb. I felt so close to him. He filled the void inside me that had gaped so wide and dark after losing my dad.

It was more than just his physical presence next to me, or even his arms holding me tight. I knew what it was like to be surrounded by people, and still feel terribly alone. With William, I felt connected again—no longer disassociated from the world.

Enjoying his warmth, I relaxed against his strong body until Edgar whined outside the bedroom door. William kissed me and said he'd take him outside—I could take my time.

I watched him get up and pull on his sweats. God, he was gorgeous. He put on a t-shirt and ran his hands through his hair, then smiled at me over his shoulder. I bit my bottom lip and smiled back, feeling a little drunk. William was more potent than any drink I'd ever had.

He left, and I closed my eyes, letting out a long breath.

I felt amazing—relaxed, warm, and happy. A pleasant ache between my legs. I lingered in bed for a while, still basking in the glow of that long-awaited orgasm. When I heard William return with Edgar, I figured I should get up.

I put my bra and panties back on. My shirt was on the floor nearby, but I grabbed one of William's and brought it to my nose. It smelled like him, and I couldn't resist putting it on. The soft cotton fabric caressed my skin. I lifted the collar to my face again and inhaled. He smelled so good, I wanted to wear this every day, just so I could keep his scent with me all the time.

Looking over to the side, I caught a glimpse of myself in the mirror. My long blond hair was down, tousled and wavy. My cheeks pink. Dressed in a man's shirt with my hair a little messy, I looked exactly like I felt—like I'd been properly fucked.

I liked this look on me.

Edgar's paws scraped against the hardwood floor. A few seconds later, someone knocked.

"Uh oh," I muttered to myself. I dug through my bag and found a pair of leggings, then tugged them on as quickly as I could. I heard William answer the door.

"Edgar, sit," William said. "It's okay, he's just protective of his mama. Come on in."

I peeked out of the bedroom. William held the door open with Edgar sitting next to him, his ears twitching.

A man in a black shirt with the sleeves cuffed stepped inside, and William shut the door. He was probably in his mid-thirties with thick hair and a beard. He carried a worn brown leather briefcase.

I moved closer, wondering if I should come introduce myself, or wait.

"His mama?" the man asked.

William looked at me and smiled that radiant kill-me-now smile. "Yeah. James, this is Ivy."

James gaped at me as I walked toward them, his eyes widening. His mouth moved like he was trying to speak, but nothing came out.

"Ivy, this is my friend James," William said, apparently oblivious to his friend's shock.

I stepped next to William, suddenly self-conscious of my she's-been-properly-fucked appearance. William gently rubbed his hand up and down my back—a gesture that was somehow both sweet and intensely possessive.

"It's nice to meet you." I started to wonder why James was staring at me like that. Did I have something on my face? Had I forgotten to put on my bra and my nipples were showing? I fidgeted just for the reassurance of the underwire against my ribs.

James blinked. "I'm sorry. Did you say this is Ivy?"

"Yes," William said.

"*The* Ivy?" James asked.

It was dawning on me that James *knew*. William must have told him about me.

"Of course," William said. "Who else would I have in my apartment?"

"Right," James said, still sounding confused.

"Come on in," William said, as if none of that had been the least bit strange. He went back toward the kitchen, leading me with a light touch on my back. "I was just about to cook dinner. Are you hungry?"

"No, I'm fine." James followed us in and set his briefcase down on the table. "I'm sorry, I didn't mean to interrupt. I've been out of town, so I have some things to go over with you."

"You're not interrupting," William said. "It has been a while, hasn't it? I'm glad you finally get to meet Ivy."

"Me too," James said, casting another bewildered glance

at me.

I took a seat on one of the stools by the counter. Edgar still sat near the front door, his body alert, his eyes on James.

William opened the fridge, then looked back at me. "I was going to make asparagus risotto with lemon. But I'm out of lemons."

"That's okay," I said. "You don't need to cook. We could just grab something later."

He narrowed his eyes, regarding me with a furrowed brow for a few seconds. "No, I definitely need to cook you dinner. James, I have to run down to the market."

James sat at the table, pulling some paperwork out of his briefcase. He glanced up. "Um… okay."

"I'll be right back." William smiled, dimples and all, and leaned in to give me a quick kiss.

Edgar padded over to me and sat, putting himself between me and James. William winked at him. He kissed me again as he walked past, then slipped on a pair of shoes and left.

James and I looked at each other, the awkwardness practically filling the room.

"I'm sorry," James said. "I just… well, to be really blunt, I didn't think you existed. Your name is really Ivy?"

I nodded. "Ivy Nichols."

"Are you… you know, *his* Ivy?" he asked. "The Ivy he's been talking about?"

"Apparently so."

"How did you meet him?" he asked.

"I think it would be more accurate to say William *found* me," I said.

"And he told you his story," he said. "About why he was looking for you."

I nodded.

He crossed his arms and looked at me for a moment.

"How do I know you're not just playing him?"

"Excuse me?"

"Look, I'm not trying to be an asshole, but William is… different. He's been obsessed with finding someone named Ivy for as long as I've known him. Maybe your name really is Ivy. But he could have met you, found out your name, and suddenly he's convinced you're the one. The guy's smart, but if you're pretending to be this woman he thinks he's going to find—"

"Wait," I said, holding up a hand. "First of all, I didn't seek him out. He saw me in a coffee shop and started stalking me. And I'm not pretending to be anything. He's the one who knows the story of my life."

"Or you're going along with it, telling him he's right about the things he thinks he knows," he said.

"Why on earth would I do that?"

He raised his eyebrows and his gaze flicked up and down, like he was noting that I was dressed in William's shirt. "You've seen him. You pretend to be his Ivy, you get *him*."

I was torn between being offended and a little bit grateful that James was looking out for William. I'd been suspicious of James, too.

"Did he tell you what the paintings are?" I asked.

"Yeah," James said, his brow creasing. "He said they're *visions*."

I pointed to the painting of the puppy. "That's Edgar the first time I saw him. He was being fostered by a couple who lived in a house with a big front window. I wasn't sure about getting a dog. My dad talked me into it. But as soon as I saw him peeking out the window at me, I knew he was mine."

James looked over at Edgar, then back at the painting. "Okay. So he painted a white puppy, and you have a white dog."

"That's my dad's office when I was little," I said, pointing to another one. "The one there is the tree in my backyard where I grew up. My dad built that swing. That one's the blanket my mother crocheted when she was pregnant with me. I still have it at home. It looks exactly like he painted it. I know them all."

"Holy shit," James said under his breath.

"I know," I said. "I can't explain it. It's like looking at a gallery of my memories."

"You're telling me this is all real?" he asked.

I shrugged. "I don't know how. All I can say is that he knows a million things about me, and they're all true."

"I didn't think William could keep surprising me, but apparently I underestimated him," he said.

"You didn't believe him, did you?"

James let out a breath and looked around at the paintings again. "I don't know. Can you really believe a person when he says he's searching for someone he's never met, but he has visions that will lead him to her?" He paused. "But he was right?"

"Yeah," I said. "At least, the things he knows about me are. His paintings are things I recognize."

"Wow," James said, rubbing his temples. "I feel like I have to rethink my entire outlook on existence."

"*We can only know that we know nothing. And that is the highest degree of human wisdom*," I said.

James raised his eyebrows at me.

"Tolstoy, *War and Peace*. Sorry. I know what you mean. He walked into my world already knowing my life story. Displaying it on his walls."

"That is a head trip," he said. "But… here you are."

I smiled. "Yeah. Here I am. How long have you known him?"

"I met him about… nine months ago? Maybe a little more?"

"Did you really ask to take his picture and then find him again and turn him into a model?"

James chuckled. "That's... yeah, that's pretty much it. I saw him and there was something about his face. He has a great bone structure, but he looks so..."

"Innocent?"

"Yeah, only not, which is such a contradiction. But I guess that's what makes his face so interesting. When I was processing the pictures later, I kicked myself for not finding out who he was. I went back to the same park a few days later, and sure enough, he was there. I guess I got lucky. I arranged to do a proper photo shoot and it didn't take long before I had interest in his photos."

"Wow," I said. "Did he live here then?"

"No, I don't know where he was living at the time," he said. "After I sold his first photos, I helped him get set up here, in this place. I know the guy who owns the unit."

"That was nice of you," I said.

He shrugged. "He needed more hand-holding when I first met him than he does now. He wasn't as... lucid. He had a hard time remembering things, but he's improved a lot."

"Is there something wrong with him?"

"Other than the fact that he paints visions that are apparently your memories?" he asked with a little smile. "I don't know. William is just... William. He's a little odd, but whatever issues he was having with his memory seemed to have gone away as far as I can tell. He's still a mystery, though. No past. No ID."

"What do you mean, no ID?" I asked.

"He doesn't have any identification," he said. "No birth certificate, Social Security number, driver's license. Nothing."

"But how does he function without ID?" I asked.

James glanced down at the papers in front of him. "I handle everything for him. The apartment and utilities are in my name. His Jeep is, too. I come over once in a while to go over everything, so he knows I'm not screwing him over, but he never pays attention. I still do it, though."

"But he drives."

"Yeah, I know. I told him he could get in trouble for it. He just shrugs and says it doesn't matter."

That sounded like William. "Do you know where he's from?"

"No idea," he said. "According to him, he's not from anywhere."

"He told me that, too. Do you think he has amnesia?"

"It's possible," James said. "The thing is, I don't think he's lying. He really believes his own story. As far as the truth? I don't know. I wondered about his past more when I first met him, but I kind of stopped trying to figure it out. It just agitated him when I asked too many questions. I suggested he see a doctor once and he looked at me like I was nuts. Said he wasn't sick."

I shifted on the stool. Edgar had laid down, but his ears were still perked up.

"Why do you do all this stuff to help him?" I asked. "It must be a lot of work to handle all his finances and everything. Does he pay you for it?"

"He does," he said. "He insists on it. Although it's the least I can do. My career was going well before I met him, but he helped me take things to the next level. It's in my best interest to make sure he's taken care of. But to be honest, the money isn't why I do it. William is…"

"He's William," I finished for him.

"Yeah," he said. "I don't know what it is about that guy. At first I just wanted to help him get settled. He was so distracted by… well, you. He hardly paid attention to anything else. I didn't know what was going on with him—if he'd lost his memory, or if he was hiding from something.

But then I got to know him. He's a good guy. Whatever his story really is, I didn't want him getting tangled up with the authorities."

"And now he models exclusively for you?" I asked.

James nodded.

"You pay him fairly for that?" I asked. "Seems like no one would know if you didn't."

"Look, I think we're both on Team William," he said. "But if he says it's okay, you can look over everything."

"Sorry, it just seems like the wrong person could take advantage of him."

"Yeah, I know. That's part of why I do all this."

I glanced around at the paintings again. "Do you think it's possible he's right? That he doesn't have a past? He just winked into existence with all this stuff in his head?"

He shook his head. "At this point, hell if I know. I didn't think Ivy was a real person, but apparently I'm looking at her. So who knows about the rest of it."

We talked for a little while longer. He asked me what I did for a living and a few more questions about the paintings. It wasn't long before William returned carrying a grocery bag. He set it on the counter and started pulling things out.

"I didn't realize you knew how to cook," James said.

"YouTube," William said with a shrug. "You can learn anything on the Internet."

James didn't stay long. I helped stir the risotto while he went over William's finances. Then he packed up his briefcase and left.

William came up behind me and slipped his hands around my waist. Leaned in and kissed my neck, just below my ear. "Will you stay another night?"

The sparkling tension between my legs was back. I turned and pressed my lips to his neck, then grazed his skin with my teeth, earning me a low groan deep in his throat. "I'd love to."

QUESTIONS

*W*illiam took me home the next morning and helped me clean up the mess. We went through my house, sorting and putting things away. Whoever had broken in had stolen the usual things thieves target—mostly electronics and other items they could sell. It looked like they'd gone through drawers trying to find cash or jewelry. Fortunately, I didn't have any of that at home. My dad had given me my mother's wedding ring, but I kept it in a safety deposit box, along with all the paperwork from my dad's estate.

I had to go back to work, but William insisted on staying the night with me. I certainly wasn't going to argue. I came home that afternoon to find him installing a new back door. I hesitated in the doorway before he heard me and watched him work. He was so sexy. There was something about a man who was good with his hands.

He'd also installed cameras at my front and back doors, as well as motion-activated lights. He showed me how to access the camera feeds from my phone, and he could check them from his too. That made me feel a little safer.

He went home, but between the cameras, the lock he'd installed on my back gate, and Edgar, I felt safe. I did have trouble sleeping, but it wasn't due to fear. I missed him— missed the warmth of his body next to mine. The feel of his arms around me, his lips on my skin.

The next day at work I was still busy catching up. I had papers to grade, which was always time-consuming, and a number of my students stopped by my office asking for help on their latest assignments.

Mid-afternoon, a man appeared in my doorway. He was dressed in a nondescript polo and slacks. "Are you Ivy Nichols?"

"Yes."

"I'm Eric Andrews from Homeland Security Investigations." He pulled out his wallet and flashed his ID. "Can I speak to you for a few minutes?"

I closed my laptop, not bothering to disguise the confusion on my face. "I suppose so. Is something wrong?"

He came in and closed the door behind him, then pulled up a chair on the other side of my desk. Leaning back, he pitched his fingers together. "Do you know a man who goes by the name of William Cole?"

A sick feeling wormed its way through my stomach. "Yes."

"What can you tell me about him?"

"I'm not sure what you mean," I said. "Is William in some kind of trouble?"

"I'm just looking for some basic information," he said. "Do you know where he lives?"

"Yes," I said, and he raised his eyebrows, gesturing for me to continue. "He has an apartment near Westlake."

"How long has he lived there?"

"I'm not sure," I said.

"What about family?" he asked.

"He doesn't have any family."

"None?" he asked. "Are you sure?"

I sighed. "Yes, I'm sure. And I'm the same. I have no living relatives. It happens."

"Has he said anything about having moved recently?" he asked. "Do you know how long he's been in the area?"

"I don't know."

"What does he do for a living?" he asked.

"He's a model," I said.

"Does he have an agent?"

I didn't want to get into the intricacies of his arrangement with James. "I don't really know. Have you talked to William?"

"Does he speak any foreign languages?" he asked.

"Not that I know of. Can you tell me what this is about? Has William done something?"

"That's what I'm trying to find out." He stood and pulled a business card out of his pocket, then set it on my desk. "Just in case."

"Just in case what?"

"I apologize for being vague," he said. "Sometimes that's the nature of my job. Keep that. If you need to call me, don't hesitate. Thanks for your cooperation."

He walked out of my office, leaving me bewildered. What had just happened? I slid the business card across my desk. *If you need to call me, don't hesitate.* Why would I need to call Homeland Security about William?

The things I didn't know about William pinged through my mind. He said he had no past—that nothing came before last year. I knew something had to have come before, but what? Who was he? James had said he had no documented identity. No birth certificate, Social Security number, nothing. I hadn't pushed him for details about his past, but what was going on that Homeland Security was involved?

I got up and shut my door, then called William.

"Hi, Ivy," he said.

Just the sound of his voice eased the knot of anxiety in the pit of my stomach. "Hey. I'm sorry to bother you in the middle of the day."

"No, you're never bothering me."

"Something odd just happened." I walked over to the small window and looked out.

"Are you okay?" he asked.

"Yes, I'm fine."

"Are you sure?" he asked. "Are you at work? I can be there in twenty minutes."

"No, I'm okay, you don't need to come," I said. "But someone from Homeland Security was just here. Do you know anything about that?"

"No," he said. "What happened?"

"A man came to my office and asked me questions about you."

"About me?" He sounded genuinely confused. "Did he say why?"

"He wouldn't tell me," I said. "He asked what I knew about you. If you had family. How long you've lived in the area. What you do for a living. That kind of thing."

"Did you answer his questions?"

"Yeah," I said.

"Good."

"I was thinking… James told me you don't have any identification. If that's true, they might think you're in the country illegally. Although someone would have had to report you for Homeland Security to be investigating."

He was quiet for a moment and when he spoke, his voice was different. Harder. "You're right, they probably think I'm here illegally."

"Could someone you work with have reported you?" I asked. "Obviously it wasn't James. Is there anyone else who would have done this?"

"No, it wasn't James," he said. "Don't worry, I'll take care of it."

"Don't worry is a ridiculous thing to say when I just had a government agent in my office questioning me," I said. "Of course I'm going to worry."

"I know," he said, his voice back to its usual nonchalant tone. "I'll talk to James and we'll get it all sorted out."

"Are you sure?" I asked. "Do you have a way to prove who you are?"

"James and I will come up with something," he said.

"This could be serious," I said. "I can't imagine they investigate any random tip they get. William please, if there's something I need to know…"

"I've always been honest with you," he said. "I don't have anything to hide."

"No, I don't mean I think you're not telling me the truth," I said. "I'm just wondering if there's something going on that I don't know about. I'm just worried about you, that's all."

"I know. I'm sure it's just a misunderstanding," he said. "James and I will get it all straightened out. I'm really sorry you had to deal with that."

He sounded so sure, although I sensed an undercurrent of anger in his tone.

"It's all right," I said. "Just… be careful."

"I will," he said. "Can I come over tonight? I miss you."

"I miss you, too," I said. "Yeah, I'd love it if you came over."

"Good," he said. "I have a photo shoot tomorrow afternoon. Do you want to come with me?"

"I'd love to, but I don't want to be in the way."

"You won't be," he said. "And mostly I'm just looking for an excuse to spend the night."

I laughed. "You don't need one. I want you to."

"I like hearing that," he said. "Okay, baby, I'll see you in a couple of hours."

"Bye."

I put my phone down, still feeling unsettled. I hoped William was right, and he and James could get this sorted out. I was getting more of a sense of why James had decided to take care of things for William. His existence was complicated, and I could imagine what William would say if he were to be questioned. He'd tell them everything. I didn't think he had a dishonest bone in his body.

But in this case, I was worried the truth would only get him in trouble.

PARTIAL

James's studio was in a loft in south Seattle. It was open and airy with high ceilings and large windows, the space filled with curtains, backdrops, lights, camera equipment, and props.

There were a number of people there, and everyone looked busy. James waved when we walked in, more in acknowledgment than greeting. He was speaking to a tall woman in a blouse and slacks. A man in a striped shirt and tight jeans was busy hanging things on a rack, and a young woman with her hair in a ponytail scurried around, looking frazzled.

Another woman, this one with a bright blue pixie cut, greeted us with a smile. "Hey, William. Good to see you."

He smiled at her. "You too. Jade, this is Ivy."

Jade held out her hand and I shook it. "Jade, hair and makeup. Nice to meet you."

"Hi," I said.

"Let's get you ready," Jade said to William. "Ivy, you can just hang out. There's a chair over here. We have drinks just through that door. Bathroom is that way."

"Thanks."

I followed them in and Jade led William to a vanity with makeup and hair supplies. Everyone else kept working in the background. I took a seat off to the side where I could watch.

"Go get your hair wet for me, big guy," she said to William.

He obviously knew the drill. He disappeared through a door and came out a few minutes later, shirtless, toweling off his wet hair. Jade got to work, putting in hair product and blow drying. She gave him a slightly fuller version of his usual careless style. It looked great.

The man in the striped shirt brought William over to the rack, then handed him a stack of clothing. William disappeared behind a curtain. A minute or two later, he emerged looking like a rugged mountain man in a plaid shirt, jeans, and boots. With his strong jaw and thick hair, he looked the part.

James got him set up in front of a white background. I guessed that the tall woman was the creative director. She conferred with James and then he started shooting.

It was fascinating to watch. James spoke in a calm voice, directing William's poses. He looked so natural, not like he was posing at all. I had a feeling that was why this designer liked him. He was beautiful, there was no question about that. But his easygoing nature made him look like a man who was completely comfortable in his own skin. He projected an air of quiet competence. Like he knew exactly how to use every inch of that exquisite body.

I happened to know he did.

They changed backgrounds and adjusted the lighting. After a while, William changed into different clothes—a short-sleeved shirt and dark pants—and came back out.

James gave him some direction and then took more

pictures. William's eyes flicked over to me and I caught a glimpse of that enigmatic smile.

"Brilliant, give me more of that," James said.

William looked at me again, this time grinning enough to show his dimples.

James glanced at me. "You need to bring her more often. I never get this expression out of you."

After a while, James had William take a break while they put together a different set. Then it was time for Jade to touch up his hair, and another wardrobe change.

He came out from behind the curtain dressed in nothing but black briefs. At first I thought they hadn't given him the right clothes for his next set of pictures, but James motioned him over.

"They want some shots of you in their new underwear line. I'm not sure if these will make it into production, since they usually use you for other things. But we'll give them some good options." James fiddled with something on his camera, not really looking up. "I'm going to need you partially erect for this. Sorry, I know it's cold in here, so that makes it a little more challenging."

William glanced down at himself and looked up again. I nibbled on my lip to keep from giggling. I felt like I had the maturity of a twelve-year-old for wanting to laugh. Although even in the chilly space, I thought he filled the underwear out quite nicely. But James knew what he needed to get the right look for the shoot.

"You can step behind the curtain." James looked over at me and raised his eyebrows. He nodded toward the curtained-off area. "Maybe this will go faster if you help?"

My mouth dropped open, but I quickly closed it again. *Oh my god, he wants me to...*

"Oh, sure." My cheeks flushed hot, so I quickly joined William behind the curtain before James could see me blush.

William grinned at me.

"Did you know he'd have you pose in underwear?" I asked, keeping my voice low.

"James probably told me, but I don't usually worry about it," he said. "I just show up."

"Well, this is… I don't even know. They need you…"

"Partially erect," he said, his tone amused.

I took a deep breath. I was not such a prude that I couldn't get my boyfriend hard, even with people on the other side of a thin curtain who knew exactly what we were doing. He watched me step closer with that little half smile on his lips.

"You're enjoying this, aren't you?" I asked.

"Isn't that the point?"

I looked up at him and our eyes locked. My hand wrapped around his cock and I squeezed lightly. It was enormously satisfying to feel him respond, his cock growing beneath my touch.

He didn't need to be fully erect—in fact, that was probably a bad thing—but his cock felt so good in my hand. My mouth watered, and I decided to take a chance and do something very unlike me… and very unexpected. I pulled his waistband down and lowered myself onto my knees in front of him.

His eyes widened as he watched me take the tip of his cock into my mouth. I sucked it gently, then swirled my tongue around.

"Oh fuck, Ivy," he said, his voice low.

Once I started, I didn't want to stop. I took him in deeper and pulled out, sliding his thickness in and out of my wet mouth. Looking up, I met his eyes. He watched me with awe, his eyes unfocused, his lips parted.

I held his shaft and ran my tongue around the ridge of his tip. He shuddered and groaned. I knew I should stop. I couldn't finish him now if he was supposed to stay partially hard. So I slowly pulled back and released him.

Licking my lips, I pulled the waistband back up. Or tried to. My little stunt had worked too well. The top of his thick erection stuck out past the underwear.

He shook his head, as if to clear it, and took a deep breath. He had to adjust his cock so it was at least contained by the black fabric. I stood and brushed my hair back.

"You ready, William?" James asked.

Meeting my eyes, he grinned and shook his head again. "Wow. That was fun."

"Sorry," I said. "I got a little carried away."

"I didn't mind," he said, his voice amused. He took another deep breath, glanced down at himself, and shrugged. Then went out to the set.

I peeked around the curtain.

James was still adjusting something on his camera. He looked up and blinked. "Oh, shit. Uh… I guess we'll wait a minute for that to… That's… wow, okay."

Part of me was embarrassed. But I had to admit, I felt a little bit proud of myself. William met my eyes and shrugged again.

James moved some things around and checked his equipment again. Looked back at William. He was still filling out those briefs more than *partially*. Everyone seemed to run out of things to do. They stood around, tapping feet and checking the time. Looking everywhere except at William.

Long minutes later, James finally determined that William looked right. They had him lie on a couch and moved one of the lights.

I stepped outside the curtain to watch. Jade darted in and fixed a lock of William's hair. James lifted his camera and William titled his face toward me. Our eyes met, and I smiled, nibbling my bottom lip.

"Really?" James asked, stepping back and lowering his camera.

William's bulge was… larger.

"She's way over there," James said, gesturing toward me. "Think about something unappealing. I'm not trying to shoot lady porn, here."

William seemed completely unfazed. He took a deep breath and looked up at the ceiling.

We all waited, again. James paced back and forth. After a few more minutes, he looked at William through his camera lens and muttered something that sounded like *finally*.

I wondered if I should hide behind the curtain, but I needed to use the restroom. I figured I'd sneak away while he was busy. I crept across the loft toward the vanity where Jade had done his hair. Pausing about halfway, I looked back. James had William standing now.

God, he looked delicious. I wasn't sure if I liked him being photographed like this. I didn't want to share him.

Our eyes met, and his mouth hooked in that subtle smile I loved so much. Feeling suddenly naughty, I brought a finger to my mouth and slowly licked it with the tip of my tongue. Then I pressed my lips around it and pulled it out, winking at him.

His smile transformed into an expression that was down-right carnal. I felt my cheeks flush and my body tingle with desire.

"Damn it, William," James said. "Forget it. We'll go with what we have."

I stifled a giggle and tried to look innocent. The wardrobe guy caught my eye and gave me a covert thumbs-up.

In the bathroom, I took a deep breath and fanned myself. My cheeks were pink, and I was warm. When I came out, William was behind the curtain changing. James looked at me and rolled his eyes. Stifling another laugh, I just shrugged.

James spoke to the tall woman again, and I thought I heard him say, "And remind me to never introduce him to my girlfriend."

William came out, dressed in his own clothes. "Ready?"

"That's quite the asset you have there," I said, running my finger down his chest. "We should hurry home, so I can finish what I started."

His eyes widened, sparkling blue. "My place is closer."

I laughed as he grabbed my wrist and pulled me toward the door.

UNEXPECTED VISITS

s much as I wanted to get lost in a world where I could spend my days—and nights—tangled up in bed with William, I had classes to teach. Between teaching, updating lecture notes for my *Survey of British Literature* class and writing test questions for the *Literature Across Genres* course I taught online, my days seemed to be over before they'd even begun. Fortunately, I had no more government visitors, and neither William nor James heard from Eric Andrews. I thought about calling him to see if he was still looking into William, but I didn't want to draw unnecessary attention to him.

Friday, I went home, mentally exhausted. I couldn't wait to curl up on the couch in comfy pants and slippers. William and I didn't have plans, but I was so tired, I didn't mind too much. The most I wanted to do tonight was flip through options on Netflix. Maybe I'd just have popcorn for dinner. That counted as a meal, didn't it?

Edgar needed to go outside and when we came back in, he immediately started growling. Someone knocked, and he barked.

"Who is it, buddy?"

I answered the door to find Blake.

"What are you doing here?" I asked.

He looked a little rumpled, dressed in a button-down and slacks, but no tie or jacket. "Can I come in?"

"I don't think so."

Edgar put himself between me and Blake.

"Please?" he asked with a wary glance at my dog. "I just want to talk to you and you won't take my calls."

"We don't have anything to talk about."

He let out a sigh and ran a hand through his hair. "I know I came on too strong before. I'm sorry about that. I didn't mean to put you off."

"Look, you apologized, and that's fine. But I don't understand why you keep trying to contact me."

"Because I want to see you again," he said.

I crossed my arms. "That's not going to happen."

"I just want another chance," he said.

"Why?" I asked. "It's not like we had a relationship. We went out a few times and nothing came of it."

"Because I can't stop thinking about you," he said. "I made a huge mistake and I've spent every day since regretting it."

My phone rang, but it was on the kitchen counter.

"Blake, I'm going to be really honest with you," I said. "Regardless of what happened the last time you came over, this wasn't going to work out. Even if I didn't have someone else in my life—which I do—my answer would still be no."

He glanced down, like he was thinking about what to say next. When he met my gaze, his eyes were hard. "You need to be careful with that guy."

"That's none of your business," I said.

"You don't realize what you're getting into," he said.

I rolled my eyes. "As if you know anything about the man I'm dating."

"Do you know who he really is?"

I wasn't going to take the bait. "Enough, Blake."

"If there's nothing going on, why is he being investigated by Homeland Security?"

"Now you're just... wait, how do you know about that?"

His demeanor shifted, the desperation leaving his features, replaced by the arrogance I'd somehow missed when I first met him. "I know enough."

"Honestly, why are you here?"

"I'm just looking out for you," he said.

God, it was like I'd stepped into a parallel universe. What was he going to say next? That he had visions about me, too? "I don't need you to look out for me."

"This isn't coming out right," he said. "I think you're making a mistake with that William guy. He's not what he seems. You're sweet and beautiful and you should be with someone who cares enough to be honest with you. How can you trust someone with no real identity? What's he hiding, Ivy?"

"What makes you think he has no identity?"

"I have connections," he said. "And if he didn't want me looking into his life, he should have stayed out of mine."

"Oh my god, what are you talking about?" I asked. Edgar growled, clearly sensing my growing agitation. "William isn't doing anything in *your* life. He's dating *me*, which has nothing to do with you."

"Then why is he following me around?"

I stopped because I didn't know how to answer that. I wanted to say that William was *not* following him around, but how could I be sure? He'd followed me. Until now, it hadn't occurred to me that he might use those stalking skills on someone else. Wasn't it just about his visions? Finding Ivy? Why would he follow someone else? Especially Blake, who was nothing to me—just a guy I'd gone out with a few times. I had no explanation for why he'd care about Blake at all. William was with me, Blake wasn't. What else was there?

"He's probably after your money," Blake said.

I rolled my eyes again. "Now you're really reaching."

"Am I?" he asked. "He came out of nowhere a year after your dad died. You shouldn't trust him."

"I have no reason to trust you either," I said.

"Yes, you do," he said. "I care about you."

"You don't even know me," I said. "Why are you making this out to be something it wasn't?"

"It's not about the amount of time we spent together," he said, his voice softening. "The first time I saw you, I knew you were going to be important to me."

I took a deep breath and touched Edgar's back. His body was tense. So was mine. "I'm sorry if you thought there was something between us. There wasn't. I've tried very hard to make that clear, but I feel like you're not hearing me. So let me say this again. I don't need you to look out for me. I'm not going out with you again. And who I'm dating now is not your concern."

"Ivy—"

"Go home, Blake," I said. "I don't understand what's fueling this, but whatever it is, get over it. Get help. Something."

His face hardened into an emotionless mask, just like when he'd brought breakfast. "I tried to warn you."

Edgar growled again, and I slipped my fingers beneath his collar, just in case he decided to get aggressive. I didn't need vicious dog accusations added to the drama that was apparently my life now. Fortunately, Blake didn't say anything else, just turned and walked back to his car. I shut and locked the door.

I released my grip on Edgar's collar and let him bark at Blake's retreating car through the window without a reprimand. My head was killing me, and my back was still tense with frustration.

"What is wrong with him?" I asked Edgar. He barked out the window again. "First I'm with Julian who won't stick around when things get hard. Then I meet someone who thinks he needs to be my personal protector after a handful of dates?"

Edgar swung his head around to look at me, his ears twitching.

"I know, when it comes to personal protectors, Blake has nothing on William." I sank down on the couch and Edgar jumped up, putting his head in my lap. I scratched behind his ears. "But William is different, isn't he? You like him. That certainly means something. And I like him, too."

I kept petting Edgar and leaned my head back against the couch. "I don't just like him, buddy. It's so much more."

The knock on my door startled me. Why hadn't Edgar barked?

"Ivy." William's voice. "Baby, are you home?"

Of course, that was why. William remained the one person who could approach my house without a warning bark from my dog. I got up and opened the door. "What are you doing here?"

He pushed past me into the house. "Where's Blake?"

"He left," I said. "How did you know he was here?"

"The camera," he said, holding out his cell phone. It was frozen on a blurry image of Blake on my doorstep.

"Oh, right," I said. "You sure got here fast."

"You didn't answer your phone."

I glanced over to the kitchen. "It was over there. I'm sorry, I forgot it rang. I would have checked it in a few minutes."

"What did Blake want?" he asked.

I went over to the couch and sat back down. "I don't

know. To win an award for being the worst at accepting rejection?"

"What did he say?"

"That he wants another chance," I said. "And that you aren't what you seem and you're probably after my money."

William looked like he was ready to murder someone. Blake, most likely.

"It's not like I believe him," I said. "He did say you were following him, though. Is that true?"

"Yes," he said.

I cracked a smile. I knew he'd tell me the truth. "Why?"

He sat down next to me. "Because I'm here to protect you."

"But do you need to protect me from Blake?" I asked. "It's odd that he won't give up, but other than that, he seems pretty harmless. What's he going to do? Annoy me to death? He was here that whole time and he didn't even try to come in the house."

"Edgar was here," he said.

"Well, yeah, but if Blake really wanted to hurt me, would Edgar be enough to stop him?"

"I don't want to find out." He brushed my hair back and kissed me softly. "And I don't think he's being persistent just because he wants another chance with you."

"What do you mean?"

"I think he's after your inheritance," he said.

"Blake?" I asked. "What makes you think he's after my money? He seems to have plenty of his own."

"I don't think he does," he said. "He has a gambling problem."

"How do you know that?"

"I hacked into his laptop."

"You just said that with a completely straight face." I

paused, waiting to see if he'd tell me he was kidding. But he didn't. "You're serious, aren't you?"

"Of course I'm serious."

I laughed a little. "So you're a model and a hacker?"

"I model to pay the bills," he said. "And you can learn anything on the Internet."

"Okay… let me work this out," I said. "Let's say Blake has a gambling problem, so he needs money. For what, more gambling?"

"No, he's in debt," he said. "A lot of debt. And I don't mean to a bank."

"A loan shark or something?" I asked.

"Something like that."

"When I was out with him once, we ran into someone he knew. He said something to Blake about *playing with the big boys*. Blake said it was just a monthly poker night."

"High-stakes poker, maybe," he said. "I know I already asked who knows about your inheritance, but is there any way Blake could have found out how much money you have?"

"I'm not his client, so he shouldn't…" I trailed off, real-izing something I hadn't considered before. "Wait, the estate had to go through his department when ownership was transferred to me. He probably had access to my information then. But how was dating me supposed to solve his problem? Was his plan to make me fall for him and offer to pay his debts?"

"Possibly," he said. "That's a lot less risk than stealing from you. His company must have safeguards against employee fraud. Maybe he thought if he wormed his way into your life, he could have the best of both worlds—get his debt paid and keep his job."

And get in my pants, I thought. But I didn't say that out

loud. "And I'm screwing up his plan because I keep rejecting him."

"Exactly, and he's getting desperate," he said. "I think he's the one who broke in to your house."

"What makes you think that?"

"I started doing some research after we saw him at Dorset," he said. "I didn't like the way he looked at you. And then there was the break-in here. It was just a gut instinct, but I had a feeling he might have been responsible. That's how I found out about the gambling debt. He owes a lot of money to some very bad people. I think they're putting a lot of pressure on him."

"So if he broke in here, what was he after?" I asked. "Personal information?"

"Yes," he said. "Passwords, Social Security numbers, maybe even copies of your dad's will or other estate paperwork. I think he was behind the break-in at Dorset, too, looking for the same thing. But in both cases, he made it look like something else."

"So he trashed the whole office instead of just Arthur's, so no one would know what the real target was."

"Right. And here, he made it look like a home invasion. He might have even paid someone else to do it, just told them what to look for."

"Do you have any proof?" I asked. "Can we go to the police?"

"Not yet," he said. "That's why I haven't said anything. I didn't want you to think I was making it up."

"I wouldn't have thought that," I said. "But you need to be careful. You have someone from Homeland Security sniffing around, and now you're telling me you've been stalking Blake, and you hacked into his computer. I don't want you getting arrested."

"I know," he said. "I'll be careful."

"I should call Arthur and make sure there hasn't been any suspicious activity on my accounts." I put a hand to my forehead. "Is this really happening? This is too crazy to be my life."

He put his hand on my thigh and squeezed. "Don't worry. I'm not going to let anything happen to you. But I don't want you to be alone right now. Especially since he showed up here today."

I smiled. "If only there was a sexy man in my life who had vowed to protect me. He could stay here and keep me warm at night."

He grinned and pushed me down onto the couch, climbing on top of me. "If only."

I melted into his kiss and in seconds, all thoughts of Blake, the break-ins, and my inheritance were far from my mind.

WE'RE IN MY OFFICE

fter Blake showed up at my house, William hardly let me out of his sight. A few days later, when I saw Blake drive past campus, I stopped telling him he was being overprotective.

So I got used to William being my shadow. He didn't go to work with me all day, but he did pop in to check up on me. And he charmed everyone I worked with. Lisa couldn't stop talking about how dreamy he was. My boss met him and later went on and on about him being so likable and engaging.

Even Jessica, who'd held onto her skepticism because of the whole stalking thing, had come around. Although she did complain that we hadn't spent any time together recently. She was right. I made it up to her by taking her out for a girl's night that weekend. Peter happily stayed home, and I pretended I didn't notice William following us the whole time.

The following Friday, William came to my office in the afternoon. I was just finishing up with a student who was attempting to persuade me to raise his grade. His name was

Danny, and he wasn't nearly as cute as he seemed to think he was. I wasn't impressed with his cocky grin and thinly veiled hints that he'd make it worth my while.

William appeared in the doorway and waited.

"Look, I'm sure we can figure this out," Danny said. "I need a better GPA or my parents are going to give me all kinds of crap. And maybe you could use… you know… a little relaxation. You work hard. You deserve it."

William crossed his arms and leaned against the door frame, looking amused. "She does deserve it. But I don't think she needs your help."

Danny whipped around and muttered, "Oh, shit," under his breath.

"Hi, baby," William said, his eyes on me. He was so good at subtlety. There was no bravado. The look in his eyes and the tenor of his voice made one thing perfectly clear—I was his.

"Danny, if you want to raise your grade, ace the final," I said. "And I'd suggest actually reading the books, rather than relying on chapter summaries you find on the internet."

He frowned, looking defeated. "Yeah. Thanks, Dr. Nichols." Shouldering his backpack, he cast a quick glance at William, then ducked out of my office. It was like watching the alpha wolf in the pack chase off an upstart young male. Only William didn't even need to bare his teeth, let alone growl.

"Hi." I leaned back in my chair and sighed out a long breath.

William came in and shut the door behind him. "That sounded like a fun conversation."

I shook my head. "I have one in every class. They don't do the reading, can't write a proper essay to save their life, but they think they can come in here and sweettalk their way to a better grade."

"They underestimate you," he said.

I smiled. "And they underestimate *you*, if they think I have any… unmet needs."

"Indeed," he said. "Do you have time to get away? I think you could use a break."

"I have a little time." I pushed my chair back and stood. "But I still have a lot to do before I can go home."

He came around to the other side of my desk and slid his hands around my waist. Leaned in and pressed his lips to mine. His mouth moved, soft at first. Then his tongue teased my lips and his hands moved lower, his fingers inching my skirt up.

I lost myself in the feel of kissing him, sparks of electricity racing through my veins. He pulled my skirt higher and slid one hand into my panties, grabbing my ass, pressing me against him.

"You feel so good, I want to kiss you all the time." He squeezed my ass, kissing me again.

"We're in my office," I said between kisses, but the more he touched me, the less I cared.

He kissed down my neck. "Do you want me to stop?"

"No."

Growling deep in his throat, he pushed my laptop aside, and set me on top of my desk. He moved his hand up my inner thigh and brushed his fingers along the outside of my panties. "Do you feel how wet you are?"

I shuddered at his touch. With my arms around his strong shoulders, I nodded.

"I want to taste you," he whispered in my ear, still rubbing me through my panties. "I want to lay you down on your desk and lick your pussy, baby. I don't want to wait. I want you right now."

"This is crazy," I breathed, but it wasn't much of a protest. I glanced at the window. The blinds were down and only partially open. Someone would have to be standing right outside to see in.

He kissed my neck and slid his tongue across my skin.

"Okay, now," I said. "Lock the door."

He left me sitting on the edge of my desk, breathing hard, while he locked the door. His eyes held me, a predator circling his prey. I didn't keep much on my desk, and he moved it all aside so I could lie down. My pussy throbbed with anticipation. He nudged my legs open and kissed up the inside of my thighs, his stubble pleasantly scratchy. When he reached my center, he took my panties off and dropped them to the floor.

The first few exploratory strokes of his tongue had me trembling. It felt like warm velvet against my desperately sensitive skin. He licked up my center and I gasped when the tip of his tongue swirled around my clit.

"Oh, god," I whispered, trying to stay quiet.

"Mm." He hummed, the vibration sending shock waves through me. "You taste so good."

He licked and kissed, little teases of his lips and tongue. Then he clamped down harder and sucked. His tongue slid in and out of my wet pussy while he gently sucked my clit.

I bit my bottom lip to keep from crying out and ran my fingers through his hair. I couldn't believe I was doing this. We were in my office, on my desk. It was insane.

But I'd never been more powerfully aroused. I moved my hips and pressed my fingers into his scalp. Pressure built deep inside, hot and tantalizing.

Looking down, I watched. Seeing my skirt hiked up around my waist and his mouth between my legs made me feel wild and free. Like I could do anything with him. I gasped as he sucked harder, then flicked my clit with his tongue.

"William, I'm going to come," I said. "Oh god, William."

Just when I thought I couldn't take anymore, he slid two fingers inside me. The added pressure and the soft strokes of his fingertips in just the right place sent me careening over the edge. My back arched, and I covered my mouth as the intensity of the orgasm overtook me.

He didn't stop, and my climax stretched out, waves upon waves of intense pleasure surging through me. I panted and writhed while he licked and sucked.

"Oh my god, stop," I said, almost breathless. "I can't... William... oh god."

Slowly, like he was enjoying the delicious torture, he stopped. I lay on my desk, trying to catch my breath after one of the most insane orgasms I'd ever had.

"I have no idea how you just did that," I said.

"I could taste you all the time," he said, his voice rough and low. Closing his eyes, he licked his lips and groaned.

I sat up, leaning back on my arms. "What are you going to do now?"

"I'm going to fuck you until you come again." He unfastened his pants and lowered the zipper.

My eyes locked on his erection, bulging through his underwear. I was so glad I'd gone back on the pill. He pulled the waistband down, releasing his cock. It sprang up, long and thick. I bit my lip and scooted my ass forward, so I was right on the edge of the desk.

I tipped my knees open and he stepped in close. Holding the shaft of his cock, he rubbed the tip along my slit. Up and down, dragging it through my wetness, teasing. His other hand went to the back of my neck, his fingers through my hair. Closing his fist, he held tight, keeping me in his control.

"I love you," he said, our lips brushing together. He kept rubbing his cock against me, the tip sliding against my clit. "And I love that you're mine. Every bit of you. I love that I get to be the man to do this to you. To taste you and touch you."

"I love you too." My tongue darted out and he groaned as I licked my taste off his lips. "I love that I'm yours. I don't want anyone else."

Voices sounded from outside the door and we paused, our eyes locked. I sat on the edge of my desk, my legs spread wide open. He stood in front of me, his pants undone, his cock in his hand. The door was locked, but I willed them to walk by.

"Shh," I whispered. *And oh my god, please don't knock*.

William's tongue flicked against my lips and I sucked in a quick breath. Slipped my tongue out to meet his, the sensitive tips caressing. He moved his cock again, rubbing it against my clit. My eyes rolled back, and I suppressed a moan.

The voices continued, just outside the door. Whoever it was, they'd stopped in the hallway right in front of my office.

With his cock settled at my entrance, he reached around and held my ass. Then he pushed in, slowly, inch by agonizing inch. I clung to him, my arms around his neck, trying not to make a sound.

"Shh," he said against my mouth. Pushed in deeper until he was buried inside me.

I wrapped my legs around his waist and he let go of my hair to grab my ass with both hands. The tension was making me crazy and I had no idea how he was controlling himself. His cock throbbed but he held still. I wanted movement, rhythm, pressure. I wanted him to fuck me—so much that I almost whispered for him to do it, and be damned who could hear us.

A muffled *see you later* came through the door. He bit my lower lip, pinching it between his teeth. I whimpered softly. Then footsteps, and a moment later, silence.

William released my lip, tightened his grip on my ass, pulled halfway out, and thrust. He drove into me, hard and fast, unleashing all his tension. I held on while he pounded me, my legs locked around his waist. The only sound he made was an occasional low grunt, and his eyes never left mine.

We watched each other, not breaking eye contact. His eyes were focused and fierce. I could see his climax building even as I felt it. See the lust and desire in his eyes. The tension rising.

It made me feel dangerous and uninhibited. The heat in my pussy grew, all sensation rushing toward the tantalizing feel of his cock sliding in and out. Pushing and pressing and grinding. Every thrust bringing me closer.

The look in his eyes intensified and his control slipped. He drove in again, his thick cock pulsing, and he buried his face in my neck to muffle his groans.

His hard thrusts as he came made me burst apart. All that heat and pressure exploded, and I held on for dear life, riding the wave of another orgasm.

He held me while we caught our breath. My mind slowly came back to reality and I blinked, looking around my office. A few pencils and pens were scattered on the floor. A stack of papers still fluttered down. My laptop had been spared, but my chair was pushed back against the shelf behind it and a few books lay nearby.

William gently kissed my lips and smiled, his dimples puckering.

"Wow," I said. "I wasn't expecting that."

He pulled away and tucked his cock back in his underwear. Refastened his pants. "Me neither."

I took a deep breath and got off my desk. He handed me my panties and I quickly slipped them on, then smoothed down my skirt.

He ran his hand through his hair, looking dazed. We

heard more voices outside my door and I covered my mouth to suppress my laughter.

My cheeks were still warm, so I fanned myself. "I need to cool down."

He brushed my hair away from my face and smiled. "I like it when you look like this."

"Yeah, but I can't let my boss see me," I said.

He laughed and kissed me. "I'll help you pick up. No one will know."

We righted my office and I opened the window for some fresh air. But I wasn't really worried. I was swimming in euphoria after two amazing orgasms.

But it was much more than that. With William, I felt free. Connected, and loved. Whatever happened, I knew he'd be with me, and that was all that mattered.

CONFRONTATION

⁊he auditorium buzzed with voices. Representatives from dozens of companies sat at their tables, passing out brochures and swag. Students meandered around the room and stopped to chat with them.

I'd somehow let my boss talk me into being there for half the day to man the graduate programs table at the Woodward Career Expo. It was a Saturday, so I didn't have classes, but I'd been hoping to use the day to catch up on grading papers. I had fifty essays sitting on my desk in need of reading. Just the thought of it made me sigh audibly.

My eyes kept darting to the Dorset Financial table. They were a large financial institution, and attended our career expo every year. Their account managers were never the ones to man their table, so I shouldn't have had to worry about Blake showing up. But I had a bad feeling that he would.

William loitered near the edge of the room, his eyes always on me. I sat behind the table with Lisa and answered questions when students approached. I glanced at my phone, checking the time. I only had another hour before someone would be here to relieve me. Taking a deep breath, I glanced in William's direction.

His body language had changed, and his face was hard, as if it had been carved from stone. I followed his gaze and my stomach turned over.

Blake stood talking to the two women at the Dorset Financial table. His eyes met mine and he smiled, lifting one hand to wave at me. I stared at him, open-mouthed.

"Everything okay?" Lisa asked.

"No," I said. "Everything is definitely not okay."

William hadn't moved, but his eyes were locked on Blake. A hint of fear trickled through my veins. He looked dangerous. I thought back to what he'd said after we'd seen Blake at Dorset. I knew the chances of Blake leaving me alone were basically zero—why else had he come?—and a sense of dread poured through me. This could get ugly.

"I might need to leave," I said. "I hate to abandon you, but... oh god."

Blake strode over to our table. He looked polished in his gray suit, but there was something in his eyes—a wildness I'd never seen before. Usually, he wore a mask of confidence, but it looked like his mask was slipping.

William made a beeline for me, wasting no time. I felt like I was in the middle of a game of chicken on a dark highway, two sets of headlights speeding toward me, neither driver willing to be the one to swerve.

I stood and put my hands up, palms out, one in front of each man. "Stop."

Blake ignored William, smiling at me as if he didn't exist. "Hey, Ivy. I didn't know you'd be here."

"Right," I said. "I'm sure it's just a coincidence that you decided to come. On a Saturday."

He shrugged and adjusted the cuffs of his jacket. "They needed someone to bring another box of brochures."

"How generous of you," I said.

William watched Blake, his posture both completely calm and enormously aggressive. To anyone else, he might have appeared relaxed, but I could see the tension in his jaw, the strength in his stance.

"I'm only here in a professional capacity. Although I'm glad I ran into you. There are some things going on at Dorset that have me concerned. I know you've worked with Arthur for a while, but…" Blake's eyes flicked to William, then back to me. "This isn't really the place to discuss it. When you're finished here, maybe I can buy you some coffee so we can talk."

"No," William said and the hardness in his voice made my blood run cold.

Blake smiled, but there was no humor in his tone. "I'm asking Ivy."

"And I'm answering," William said. "You can go now."

"She doesn't need you to answer for her," Blake said.

"Fine, I'll answer." I didn't believe his story for a second. "No thanks."

Blake didn't acknowledge that I'd spoken. "William, is it? That's what you're going by?"

William's eyes were cold steel.

"Easy to fly under everyone's radar when you're off the grid, isn't it?" Blake said. "Who the fuck are you?"

"Blake," I said. "Stop."

"I'm nobody," William said.

"That's probably the first honest thing you've said." Blake shifted, turning to face him.

William's arms were loose at his sides, but he looked like a coiled spring. "You need to leave."

"Actually, you're the one who doesn't belong here," Blake said. "I'm just trying to have a simple conversation with Ivy."

"It's not going to work," William said.

Blake looked at him like he must be insane. "What?"

"I'm onto you," William said. "And you're wasting your time."

"You don't know what the fuck you're talking about," Blake said.

"Blake, keep your voice down," I said.

I noticed two campus security guards moving closer. The tension between the two men was escalating quickly. I needed to get us out of here.

"William, let's go. It's almost time for me to leave anyway." I picked up my purse and cast an apologetic glance at Lisa. "Sorry."

"It's okay," she said, her eyes wide.

I stepped around the table, but Blake was in between me and William. I tried to go around him, but his hand darted out, grabbing my arm. His grip was tight. I twisted my arm, trying to break free, but I didn't want to cause more of a scene.

William's voice was low and dangerous. "Let go."

"Back the fuck off," Blake said.

A look of resignation passed over William's face, then all hell broke loose.

Blake tried to yank me backward, but William's fist flew toward his face. He let go of my arm and I stumbled, bumping into the table. I looked up in time to see William connect another punch, sending Blake's head twisting to the side.

Lisa screamed, and security came running. People moved back, tables and chairs scraping. Someone tripped trying to stay out of their way and almost ran into one of the security guards.

I yelled for them to stop, but there was nothing I could do. Blake's face was twisted with fury, his eyes wild. William didn't take another swing, just strove to control Blake, keeping him away from me. He deflected Blake's punch, using Blake's momentum against him. Blake rushed forward, but William took a small step to the side and turned his body, letting Blake stumble past.

One of the security guards tried to grab Blake from behind, but he shoved him off. He swung at William again. William deflected, grabbing Blake's wrist. He twisted his arm around and slammed him down onto a table.

"Stay away from her, or I'll fucking kill you," William said, leaning down to speak low into Blake's ear. Blake winced as William wrenched his arm harder.

A security guard grabbed William by the shoulders and hauled him backward. William released Blake and put his hands up in front of him. Another guard was there to restrain Blake.

I watched in horror, my stomach sick and heart pounding.

"Outside," one of the security guards said. "Let's go."

Ignoring the huge crowd of people staring at us, I followed the security guards out the side doors. One of them pulled out a walkie-talkie. I heard the word *police*.

"Wait," I said, panic threatening, making my voice come out high-pitched. "Things just got out of hand. You don't have to call the police."

"No, call the police," Blake said. "Please."

"Shut up, Blake." I looked at the security guard's name tag. *Matt*. I knew some of the guys who worked campus security, but I didn't know him. "Matt, listen. The police don't need to be involved. It's over now. We'll all just go."

"Sorry," Matt said. "Campus policy."

Blake's face was red, and he had the beginning of a black eye where William had hit him. William stood with his arms crossed, his expression calm. I didn't understand how he could appear so relaxed when the police were on their way.

185

What was he going to tell them when they asked for identification? That he didn't have any? That he before last year, he didn't exist? That would go over well.

Within minutes, two police officers arrived. They spoke with the security guards, but I couldn't hear what they said. Blake tried to interject himself into their conversation, but one of the officers snapped at him to wait, and he shut his mouth.

The two officers approached William and Blake, pulling out handcuffs. I put my hand over my mouth, afraid I might vomit.

"Wait, what's going on?" Blake asked, his voice panicky. "I didn't do anything wrong. He attacked me. You can't arrest me."

The officer ignored his protests while he read him his rights and handcuffed him. William didn't say anything as the other officer did the same—just kept his eyes on Blake, his gaze cold.

"It was just a scuffle," I said. "Do you really have to arrest them?"

"We'll work it out at the station," one of the officers said. He led William to his car and put him in the back seat.

Blake tried to argue with the officer until he threatened to charge him with resisting arrest.

I stood on the sidewalk, my heart pounding, and watched them drive away.

I EXPLAINED EVERYTHING

The police wouldn't let me see William, but they didn't kick me out of their waiting room after I gave a statement about what had happened, so I stayed. I sat in a faded chair, my legs crossed, and tried not to lose my mind.

What were they asking him? I half-expected to see Eric Andrews from Homeland Security waltz in. I imagined him hauling William off to some undisclosed location for interrogation.

I chewed on my fingernails and tapped my foot. The minutes ticked by, one by one. It felt as if time had ceased to have meaning, the seconds stretching out in unbearable agony.

Eventually, Blake emerged. He was no longer handcuffed, although his clothes were rumpled, and his black eye had darkened. His eyes widened in surprise when he saw me, but a second later, his expression smoothed over. He straightened his jacket and walked out without saying a word.

I breathed out a sigh. If they'd let Blake go, maybe William wouldn't be far behind.

My relief was short-lived. Another hour went by, and still nothing. The sick feeling in my stomach grew. I texted Jessica to tell her what had happened. Thankfully, she didn't press me for details, just asked if I needed her to go see to Edgar. I thanked her.

Finally, an officer came out—the same one who'd arrested William at Woodward.

The look on his face made my heart sink with dread. It was not the look of someone bringing good news.

"Are you Ivy Nichols?" he asked.

I stood. "Yes. Where's William?"

"He's being transferred to a different facility," he said.

"What facility? Why? Is he under arrest?"

"No," he said. "But we determined he needed to be detained for evaluation."

"I don't understand," I said.

"He's been sent to Northwest Hospital," he said. "He's being put on a seventy-two-hour hold so doctors can evaluate his mental state. We need them to determine if he's a danger."

"Danger?" I asked. "William's not dangerous."

"His answers to our questions indicate he is," he said. "And based on some of his responses, we have reason to believe he's not mentally stable. I'm sorry, but this is for his protection as well as yours."

"William is not crazy," I said. God, what had he told them? "And he's not dangerous.""

"Miss, I'm sorry, but this isn't something we take lightly," he said.

"Is he gone already?"

"He is. But he asked me to give you a message." He held out a folded piece of paper.

I took it, but decided to wait to read it until I was alone. "Will I be allowed to see him?"

"Eventually, yes," he said. "But the doctors there will need to conduct their evaluation first. If you want my advice, go home. Get some rest. He's safe where he is."

Safe? William was *not* safe. Not locked up in a mental hospital against his will.

The officer left, and I went back to my car. My hands trembled as I opened the note William had written.

Ivy,

Please don't stay at home tonight. Go to my place, or stay with Jessica and Peter for a few days. Don't worry about me. I explained everything to the police. It will be fine.

William

I stared at the neat handwriting. Explained everything? I wanted to throw up all over again. Had he really told them *everything*? About me and his visions? About being sent to save me? Oh god, no wonder they'd locked him up. His story did sound crazy, especially from the outside. If he hadn't actually known so many things about me—if his paintings hadn't been so true—I wouldn't have believed him. I would have thought he was crazy, too.

I drove over to Northwest Hospital, but the officer had been right. They wouldn't let me see him until at least tomorrow. I tried everything I could think of, short of bribery or getting down on my knees and begging. They wouldn't let me past the front desk.

It was all I could do to keep myself from crying as I

walked back to my car in defeat. The enormity of it all threatened to crush me. I was terrified for William. I didn't know what they would do to him. Glancing behind me at the imposing hospital, I was tempted to camp outside in my car. I wanted to stay close to him, even if there were walls and a maddening group of hospital staff keeping us apart.

But I knew that more than anything, he wanted me to be safe. I didn't know if he had access to his phone, but I texted him, just in case, letting him know I'd stay at Jessica and Peter's tonight. If I could alleviate any of his worry and make his night easier, it was the least I could do.

Jessica and Peter were both at my house when I got there. They were quietly sympathetic, helping me get a few things ready for Edgar while I packed a bag for myself.

Edgar seemed to sense my distress. After we got to Jessica and Peter's, he stayed close to me, curling up with his head on my lap. I was about to tell him to get off Jessica's couch, but she stopped me.

"He's fine. You've had a rough day." She handed me a mug of steaming tea and sat down. Peter sat in a chair next to the couch. "Do you want to talk about it?"

"Blake showed up at the career expo," I said. "He wanted to talk to me, which didn't make William happy. I tried to leave, but Blake grabbed my arm. He wouldn't let go."

"Oh hell no," Jessica said.

"Then William hit him."

"Good." She glanced at Peter as if she expected him to disagree, but he nodded.

I sighed. "That turned into a fight. Campus security broke it up and took them outside. They called the police and both of them got handcuffed and taken away."

"So are they being held?" she asked.

"No, they let Blake go."

"But not William? Why would they put him in jail and not Blake? Because he threw the first punch?"

"He's not in jail," I said. "They sent him to a mental hospital for evaluation."

"What, now?" Jessica asked. "What the hell did William do?"

I sighed and swallowed hard, trying to hold back the tears. "There's something you need to know about William."

I told them everything. Why he had been following me. His belief that he'd been sent to save me. The things he knew. His paintings. The lack of knowledge of his past, and his insistence that he didn't have one. Peter listened without comment, but I could tell by the strain in Jessica's expression that she was having a hard time holding back.

"You have rendered me speechless. And I can't remember the last time that happened." She glanced at Peter. "Don't comment on that."

Peter held up his hands. "I didn't say anything."

"His note said he told the police everything," I said. "Judging by the fact that he's being held in a psychiatric facility, I guess he meant *everything*."

Jessica looked down at her tea. "Honey, don't take this the wrong way, but… what you just described is more than a little bit crazy."

"People can't be involuntarily committed without reason," Peter said. "The authorities have to believe the person is in danger of causing harm to themselves or others. That means they had reason to believe he's mentally unstable, as well as dangerous."

"He told Blake he'd kill him if he came near me again," I said. "But is that enough to have him held like this? People say things when they're angry. And William clearly had the upper hand in that fight, but he didn't really hurt Blake.

Aside from a black eye. But there was no sign he was going to do any permanent damage."

"But we don't know what he told the police," Peter said.

"Exactly," Jessica said. "I'm not saying he deserves to be held against his will. But, you don't actually believe his story, do you?"

"The paintings are real, Jess," I said. "I can't explain it, but he knew me inside and out before we ever met."

Jessica and Peter shared a look. "Or, he found out things about you," she said.

"No, he couldn't have."

"Are you sure?" she asked. "We already know he was stalking you. And didn't you say he looked into Blake's life? How did he do that?"

I glanced away. "He followed him. And hacked into his computer."

"So, he couldn't have done that to you?" she asked. "He could have seen the photos on your computer and painted some of them."

"That doesn't explain all of them," I said. "Some were things I don't have photos of."

"You'd be surprised how much information someone can find if they dig long enough," Peter said. "He could have started with your computer files and kept following the trails back in time. Old addresses, places you've been."

"You said he painted a picture of the tree in the backyard of your childhood home," Jessica said. "What if he found out where you used to live and went there? He could have seen it. Taken pictures. That's how he painted things from your past."

"But why would he do that?" I asked.

"Ten million dollars is a lot of money," Jessica said.

"William is *not* after my money."

"And Blake is?" she asked.

"Yes," I said. "At least that makes a little bit of sense. If William is right about Blake's gambling debt, he could very well be after my inheritance. It explains the break-ins, and why he's been so persistent."

"But you have to take William's word for everything," Jessica said. "Maybe he's just trying to pin the blame on Blake for what he's doing."

Edgar lifted his head and snorted. I rubbed behind his ears and he settled down again.

"I just can't believe that William has been lying to me," I said. "He never lies. Every time I ask him a question, he gives me the truth, no matter what it is. I asked him if he'd been following me, and he admitted it. He never tries to hide anything."

"Or he's a very good liar," Jessica said, her voice soft.

I shook my head and looked down.

"Honey, I'm sorry. I like William. I loved seeing you happy. But I think there are really just two possibilities here. Either he's a very talented con-artist who's been playing you from the start. Or he's not mentally stable and needs medical help."

Peter gave me a sympathetic smile and nodded.

Tears burned my eyes. I sniffed and swallowed, trying to keep them from spilling. I didn't want to believe that William had been lying to me. I didn't want to believe he was crazy, either.

But the truth was, I'd allowed myself to overlook the impossibility of his story for one simple reason: I liked him. From the first time we'd met, I'd been taken with him. Not just the mystery of who he was, although that had been enticing in the beginning. He drew me in. For the first time in a long time, I didn't feel alone.

Had I allowed my attraction to him to overshadow my

good judgment? Was I willing to ignore the warning signs because I didn't want to see the truth?

I honestly didn't know.

And the worst part was, I'd fallen for him. This went well beyond attraction, physical or otherwise. I was in love with him. And now I was faced with the distinct possibility that I'd either fallen for a con-artist, or someone who was legitimately crazy.

I wished I could see him. Things always made sense when I was with him—even the things that didn't. His calming presence made the impossible parts seem like trivial details. Things I could live with if it meant I could be with him.

But now I had to face reality. Who was William Cole? How had he painted these scenes from my life? And why? I didn't know if Jessica was right and there were only two explanations. I desperately wanted to believe there was a third—a reason that didn't involve William being a criminal out to steal my inheritance, and leave me heartbroken in the process, or being so mentally unstable he needed to be in that psychiatric hospital.

"Listen, honey, we're here for you," Jessica said. "And we're not going to get any answers tonight. Maybe you can talk to the doctors tomorrow. See what they have to say."

I nodded. "Thanks, you guys."

I stayed up with them for a while longer, sipping tea. But my mind kept drifting to William. Was he okay? Were they treating him well? I hoped he wasn't worried about me, but I had a feeling they'd confiscated his phone. I went to bed in Jessica and Peter's guest room, heartsick and worried. Wondering what tomorrow would bring.

DIFFICULT TRUTHS

❦

I was at the hospital early in the morning. I'd already decided I wasn't leaving until they let me see William. If that meant I had to spend the night in a chair in the lobby, that's what I was going to do. Jessica and Peter had offered to take Edgar for as long as I needed, and I didn't care about anything else. Not my job, my house, none of it. All that mattered was him.

After a few hours, the receptionist took pity on me and brought me coffee and a granola bar. She couldn't give me any information, but she assured me someone would speak to me soon. I noticed she didn't say I'd be able to see William, but I didn't let that deter me.

I finished my coffee and used the restroom, then went back to my seat. A few minutes later, a man came in. He glanced at me and my heart sank. It was Eric Andrews, from Homeland Security Investigations—the man who'd come to my office asking questions about William. I had a feeling William's situation was about to get worse.

"Dr. Nichols," he said.

"Mr. Andrews?" I asked. "What are you doing here?"

"Please, call me Eric," he said. "I came to see if I could speak to William."

"Now is when you choose to come question him?" I asked. "When he's being held against his will in a psychiatric facility?"

"I'm not conducting an official investigation." He sat in the chair next to me.

"Then why are you here?"

"You might say I'm here for personal reasons," he said. "William Cole has become something of a thorn in my side."

I glanced at the receptionist, but she wasn't paying attention to us. "So, if you're not investigating him now, will you tell me why you were? Did he do something?"

"No, William didn't do anything," he said. "I was given false information. Granted, I can't find proof of his identity. But I was led to believe he might be involved in an international crime ring. Human trafficking, that sort of thing."

My mouth dropped open. "What? Why would anyone think William was involved in something like that?"

"Knowing what I know now, it's obvious the person who contacted me about him was lying," he said. "It was clear after just some cursory research that there's no evidence of William doing anything illegal. Someone wanted to make trouble for him, and tried to use me to do it."

"Is there any chance you'll tell me who that someone is?"

"I think you can guess," he said.

"It isn't Blake Callahan, is it?"

He nodded. "Afraid so. And I've put myself in a risky position, professionally speaking. I know Blake. We went to college together. So when he called me and asked if I'd investigate someone, I should have passed him onto one of my colleagues. But I said I'd do it as a favor."

I shook my head. "Oh my god, that asshole. I can't believe him."

"I owe you an apology," he said. "I'm sure my visit to your office caused a fair amount of distress."

"It did, but I guess I'm glad to hear William isn't under investigation. Although, now…" I gestured to our surroundings. "How did you know he was here?"

"I have access to that type of information," he said.

"So, Blake tried to get rid of him," I said. "You know, I wondered if it was him. He said something about William's identity, and that he had connections. Is there anything you can do about him giving you a false report?"

"Unfortunately, no," he said. "Blake contacted me privately and I didn't open an official investigation. I wanted to see if his story checked out before I got other resources involved. The silver lining is that William isn't flagged by my department. That could have come back to haunt him later. But there isn't a record of any of this."

"I suppose that's a good thing," I said. "So why *are* you here? What sort of personal interest do you have in him?"

"Two reasons," he said. "I've been trying to put together the connection to Blake. I haven't seen him socially in years, but frankly I was shocked to realize he fed me false information. I wanted to talk to William to see if I could find out why."

"Well, it's either because Blake is obsessed with me and he's a sore loser, or he's after my inheritance."

"I take it you and Blake had a relationship?" he asked.

"Not even that," I said. "We went out a few times. But he doesn't seem to know how to take rejection."

He nodded slowly. "I see."

"What's the second reason?"

"Curiosity," he said. "I didn't find anything that connected William to any illegal activity. But I also didn't find any evidence of his identity. The man you know as William Cole doesn't exist on record anywhere. I'd like to see if I can find out why."

"I can tell you what he'll say. He'll tell you he didn't exist before last year. That he doesn't have a traceable identity because there's nothing to trace. He's just William."

"No offense intended, but perhaps that's why he's here?"

"His story is more complicated than that," I said. "But yes, I'm sure that's part of it."

"Do you still have my card?" he asked.

"Yes."

"You've answered a lot of my questions, so I won't bother William today," he said. "But I'd still like to speak with him, if he's willing."

"Okay, I'll let him know."

Eric stood, and I followed. He shook my hand. "Thanks for your time, Dr. Nichols."

"Ivy," I said. "And you're welcome."

"Good luck," he said.

"Thank you."

Eric left, and I went back to waiting.

It was well into the afternoon before a nurse came out and led me to an office. Framed certificates and plaques decorated the walls and there were bookshelves packed with thick medical and psychiatry texts. A middle-aged man in a white coat sat at the desk. He greeted me with a warm smile as I took the seat across from him.

"You must be Ivy," he said. His voice was soft, almost soothing. "It's nice to meet you."

"Thank you," I said. "When can I see William?"

"Soon," he said. "He's meeting with another of our specialists right now. I'd like to talk with you first, before you see him."

I crossed my legs and folded my hands in my lap. "Okay."

"As you may or may not be aware, William has a number of psychiatric issues that need to be addressed," he said. "First, the amnesia. What he's experiencing is not a typical presentation. Patients who have experienced brain trauma might lose the memory of the incident that caused the damage, and a short time after. Others will have difficulty making new memories, making them appear forgetful and distracted. But it's extremely rare for someone to lose access to the memories of their entire past."

"Then why do you think he has amnesia?"

He looked surprised by my question. "Well, he has no recollection of his past. I'd say that qualifies as a severe case of amnesia."

"Can you determine the cause?"

"Not at this point," he said. "William's apparent lack of memory makes it difficult to determine if he had a brain injury. And his tests so far have come back normal."

"Is there another explanation?"

"The other explanation is that he's lying." He opened a folder and continued before I could argue that point. "He's also experiencing a very detailed delusion that involves you. I assume you're aware of this?"

"Delusion is your word, doctor," I said.

"He believes he is something other than a normal man, who was sent here to save you from an as yet unknown calamity," he said. "That's certainly a delusion. Or again, he's a very skilled liar."

I dug my fingernails into my fists at hearing the word *liar* again. "I realize his story sounds impossible. But there are pieces of it that are very true. Pieces that I can't explain."

"His paintings," he said.

"Yes."

"He accurately painted scenes from your life?" he asked. "Is that what you're telling me?"

"Yes, he did," I said. "And they aren't things just anyone would know."

"Does he paint other things?" he asked.

"There's one painting I don't recognize," I said. "I'm not sure what it means, if anything."

He looked at me for a long moment. I tried not to fidget.

"I have a number of concerns for William," he said. "Not the least of which are his violent tendencies."

"William isn't violent," I said. "Getting into a fight with someone who is harassing his girlfriend does not make a man *violent*."

"It's not the fight I'm referring to," he said. "He has threatened, several times now, to kill this man, Blake Callahan."

"He's just angry because Blake won't leave me alone," I said. "He barely even hurt Blake, and believe me, he could have. He was in control of that fight the entire time. If he was really in danger of committing murder, don't you think he would have done worse?"

"Perhaps," he said. "Or perhaps he's planning something more subtle. Maybe when his girlfriend isn't watching."

Once again, William's words after the break-in at Dorset ran through my mind. *If he touches you, I'll end him.* But I was sure that didn't mean he'd plot a murder. He simply meant he'd defend me, physically if necessary. "I don't believe for a second that William is a murderer."

"Here's what you need to understand. William has built an entire reality based on his belief in himself as your divinely-sent protector. He sees himself as something like a guardian angel, only not religion-specific. Since he's not tying his created reality to an outside source, such as the belief structure of a religious tradition, his mind is free to make up rules as he sees fit. In effect, he's created his own moral code. Now, if anyone suggested he was a danger to you, I would disagree vehemently. That would grossly violate the moral code he's built for himself. But killing someone he believes is a threat to you won't even register as wrong in his mind. He sees it as an action that is completely justified. His internal logic is driven by his delusions, and his amnesia completely supports his created self-concept."

"Is that why you're holding him here?" I asked. "Because you think he's going to murder Blake Callahan?"

"He's being held because he told the police officer who questioned him a very bizarre story about who he believes himself to be," he said. "And that included specific threats on Blake Callahan's life. This led them to determine he might be a danger to others and needed to be evaluated."

I let out a breath and brushed my hair back from my face. "You said you had several concerns, is that right?"

"Yes," he said. "My other concern is you."

I straightened in my chair. "Excuse me?"

"Do you understand what enabling is?"

"Yes," I said. "When someone protects another person from the natural consequences of their actions, thus removing potential motivations for change."

"Well stated," he said. "But enabling can also mean feeding into a person's misguided or skewed self-concept. Indulging in false beliefs."

"So how am I enabling him?"

"By playing along with his story," he said. "You're allowing him to believe that you are, in fact, the Ivy of his imagination."

"I *am* his Ivy," I said. "His apartment is filled with paintings of my memories."

"The issue here is that you are the centerpiece of his delusion," he said. "And I'm concerned that your presence in his life is obstructing any chance he has of getting better."

I stared at him, my heart racing, my cheeks flushing with the heat of my anger.

"I can see I've upset you," he said. "And I apologize. But I'm not doing either of you any favors by holding back the truth."

"The word *truth* implies objectivity," I said. "What you gave is your opinion."

"If you want to argue semantics," he said. "But it's my *professional* opinion, and I've been doing this for twenty-five years."

"Can I see him now?"

He took a deep breath. "He'll be ready to see you shortly."

"When can he leave?"

"We can only hold him for seventy-two hours," he said. "After that, it's up to him."

I heard the implication in his voice—that he hoped William would admit himself for treatment.

"We want to help William," he said. "This hospital is not the enemy."

Logic and emotion warred in my mind. There was a certain level of reason in what the doctor was telling me. I couldn't deny it completely. But I hated the idea that I was bad for William—hated it with every cell in my body. Every ounce of my soul. And I knew William wasn't crazy. He might have amnesia, but he didn't need to be in a psychiatric hospital.

"I just need to see him," I said. "Please."

"All right," he said. "I'll have someone take you back."

* * *

AFTER MAKING me wait another twenty minutes, the nurse led me to what appeared to be a common area. Patients sat at circular tables, some playing games or working on puzzles. Two couches and several armchairs faced a TV in one corner, and windows lined the adjacent wall. A few hospital staff lingered around the edges, watching. Another sat with a patient, speaking to her in a quiet voice.

William stood alone in front of a window, looking out over a view of a concrete courtyard. He was dressed in gray sweats and a white t-shirt, gray socks on his feet.

My throat felt thick and my chest tight at the sight of him. He turned, and his face lit up with a smile.

"Ivy," he said. "I've been so worried about you."

I hurried to him and landed in his arms. I held him tight, putting my face in his neck. Inhaled his scent. He rested his cheek against my head and rubbed my back.

"Are you okay?" I asked.

"I'm fine," he said. "They gave me something, so I'm a little out of it. I keep telling them I'm not sick. Did you stay with Jessica?"

"Yeah, I did. Edgar's still there."

"Good," he said.

I decided now wasn't a good time to tell him about my conversation with Eric Andrews. His eyes were glassy and unfocused. And I wanted to make sure they'd let him out when the seventy-two hours were over. I knew they couldn't continue to hold him just because of his supposed delusions about me. But I needed to make sure he wasn't fixated on Blake—or talking about killing him. That had me worried. Giving him more reasons to hate Blake didn't seem like a good plan at the moment.

"Listen," I said, taking his hand and pulling him to one of the tables. We both sat down, and he kept my hand in his. "I think the main reason they brought you here is because they're worried you're dangerous."

"They just don't understand," he said, and I could hear the frustration in his voice.

"I know. But I think it will help if you explain to them that you're not going to murder anyone."

"What are you talking about?" he asked.

"They think you might be planning to murder Blake," I said. "Or at least capable of it."

He met my gaze and his eyes seemed to come into focus. "I'm not planning to murder him. But I'll do what has to be done to keep you safe."

"But see, when you say that to the police, or the doctors here, they think that means you're dangerous," I said.

"I'm only a danger to someone who's a threat to you," he said.

I tucked my hair behind my ear and looked down at the table. This was what the doctor had been referring to. His self-created moral code. "Yeah, but you can't just say you're okay with killing someone."

"Ivy, I'm not some psycho who's going to start chopping people up," he said. "You know me. You know why I'm here."

"Yes, I know, you think you're supposed to save me."

He pulled his hand away. "I *think* I'm supposed to save you?"

"I just mean, yes, I know. You've told me."

"That's not what you mean." He sat up straighter and leaned away. The change in his body language was subtle, yet it screamed at me.

"I'm just trying to help you," I said.

He stared at me for a second, his face frozen. "You don't believe me."

His voice held such a mixture of shock and desolation, it sucked the air right out of my lungs. I nearly gasped for breath.

"William—"

"No," he said, shaking his head slowly. "You don't believe me. You think it's all a lie."

I put my hand over his, but he snatched it away. "No. No, I don't think it's a lie."

"Then what is it?" he asked. "Why do I have your paintings all over my walls?"

"I don't know," I said, my voice choking with tears.

"You don't know because you don't believe it's real."

"It's not that simple," I said. "I know your paintings are true. I just don't understand how."

"They led me to you," he said, tapping the table with his finger. "I knew they would, and they did. My visions told me what I needed to know to find you. And they were right."

"Yes, they were right," I said. "But who were you before? There could be an entire life you're missing."

"There isn't," he said. "There's nothing before. I was created for this."

"But how can someone just appear out of nowhere?" I asked. "It doesn't make sense."

"I thought you understood," he said. "But you don't, do you? You don't believe in me."

The hurt in his eyes gutted me. Cut me like a knife to the back. Except I felt the blood on *my* hands, the knife falling from my limp fingertips. The wound was William's, and I'd inflicted it.

His eyes moved from mine, coming to rest on the table. His shoulders slumped, like I'd taken all the fight out of him. "You can go."

"No, William, please."

"Maybe they're right," he said, his voice quiet. "Maybe I am crazy."

I put a trembling hand to my lips. "No. William, you're not. Please don't say that."

"I guess it's a good thing I'm here." He stood, slowly, like he barely had the energy to stand. A nurse in blue scrubs appeared, as if from nowhere, and put a hand on his arm.

"William, wait."

He didn't look at me. He just let the nurse lead him away,

his feet shuffling across the floor, soft whispers of sound coming from the bottoms of his socks.

I watched him go, tears streaming down my face. My skin was prickling cold, the weight on my chest so heavy I could barely breathe. Shaking with the effort of holding in my sobs, I gathered up my purse and left.

PICTURES OF CHILDHOOD

To be *filled with emptiness* was something of an oxymoron, but one I'd never felt so keenly as I did now. I left William in the psychiatric ward of a hospital, his heart crushed. In breaking his, I'd torn apart my own. I felt hollow, and yet consumed with guilt. Empty, but filled with confusion and sadness.

I went back to Jessica and Peter's, but I didn't tell them what had happened. I couldn't. Instead, I took Edgar for a long walk, hoping the fresh air would help clear my head.

My conversation with the doctor weighed heavily on me. I didn't want to believe he was right—that I was a barrier to William getting better. I could no longer imagine my life without him. I'd lost my mother when I was too young to know her. Lost a man I'd thought I might marry when he'd decided I wasn't worth waiting for. Lost my father, the only family I'd ever had.

Now I'd lost William. The man who'd brought me back to life.

When I got back to their house, my nose was cold from

the night air. And I wasn't any closer to finding answers, my mind as muddled as ever.

The next morning, I took Edgar out, then came back in and sat at the kitchen table with a mug of coffee. Jessica and Peter had already left for work. I didn't know what would happen with my job, but it was hard to care. I had too much on my mind. And worst-case scenario, it wasn't like I needed the money. I loved what I did, but if I got fired, at least my inheritance afforded more than enough resources to live on.

I couldn't stop thinking about William's paintings. If the doctor was right, and it was all a delusion, how had he seen those things to paint them? How had he known?

Was he a con-artist, like Jessica had suggested? Had he spent time researching me, visiting places I'd been, taking pictures? Had he concocted an elaborate ruse to draw me in and seduce me? It seemed like an enormous amount of effort to undertake, even for ten million dollars.

No matter how I looked at it, the paintings didn't make sense. If he was crazy, and it was all a delusion, how had he painted them? Even the doctor had glossed over that part. He hadn't really responded when I'd told him the paintings were real.

But if he was conning me, why had he taken such elaborate measures? Was money enough motive? Was there something else fueling such intricate lies?

His paintings were the key. They were the anomaly—the part of this puzzle that didn't fit. So maybe we were trying to build the wrong picture. But if we were, I had no idea what the real puzzle was supposed to look like.

"There might be a way to find out," I said to Edgar. His ears swiveled, and he blinked his eyes open. "Or at least give me a clue. You want to go for a ride in the car?"

He sprang to his feet, looking spry for an old man. I grabbed a few things and we headed out to my car.

* * *

NINETY MINUTES LATER, we arrived at our destination and I parked on the street. The house still looked so familiar—so much like it had when Dad and I had lived here. Sage green siding with white trim and a white door. A long driveway lined with dark green shrubs.

I took a deep breath. If William had researched me, this was one of the places he would have come. He'd painted the tree in the backyard of this house—my childhood home.

"Stay here for a little bit, okay, buddy?"

Edgar settled down on the backseat, his head resting on his front legs.

"Such a good boy."

I gave him a Nylabone to gnaw on, cracked the windows so he'd have enough air, and went to the front door of the house I'd grown up in.

Another deep breath, and I knocked.

A few seconds later, the door opened. An older woman with graying hair answered. She was dressed in jeans and an oversize t-shirt.

"Can I help you?" she asked.

"Hi," I said, feeling suddenly awkward. "I'm sorry to bother you. This might seem strange, but I used to live here."

Her smile put me at ease. "Well, I'll be. I remember you. You must be Dr. Nichols' daughter. You were younger the last time I saw you."

"You knew my dad?"

"He was an acquaintance," she said. "We bought the house from him. That must have been what, fifteen years ago?"

"Yes, about that," I said. "You've lived here that long?"

"We have," she said. "How is your father?"

"Oh, he passed away last year."

"I'm so sorry to hear that," she said, her voice full of sympathy. "I didn't realize."

"Thank you," I said.

"I suppose you're here for the memories?" She opened the door wider. "Come on in. I bet it's different from when you lived here, but you're welcome to look around."

"Are you sure?" I asked. "I don't want to intrude too much. I thought maybe I'd just look around outside. But I didn't want to trespass, so I figured I'd ask."

"Nonsense," she said. "Come in. I don't mind a bit."

"Thank you."

I stepped through the door and looked around. It did look different, but much of it was still familiar. The flow of the rooms. The way the kitchen had a pass-through into the dining area. The back door leading into the yard.

"I'm Alyssa," she said. "Alyssa Redmond."

"Ivy Nichols," I said.

"Can I show you around?"

"Sure, that would be great."

I followed Alyssa through the house. She opened bedroom doors and I peeked inside. My old bedroom was now a craft and sewing room, with a large work table and bins and shelves along the walls. I seemed to remember it had once been carpeted, but it now had hardwood floors. The kitchen had been updated, with new countertops and appliances. The room my dad had used for his study was their guest room—instead of being crammed with books, it had a bed with a patchwork quilt.

"This is so nice of you," I said as she led me back into the main living area. "I appreciate it so much."

"It's my pleasure," she said.

"Can I ask you what might be an odd question?"

"Sure," she said.

"Has anyone ever come by asking about me or my father? Particularly in the last year or so?"

She shook her head slowly, as if she was thinking. "No, I don't think anyone has ever come here asking about him, or you. That sounds worrisome. Who might it have been?"

"No one you need to be concerned about," I said. Had William been here? Maybe he hadn't spoken to the owners. It was only the tree he'd painted. He wouldn't have had to come inside to have seen that. "Do you mind if I look around outside?"

"Be my guest," she said.

Alyssa followed me outside. The familiarity of the back property was more poignant—so similar to what I remembered. The freshly clipped grass. The concrete patio. The creek at the edge of the property. But one thing was strikingly missing.

"What happened to the tree?" I walked toward a large stump next to the creek. "This tree used to be huge. The branches hung over the creek, and my dad built a swing."

"Oh, we had to take that tree down years ago," she said. "In fact, I think it was right after we moved in. I remember it well because I was so disappointed. That tree was one of the reasons I wanted to buy this house. But it had a disease of some kind. Rotting from the inside. It was so big, we didn't want to risk it falling, or one of our kids climbing in it and a limb breaking. So we had it cut down."

"You cut it down fifteen years ago?"

She nodded. "We did. I'm still a bit sad when I think about it."

I stared at the stump. The top was weathered smooth, the wood faded and old. If they'd cut this tree down fifteen years ago, there was no way William could have seen it. The tree wasn't here.

Oh my god.

"Do you mind if I take a picture of this?" I gestured toward the stump.

"Not at all."

I pulled out my phone and snapped a few pictures, then texted one to Jessica.

"Thank you so much for your time, Alyssa," I said. "I really appreciate it."

"You're quite welcome," she said. "Would you like to stay for lunch?"

"That's so nice of you to offer, but I'm afraid I can't," I said. "I have to get home. But thank you again."

My mind was racing as I said my goodbyes and went around the front to my car. Jessica had already texted back with a series of question marks. I clipped on Edgar's leash and let him out of the car, then called her.

"Hello? Ivy, why did you send me a picture of a tree stump?"

"That's the tree," I said. "From my childhood home. The one with the swing."

"I'm not following."

"The tree William painted," I said. "He couldn't have seen it in person, Jessica. It was cut down fifteen years ago."

"What are you saying?"

"That he didn't come here," I said. "He couldn't have seen that tree. And I know I don't have any photos of it. Not a single one."

"Well, maybe he just painted a tree with a swing," she said. "How do you know it's that specific tree?"

"It is, Jess," I said. "Every detail is the same, just like I remember it. He even painted me sitting on the swing reading a book."

"So, okay, that means what?" she asked. "He didn't research you? He's not lying?"

"It means he's not lying, *and* he's not crazy," I said. "At least, not the kind of crazy they think he is."

"Then how did he know what the tree looked like?" she asked.

"I have no idea." I was practically laughing. "Oh my god, I'm right back where I started. I have no explanation. But he was right all along."

"Right about what?"

"Saving me," I said. A tear broke free from the corner of my eye. "He was right about saving me. I just hope I'm not too late to return the favor."

PURPLE HYACINTH

❦

I waited until the next day to go back to the hospital. His seventy-two hours were almost over, and I wanted to be able to take him home with me. If he'd come. I had to face the very real possibility that he wouldn't. But I couldn't give up on him now.

On the way over, I stopped at a florist and bought a single flower, a purple hyacinth. In the language of flowers, it had represented a plea for forgiveness. I wasn't sure if he'd know what it meant, but it felt like the right thing to do. I'd spent too much time trying to follow my head, and that had gotten me into this mess. It was time I followed my heart. And my heart said to bring the flower.

I waited at the front desk for them to let me back, my stomach fluttering with nerves. Would he see me? Or would he tell them no?

Finally, a nurse came and led me back. I spotted William instantly, sitting alone at one of the tables, still dressed in a t-shirt and gray sweats.

He glanced up at me as I approached, then looked away.

CLAIRE KINGSLEY

His blue eyes were dull and lifeless. It broke my heart all over again. I couldn't imagine what his felt like.

I put the flower on the table. His eyes flicked to it, but he looked away again. And he still didn't say a word.

"It's a purple hyacinth," I said. "It used to mean—"

"Please forgive me," he said, his voice soft.

"Yes," I said. "Can I please talk to you?"

He didn't respond, just kept his eyes locked on the table, his head tilted to the side. But he didn't say no, either.

I pulled out the chair next to him and sat. "William, I'm so sorry for doubting you. Everything inside me has been telling me to believe you. From the first time we met, I've trusted you. Even when I didn't know you, and it didn't make any sense. When I should have been afraid of you. Do you know why?"

He silently shook his head and absently touched the flower petals.

"Because you're William."

He looked at me then, and the flicker of hope in his eyes hit me like a lightning strike to the chest.

"You told me you've been sent to save me," I said. "I'll be completely honest. I don't know if someone, or something, sent you. But you've been right all along. You did come into my life to save me. You already have."

"No, I haven't."

"Yes, you really have," I said. "Do you know how lonely I was before we met? How disconnected? Most people have someone to turn to when they're sad or alone. I had my friends, but it wasn't the same. Jess and Peter have each other. They care about me, but I've always been their third wheel. But then I met you. And it was like these little threads started to stitch us together, connecting us."

He nodded.

"And the remarkable thing isn't that you know things

216

from my past. It isn't that you painted things that only exist in my memories. You don't just know things *about* me. You know *me*. Who I am, deep down. That's not because you had visions, or because of something you painted. You see me. You see every part of me, right down to the core of who I am."

I reached out and took his hand, my heart soaring when he didn't pull away.

"I went to the house with the tree yesterday," I said. "The tree you painted. Do you know what I found?"

He shook his head.

"The tree is gone," I said. "It's just a stump. The people who bought the house from my dad had to cut it down fifteen years ago. You've never seen that tree with your own eyes, and I've seen the picture you painted. I can't explain how that's possible with any sort of logic. But when I saw that old, weathered stump, I realized what you've been trying to tell me this whole time. *How* it's possible isn't important."

"Then what is?"

"Us," I said. "Whatever brought us together, it was for a reason. Because I was meant to be yours, and you were meant to be mine. And maybe someday we'll know more, and maybe we won't. But that doesn't really matter. The only thing that matters is that I love you, and I need you in my life."

He looked deep into my eyes, as if he could see straight through me. My heart beat fast. Dread and hope warred for dominance, making my stomach clench and my mouth go dry.

Wrapping his fingers around my hand, he squeezed. "I love you too."

"Please come home with me," I said.

He nodded, and I sighed out a deep breath, my body trembling with relief. We stood, and I reached for him, pulling him close. He held me in his arms, burying his face in my neck.

Someone began to clap, and a few more people joined in. William either didn't notice, or didn't care. He squeezed me tighter, nearly picking me up off my feet.

* * *

WE HAD to wait for them to return William's personal belongings and have him sign the necessary paperwork before we could leave. The doctor came to speak with him before we left, urging him to seek treatment. With his usual confidence, William assured him that he was fine.

On the way to pick up Edgar from Jessica and Peter's house, I told William about Eric Andrews from Homeland Security. How Blake had turned William in using a false story. I expected him to get angry, but he just shook his head.

"See? Desperate," he said. "It won't be long and Blake is going to dig himself into a hole he can't get out of."

"I just hope it's a hole that's far away from us," I said. "So, Eric tried to find out more about who you are, but he couldn't. He'd like to talk to you. I think he sees you as a challenge."

William shrugged. "He's welcome to look all he wants."

"You don't think he'll find anything."

"I know he won't," he said. "There isn't anything to find."

I took a deep breath. "Listen, I know you're not lying to me. I never thought you were. And I don't think you're crazy either. But aren't you curious? Don't you wonder if anything came before, and you just can't remember?"

"No."

"Okay." I wasn't sure I wanted to give voice to my thoughts, but there was something I could no longer ignore. "But could you understand that maybe I'd like to know? Let's entertain the possibility that you do have a past, just for a second. What if you had a family? What if you had someone else in your life? Maybe even a wife."

He looked at me, his expression serious. "No, Ivy, that's not possible."

"Why not?"

"Because it's not."

I flicked on the blinker and turned a corner. "I appreciate your confidence, but I'd like to be sure."

"Why?" he asked, and there was something in his tone. He wasn't angry or frustrated that I was pushing this issue. He sounded… amused.

"Why do I want to know if you have a wife somewhere?" I asked. "I think that's pretty obvious."

He held out his left hand. "I don't have a ring."

"You don't have a birth certificate."

"Fair point," he said.

"I'm just wondering if you would mind if I told Eric that it's okay to do some more digging," I said. "I know you don't think he'll find anything. And if he doesn't, that's fine. I just want to be sure there isn't something we're missing."

"Like my wife and kids?"

"Stop," I said, reaching over to smack him playfully on the arm.

He laughed. "All right. If it makes you feel better."

We picked up Edgar, who was downright joyous at seeing William. His tail whipped back and forth so hard he knocked things off a shelf before we got him outside.

When we got back to my house, I wanted to crumple with relief. Everything felt right with him there, and I knew I was never letting go of William again.

HOSPITAL

*L*ife quieted down after William's forced hospital stay. I went back to work. My boss had granted me personal leave after the incident at the career expo. Word had spread across campus, and on my first day back, I could tell my students were dying to ask what had happened. Rather than leave them to wonder and spread more rumors, I addressed it as simply as I could. In several of my classes, it turned into a good discussion about boundaries and harassment.

I was happy to get back to a normal routine. William all but moved in with me, even bringing his painting supplies, easel, and canvases to my house. We moved some furniture around and set up a painting area for him near a window.

His vigilance hadn't diminished. He still wanted to take me to work and he met me for lunch regularly. But there was no sign of Blake. I spoke with Arthur, who assured me there was nothing to be concerned about when it came to my accounts. He also said Blake had taken an unexpected leave of absence. I hoped that meant it was over and I wouldn't hear from him again.

Early on a Saturday morning, while William was busy painting and I sat at the table reading over coffee, I got a text from Eric Andrews. I'd called him shortly after William came home from the hospital, letting him know William didn't mind if he did a little digging. Eric had spoken briefly to William, and said he'd get back to us if he found anything.

I stared at the text.

"Is everything okay?" William asked.

"It's from Eric." I looked up at William. "He thinks you might have been treated at Saint Peter Hospital in Olympia last year."

His brow furrowed. "I've never been there."

"Well, what if it was before? Before the park, and before you met James?"

He opened his mouth and I was sure he was going to argue with me. But he closed it again and came to sit next to me. "Would it make you feel better if we go there? Find out for sure?"

I nodded.

He took my hand and brought it to his lips. Kissed the backs of my fingers. "Then let's go."

"Thank you."

I glanced down at the text again and my sense of unease grew. This might be the first step to finding some real answers about who William really was. Part of me was afraid to find out—afraid of what lurked in the shadows of his past.

But I knew that wasn't the only source of tension in my back and anxiety churning in my stomach. Saint Peter Hospital was where my dad had spent his last months. Where I'd held his hand as he died. I hadn't been there since the day I'd lost him, and I wasn't sure how I felt about going back.

* * *

My heart fluttered with nerves as we walked into the hospital. William held my hand, his body relaxed. He'd been quiet on the drive. I knew he was doing this to indulge me. He didn't expect to find that he'd been here. I wasn't sure what we would discover, but the closer we got, the more I hoped we'd leave with more answers.

A woman at the front desk smiled at us. I'd gotten to know a lot of the hospital staff during the months my dad spent here, but I didn't recognize her.

"Can I help you?"

"Possibly. We're trying to find out if he was treated here last year." I gestured to William. "His name is William Cole."

"Can I see some ID please?" she asked.

"I don't have any," William said.

"Um…" She blinked a few times. "Well, I can't release patient information without identification. It's confidential."

I'd wondered if this would be a problem. "Could you just tell us if you had a patient by that name? That would at least be a start."

"I can ask the hospital administrator," she said. "But I don't think I can give out any information."

"We'd appreciate it if you could ask," I said. "Thank you."

We waited while she called someone. William gently rubbed my back and looked around. If he did have amnesia, and he had been here, he was showing no signs of recognition.

The large automatic doors to the side of the reception desk opened and a nurse in blue scrubs came out. I recognized her from when my dad had been here. She glanced at us with a polite smile, then stopped in her tracks.

"William?" she asked.

He looked around, as if to see if she might be speaking to someone else. "Yes."

"Look at you." She walked slowly toward us. "You look amazing. We've been wondering what happened to you. How have you been?"

His body went stiff and I clasped his hand. He stared at the nurse but didn't say a word. It didn't take long before the smile left her face.

"I'm sorry," I said. "You know him?"

"Of course I do," she said. "He was on my floor for months."

"You're sure it was him?" I asked.

Her forehead creased. "Yes, I'm sure. I couldn't possibly forget William. He had the entire staff rooting for him. You look familiar too, although William never had visitors."

"No, but my dad was here for a while," I said. "I spent a lot of time visiting him."

William squeezed my hand. "Ivy, this isn't right."

I put my other hand on his arm, trying to offer him reassurance. "Maybe it is. She knows you."

"I wasn't here," he said. "I've never been here."

I turned back to the nurse. "He doesn't remember this."

She nodded, her eyes full of sympathy. "He was having memory problems, but we hoped with proper treatment, he'd improve."

"Can you tell us what happened?" I asked. "Why he was here? What happened to him?"

"Yes, of course," she said. "Why don't you come with me."

She led us back to a small waiting room. William was silent, his eyes moving over everything. I couldn't tell what he was thinking. Was he looking for something familiar? We sat at a table and waited while she left for a moment, then came back with a tablet.

"All right, let's see," she said, tapping her tablet screen. "The Coast Guard rescued you about two miles off the coast and—"

"Wait," I said. "You mean he was in the ocean?"

She nodded.

"Does it say how he got there?"

Her eyes scanned the screen. "No, the note here says *origin not determined*. It looks like there had been a storm that night, and the Coast Guard had to respond to multiple emergencies. They didn't know where he'd come from."

"Wow," I said. "I'm sorry, go on."

"You were revived on board the Coast Guard vessel, and airlifted here due to the severity of your condition," she said. "When you arrived, you were breathing on your own, but unconscious and unresponsive. You remained in that state, so you were admitted."

"Do you mean he was in a coma?" I asked.

"Initially," she said. "That progressed to what's known as a minimally conscious state. He wasn't fully conscious or aware of his surroundings, but his cognitive function began to show signs of improvement."

"And eventually he woke up," I said.

"Yes," she said. "It happened more rapidly than the doctors could explain. He started responding normally to external stimuli and within a couple of days, he was speaking. Answering questions. Most people who spend time in a coma, or with another consciousness disorder, never fully recover. But once he woke up, so to speak, he improved quickly. Then we worked on getting him mobile again. Physical therapy for muscle atrophy and so forth."

"How did you know his name?" I asked. "Did he have any identification when he was brought in?"

"No," she said, "We called him John, as in John Doe, until he woke up and told us his name was William Cole."

"And he was having problems with his memory?"

She nodded. "He was sure about his name, but that was about all he could tell us. He had trouble with his short-term memory too. His brain had difficulty making new memories. But we were seeing improvement with that. Unfortunately, once he was strong enough, we had to discharge him. We were working with social services to find a place for him to go, but he insisted he didn't need help. He left before his patient advocate could make sure he had somewhere to go."

"He's been doing fine," I said.

"Good. It's such a relief to see you," she said to William. "Not a day has gone by that I haven't wondered what happened to you."

William looked down at the table, his face a stony mask.

I rubbed his arm. "Are you okay?"

"I don't remember this," he said. "I wasn't here."

"Would you like to look around?" she asked. "Maybe seeing the room you were in would help."

He met my eyes, and although I could feel his confusion, he nodded.

The nurse led us upstairs to the third floor. She greeted the other hospital staff and several of them stared at William. It was clear they recognized him. We turned a corner and went down another hallway, half-open doors on either side. Monitors beeped, and the air had the all-too-familiar tang of harsh soap and cleaning chemicals. Turning again, I felt like I was losing my sense of direction. Hospitals always seemed like mazes to me.

She stopped in front of a partially open door. "This was your room. It's occupied right now. We're always short on beds, it seems. But you can peek inside if you want."

I stared at the number beside the door. Three twenty-two.

"Are you sure this is right?" I asked. "This is the room William was in?"

"Positive," she said.

I covered my mouth with my hand. It couldn't be.

William turned toward me and touched my arm. The disoriented look in his eyes was gone. He was focused—concerned. "What's wrong?"

"My dad was in this room," I said in a shaky whisper.

He took my hand. "Is this where he passed?"

I nodded. But it wasn't being faced with the room where I'd lost my father that had me reeling. The pieces of the puzzle that was William Cole were clicking into place.

Someone walked by, pushing a large cart, and we had to step aside.

"Let me take you to the waiting room on this floor so we're not standing in the hallway," the nurse said.

We followed her down the hallway, but I remembered this, now. We'd come upstairs from a different direction, so I hadn't recognized where I was. But this route was embedded in my memory. The restroom on the left. Vending machines on the right. Elevators around the corner. A waiting room with couches and armchairs, and a TV always showing daytime soaps or news. I'd spent months in this section of the hospital, coming to visit my dad almost every day.

"I think I know what happened," I said. "Can I see the dates William was here?"

William nodded, so the nurse held the tablet so I could see. She swiped through a few screens, but it said exactly what I expected.

"Thank you," I said. "You've been so helpful."

She smiled. "You're welcome. Let us know if there's anything else we can do. Take care, William. It was great to see you."

The nurse left us alone in the waiting room. I touched my fingers to my lips, staring at William.

"Ivy, what's going on?" he asked.

"I think I know where your visions came from."

"What do you mean? Where?"

"My dad had cancer, and he'd been fighting it for a couple of years," I said. "That's when he had a stroke. I'd moved in to help take care of him, but after the stroke, he was hospitalized. Here. In room three twenty-two."

"So if I was really here like she says, we were in the same room," he said.

"Not just the same room," I said. "You were here at the same time. I knew there was someone else in the room, but I never paid much attention. The second bed was always curtained off, so I never saw who it was. But William, it was you."

"Why do you think that explains my visions?"

"Because I spent three months sitting by my father's side, talking to him," I said. "I came almost every day to keep him company. He couldn't speak anymore, so I did. I sat next to his bed and told him stories. Memories. I talked about everything, all the wonderful things I could think of from my childhood. I read books aloud. I talked about my life and what I was feeling. I poured my heart out to him day after day. And you were right next to me the entire time."

"You think that's why I know the things I do?" he asked. "I heard you?"

"You told me once that my voice has been in your mind for as long as you can remember," I said. "What if that's why? What if you heard me talking to my dad? For some reason, your brain took all that in—all those months of listening to me. That's why you knew things, why you knew my name and my voice. For some reason, when you woke up, that's what stuck. That's what was left in your head. No wonder you thought you had to find me."

"But if I heard you when I was unconscious, why don't I remember anything else?" he asked. "I've been walking around this place, listening to that nurse tell me she knows me. That I was treated here. But nothing here is familiar. Not a single thing."

"I don't know," I said. "I don't know why you would have heard me, or why you'd remember. But you did. And it felt like visions to you because you couldn't explain where it had come from."

He backed up a few steps. "I don't understand this, Ivy. That isn't what happened. It can't be."

"But William, don't you see how amazing this is?" Tears filled my eyes. I blinked them away. "I looked at the dates. You started to regain consciousness the day after my dad died. The first day I didn't come to the hospital. It's like you knew I wasn't here, so you started to wake up. You already knew you had to find me."

"But you're telling me it didn't mean anything," he said. "I just heard you talking and my brain latched onto what I'd heard. I wasn't sent to save you. If I'd just wandered back to wherever I came from, it wouldn't have made a difference."

"How can you say that?" I asked. "You did save me. You've saved me a million times over. I can't imagine my life without you. Losing my dad was awful, but if it led you to me, then at least something good came of it all."

He stared at me for a long moment, his brow furrowed. "Come here," he said finally, opening his arms. He grabbed me and pulled me close, wrapping me in a tight embrace. "I love you."

"I love you, too." A few tears trailed down my cheek and I sniffed. "And who knows? Maybe someone did send you. Maybe it was my dad."

He pulled away and brushed the hair back from my face, then cupped my cheeks with his hands. "Maybe it was. And I'm the one who kept insisting how it was possible didn't matter. What matters is us."

I nodded as he leaned in to kiss me, his lips soft and warm.

"I wouldn't have done anything differently, even if I could remember it all," he said, his hands still against my face. "If I'd woken up knowing who I was before, I still would have come for you."

"I know," I said. "And I'm so glad you did."

PIECES OF THE PUZZLE

*W*illiam appeared to adjust to his new reality fairly quickly. Although he still couldn't remember anything from his past, he accepted that he had been someone before his accident—that a past existed. He even told James about Saint Peter Hospital, and how hearing me talk to my dad was responsible for his visions. James told him that knowing the source of the visions didn't make them any less of a miracle. I whole-heartedly agreed.

Weeks went by after the hospital visit, and we didn't find any more clues to William's past. Eric was convinced William Cole wasn't his real name. He'd been unable to find any records that matched. But without any hints as to what his name might have been, it was difficult to know where to look.

William seemed amused by Eric's quest to find his real identity. He answered Eric's questions as best he could with his typical nonchalance. I wondered why William didn't seem concerned over whether or not we discovered who he'd been. When asked, he simply shrugged and said if there was something he needed to remember, he would. But he was happy now—happy with me—and that was what really mattered.

But beneath his serene exterior, I sensed restlessness. Perhaps he was coping with all the new information, reframing his self-concept in light of what we now knew. Or maybe he was beginning to remember things. I wasn't sure. But I didn't ask—not yet. I knew he'd tell me what was on his mind when he was ready.

Saturday morning, I woke early, alone in my bed. The sheets were still warm from where William had been sleeping. He often woke at odd times, so I wasn't alarmed. I listened and heard faint sounds coming from the other room. His hushed voice, talking to Edgar.

Rolling over, I took a deep breath and stretched. Then got up and went in search of William.

I found him behind his easel, shirtless in his paint-splattered sweats. Just like I had after the first night I'd spent with him in his apartment.

"Morning," I said.

He twitched, blinking at me as if I'd started him. "Hi."

"Is everything okay?"

His eyes went back to his painting and he rubbed his forehead with the back of his hand. "Yeah, fine."

"What are you working on?"

"It's nothing." He fidgeted with his palette and rubbed his forehead again.

"Are you sure you're okay?" I came closer. "You seem really jumpy."

He looked at me with his brow furrowed. His eyes darted between me and his painting.

"What is it?" I asked.

Stepping back, he watched me with a mix of resignation and worry. It reminded me of the first time I saw his apartment, when he'd been so concerned about how I'd react to his paintings.

I moved to where I could see what he was working on. It was the brick building covered in ivy.

"You're painting this again?" I asked.

"Yes."

"Why?" I asked. "You already painted it."

"I can't get it out of my head."

"You keep seeing it?" I asked. "Do you mean when you're dreaming? Or when you're awake?"

"Awake. This one has always been different. I don't know how to explain it. It feels different." He put a hand to his chest. "In here. I don't know why, but I know it means something."

I studied the painting, looking for anything that might be familiar. I knew I hadn't described a building like this when I was visiting my dad. William couldn't have heard me talk about it. This had to have come from somewhere else.

"Maybe it's just my name," I said. "You remembered my name when you woke up. Maybe this is a representation of that. You kept hearing Ivy, and your mind came up with this picture. Ivy often grows on buildings like this."

He shook his head. "No. I know I was wrong about things before, but I'm telling you, this is important. And I need to figure out why."

I glanced at the other canvases leaning against the wall nearby. "What are those?"

His worried brow-furrow came back. "Nothing."

"You really won't show me?"

He sighed and turned them around. Moved them one by one so I could see. They were all the same, every one. All the same brick building, ivy trailing up the façade.

"I can't get it out of my head," he said again.

"Okay," I said, looking him in the eyes. "It means something. Let me help you figure it out. I'll start looking online to see if I can find a building like this. Maybe if we find out where this is, it will make more sense."

His relief was palpable. He put down his brush and palette and pulled me in for a hug. "Thank you," he whispered against my hair.

* * *

MY EYES WERE dry and gritty, and every brick building was beginning to look the same. I'd spent hours searching, looking at photos, trying to find one that matched the building William kept painting. His building was odd in that it appeared to be the front, but there was no door. If there were windows, they were obscured by the ivy. The rest of the scene was always hazy and indistinct, not offering any additional clues as to where it might be. Were there more buildings nearby? Was it on a hill, or near a street? Neither of us had any idea.

I'd found a large brick structure in Connecticut that was similar, but William was sure it wasn't the one. It had a wide double door, although ivy covered the windows. He was convinced his painting was accurate—that the building looked just like he'd seen it, the door obscured.

Needing a break from the endless stream of ivy-covered brick, I opened my email. I had a message from Eric. My heart started pounding as soon as I read it. There was a link to a website and the words, *I think I found him.*

My hand trembled as I clicked on the link. It was a site for a hunting and fishing guide service in Alaska, operated by a man named Jack Morton. The *About Us* page included profiles of several guides, but I didn't see anything connected to William. What was Eric talking about?

I went to the photo gallery and my heart nearly stopped.

On the first page a pair of intense blue eyes looked back at me. A picture of William.

His beard was thicker than he kept it now, and he was dressed in a dark brown coat and knit hat. He had that enigmatic half-smile I knew so well. There was no doubt it was him.

The caption simply said, *Hunting guide Will Green.*

Clicking through the pages of photos, I found more. William and another man crouched behind the body of a large elk. Standing in front of a river, holding a silver fish. Holding a bow and arrow, the bowstring drawn back. Looking back at the camera, a large ax in his hands.

Most of them just had the name Will Green beneath them. But finally, I found a photo with a longer caption.

WILL GREEN HAS BEEN a hunting and fishing guide since he was eighteen years old. His sharp natural instincts combined with years of mentoring and practical experience make him an ideal choice for your next trip. Will is known throughout the region for his excellent tracking skills and remarkable stealth.

I TOOK A FEW DEEP BREATHS, trying to calm my racing heart.

"William?" I called out into the other room.

He peeked through the door. "Did you find something?"

"Not the building," I said. "But I think Eric might have found you."

"What?" He stepped into the room and looked at my screen.

"He sent me this."

I moved so he could take my seat and waited while he clicked through the website, looking at the photos. He stared at the screen, his face unreadable.

"It looks like me," he said, his voice soft.

"It is you," I said. "Unless you have a twin named Will."

He laughed softly.

"How would you feel about me calling them?" I asked.

He met my eyes and his mouth hooked in a little smile. "You want to make sure he lets my wife and kids know I'm alive?"

"That's not funny," I said.

He stood and kissed my forehead. "It's a little funny." He kissed me again. "I don't mind if you call. I think it's better if it's you. It's hard to talk to someone who might know me when I don't remember them."

"Okay."

William touched the side of my face and kissed me, soft and slow. "I'll take Edgar for a walk."

I nodded. "I'll see what I can find out."

He left, closing the door behind him.

I got the phone number from the website and called.

A man's voice answered, "Backcountry Guide Service."

"Hi, can I speak with Jack, please?"

"You're talking to him."

"My name is Ivy Nichols and I'm calling about a man named Will," I said. "I think you know him as Will Green."

"Yeah, what about him?" he asked.

"Well, this is going to sound odd, but I think the man I know as William might be him," I said. "Only, he was in an accident and lost his memory. I'm just trying to connect the dots to see if I can find out who he was and where he came from."

"No shit," he said. "Yeah, I know Will. Known him most of his life. Is he okay?"

"Other than his memory, he's fine," I said.

"That's good to hear," he said. "What sort of accident?"

"Well, we haven't figured out the details, but he was

picked up by the Coast Guard," I said. "He was in the water, but we're not sure how he got there. They brought him in and he was taken to a hospital. He was there for a while before he woke up."

"And he doesn't remember anything before that?" he asked.

"Actually, his memory begins even later," I said. "He doesn't remember the hospital at all, although he was there for months."

"Jesus," he said.

A wave of nervousness hit me. I was so afraid of what I'd discover. "Does he have any family?"

"No," he said. "His dad was out of the picture and his mom died in a plane crash a couple years back—small plane, had trouble with the landing. She didn't have any other kids, and Will didn't have any other relatives that I'm aware of."

"Was there... anyone else in his life?" *Please say no.*

"Nah, Will was kind of a loner," he said. "Nice guy, everyone liked him. Always had a few girls chasing after him, but he never seemed serious about any of them. Liked his space, I think. But he was always kind of an odd kid."

Oh thank god. Relief washed over me. No wife or kids. "So, he worked for you as a hunting guide? Is that right?"

"He was one of the best," he said. "Good instincts. He could track anything."

"Somehow he wound up in Washington," I said. "Do you know anything about that? Did he tell you he was leaving?"

"Yeah, he did," he said. "It was out of the blue, but that was Will for you. Said he was heading south for a while."

"Did he say why?"

"Not specifically. He just said he felt like it was something he needed to do. That was like Will, though. I wasn't surprised he needed to get out in the world a little bit. See

CLAIRE KINGSLEY

some things. Maybe some of those things he was always painting."

"He painted when he lived there?"

"Yeah, talented guy," he said. "Painted some beautiful stuff. He gave one to my wife the year before he left. It's the view from our porch. So, you say he lost his memory? Completely?"

"Most of it," I said. "Although he seems to know his name, or at least his first name. He told the hospital staff that his name is William. But he said William Cole, not William Green."

"Did he? That's interesting."

"Why? Does Cole mean something?" I asked.

"That was his mother's maiden name," he said. "Suzanna Cole. His father was Phillip Green. What a bastard he was."

"Oh?"

"Yeah. He put up a good front so none of us knew what was really going on in that house," he said. "But he was hard on Suzanna and Will. Hit the both of them a fair bit, I think. First Suzanna, but they always hid it. I think he started in on Will when he tried to get the piece of shit to stop hitting his mom. Sorry, pardon the language."

"Oh my god, that's terrible," I said. "You said his dad wasn't in the picture. What happened?"

"Will got big enough to fight back," he said. "He must have been fourteen or fifteen. Rearranged his dad's face, then kicked his ass out. Suzanna and Will stayed with us for a little while after that. We helped Suzanna get a restraining order filed. Divorce went through later. Phillip left town and he's never been back."

"Wow," I said. "This is… I don't even know what to say."

"Will loved his mom," he said. "Took good care of her after they got rid of his dad. He got pretty reclusive after she died. Even more than before."

My heart broke for William. I knew what it was like to lose a parent. But I'd known my dad's death was coming. He'd been sick for a long time. William had lost his mom suddenly. That must have been a terrible thing to live through.

Maybe that was part of why he couldn't remember. He didn't want to.

"That sounds like him," I said. "He's a good man."

"That he is," he said. "You're sure he's all right?"

"Yeah, he is," I said. "He's living in the Seattle area now. He works as a model. I guess that's a far cry from a hunting guide."

Jack laughed. "I always teased him about having a pretty face. Do you mind if I ask about you? Are you a friend of his, or…"

"I'm his girlfriend."

"Good for Will," he said. "He needed to settle down with a good woman. It's a shame about his memory, but I'm glad to hear he found you."

"Me too."

"Anytime you two want to come up here, just give me a call," he said. "I've been checking on his cabin from time to time, so it's in good shape. Or you'd be welcome to stay with us. We have room."

"Thank you," I said. "I appreciate that. I'll let him know."

"Who knows, maybe seeing where he grew up might help," he said.

"It might," I said. "Thank you so much. This was really helpful."

"You're welcome," he said. "Tell Will I said hello."

"I will."

I ended the call and set my phone down. The picture of William—of Will Green—smiled back at me from my computer screen.

William was still out, so I replied to Eric's message, filling him in on what Jack had told me. He replied, letting me know he had a lead on how William ended up in the water. He'd call me as soon as he knew for sure.

I clicked through the photos again. There was a question nagging at me in the back of my mind. Something I'd almost asked Jack, but hadn't. It was probably crazy, but I decided I ought to find out. I dialed his number again and called.

THE PAST

William and Edgar were gone for over an hour. I talked to Eric again and we compared notes. It seemed we had finally fit all the pieces of the puzzle together—or most of them, at least.

When they came back, William wasn't interested in talking. He gave me that smoldering look that made me want to drop my panties, and backed me up into the bedroom.

I let all the worries about the past—about Alaska, paintings, and brick buildings—fall away while he made love to me. His strong body and masculine scent were intoxicating. He was feverish and intense, driving into me with ferocity and passion. I loved the way he felt, his body connected to mine. His stubble scratching my skin. The way he lost control, growling in my ear as he came.

Afterward, we lay together for a while, tangled in the sheets, catching our breath. I got up and used the bathroom, then slipped back into bed with him.

"I guess that means I'm not married to someone else," he said.

I laughed and snuggled against him. "No, you're not married."

"I told you I wasn't," he said.

"Do you want to hear what I found out?"

He took a deep breath, his muscular chest expanding against me. "Yes. I think I'm ready now."

"Your name was Will Green, and you worked as a hunting and fishing guide in Alaska," I said. "You realize that's kind of funny, right? When you first found me, you were using skills you didn't realize you had."

"I was hunting you," he said.

"Yep, you were." I slid my hand along his chest. This part was going to be harder to tell him. "When you were a child, your father abused your mom. You tried to stop him, but he hurt you too. When you got big and strong enough, you put a stop to it. It sounds like you beat the crap out of him. He left town, and your mom divorced him. She's where your last name comes from. Her maiden name was Cole."

"She died, didn't she?" he asked.

"Yes," I said, almost a whisper. "Do you remember any of this?"

"No," he said. "I could tell by your voice."

I took a deep breath. "She was killed in a small plane crash. Jack said you loved her, and you were pretty reclusive after losing her."

"Why did I leave Alaska?"

"He wasn't sure," I said. "You told him it was something you felt like you needed to do. And then you came down here."

"Do you know why I was in the water?" he asked.

"Yes," I said. "According to what Eric could find, you were probably en route from Alaska on a fishing boat that was being moved to Washington. Maybe you knew one of the crew members, or just arranged to go with them. We're not sure. The boat was in an accident and none of the other crew survived. When the Coast Guard picked you up, they didn't have any way of knowing who you were. If you had a wallet or ID on you, it got washed away in the water. And since you weren't part of the crew, there wasn't any record of you being on board. So your identity was a mystery."

"And the Coast Guard sent me to the hospital," he said. "Where I spent several months unconscious in room three twenty-two."

"Yeah."

"So that's all?" he asked. "I was an Alaskan mountain man, and on a whim, I decided to come down here?"

"There's one more thing." I sat up, holding the sheet over my chest, and grabbed my phone off the nightstand. "I had a feeling about something, so I asked if Jack would mind checking for me. He sent me this."

I handed William the phone, open to the picture I'd asked Jack to send. A painting of a brick building, ivy crawling up the façade.

"This is the building," he said. "Where did this come from?"

"You painted it," I said. "Jack said it was still sitting on your easel, like you'd been working on it just before you left."

He put the phone down and stared at me. "I painted this before."

I nodded.

"So it's not because of the accident," he said. "It's not from hitting my head."

"No. I think this might be why you left Alaska."

He picked up the phone and looked at it again. "I've never wished I could remember until now. I wish I knew what I was thinking when I painted this the first time."

"Me too," I said. "Maybe you saw it in a dream, or maybe it was a vision like you have now. But, you know, if this started before you were in the hospital, it might not have anything to do with me."

"No, it does," he said. "I'm sure of it."

I settled back down against his chest. "Then we'll keep looking until we figure it out."

BRICK AND IVY

he evening air was crisp, the sun just finishing its trip across the sky. Streetlights began winking to life in the fading light as William and I walked, hand in hand.

We'd spent the afternoon with Jessica and Peter at a new wine tasting room in Seattle near Queen Anne. Jessica had been dying to go for weeks. The winery owners had partnered with local artists to showcase their work, which made her art-loving heart blissfully happy. Art and wine, as she'd said, was a perfect pairing.

The wine had been lovely, and we'd all enjoyed sampling a variety of hors d'oeuvres. Cheeses, olives, bacon-wrapped dates. Fresh crusty bread and smoked salmon. We'd left the tasting room relaxed from the wine, and very full. After saying goodbye to Jessica and Peter, we'd decided to take a walk before heading back to William's Jeep.

"Jessica still looks at me funny," William said.

"No, she doesn't," I said. "Does she?"

"Sometimes," he said. "It's not like she's still suspicious. But I think she's trying to figure me out."

"Maybe she's trying to picture you in a plaid shirt, chopping wood," I said. "Or dressed in camo, tracking elk."

He shook his head and we turned a corner, walking up a hill. "Maybe. Oh, I forgot to tell you. I went to see a guy who teaches archery the other day."

"Did you? Why?."

"Jack's website has a picture of me with a bow and arrow," he said, "I was curious if I still knew how to shoot one. He let me test one out."

"And?"

"I'm very good at it," he said.

I laughed. "Are you serious?"

"Yes," he said. "I don't remember ever having done it before, but I knew exactly what to do. And I'm a great shot."

"Next thing I know, I'll come home, and you'll be skinning a deer in the front yard."

"I hear venison is delicious," he said.

I laughed again but William stopped, his hand tightening around mine.

"What's wrong?"

His eyes were wide, and he pulled me closer. "That's it."

"That's what?"

"It wasn't a building."

"What?" I glanced around, but the street was deserted. Then I realized what he was looking at. Flanking the street, right next to us, was a tall brick wall, covered in ivy. It straddled the distance between two buildings, most of its surface covered in the leafy green vines.

It looked exactly like William's painting.

My heart started racing and my limbs tingled with the sudden surge of adrenaline. William looked around, his jaw clenched tight, still keeping his grip on my hand.

"Maybe we should keep walking," I said, my voice small in the growing darkness. "Get out of here."

He nodded but just as he pulled me forward, a man with a hood drawn up over his head, his hands in his pockets, stepped around the corner.

It felt as if everything began to move in slow motion, but it all happened in an instant. The hooded man looked up, still walking toward us, and pulled his hand out of his pocket. Raised it, pointing something at me. William let go of my hand and shoved me hard toward the ivy-covered wall.

I heard an odd metallic swish. William grunted, his body jerking backward. There had hardly been a sound. My shoulder hit the wall, pain radiating down my arm. William staggered, then straightened. His left arm hung limp at his side, but he stalked toward the man.

Another swish, then a ping. William kept walking.

"Fuck," the man said. A voice I recognized.

He raised the gun again—I could see it now, the barrel long and round. I screamed. William walked straight for the gun, unflinching. Before the man could fire another shot, William grabbed his arm and stepped in closer.

They struggled, William with one arm hanging useless at his side. The man's hood fell backward, but I already knew who it was. Blake's face contorted in an angry grimace and he landed a blow across William's jaw. William's head barely moved, and he twisted Blake's arm.

With shaking hands and a pounding heart, I fumbled for my phone, trying to get my handbag's zipper open.

The two men stumbled backward, out of the circle of light cast from the streetlight above. I could see them moving, struggling for control. Low grunts and growls. Another metallic swish and one of them hit the ground, the other standing above him.

I couldn't take a breath, like the air had been kicked from my lungs. *Oh my god, please no.* With my heart in my throat, I rushed to them.

CLAIRE KINGSLEY

William looked back at me over his shoulder. Blake lay at his feet, unmoving, his body a crumpled heap. The gun fell from William's hand and clattered on the pavement. His eyes met mine and for the barest hint of a second, he smiled.

Then his legs buckled, and he collapsed onto the ground.

I was at his side in an instant. Blood soaked his shirt, running down his arm. I kicked the gun farther away, but Blake wasn't moving.

"William." I cradled his head in my lap. "William, please. Baby, please don't leave me. Please don't die."

HERE WHEN YOU WAKE

❦

I stroked William's hand while he slept. Held it and rubbed my thumb up and down. I turned it over and looked at his palm. Slid my fingers over the callouses at the base of each finger.

Please wake up.

The monitors beeped, and a nurse came in to check on him. She didn't have much to say. I knew he'd come to after surgery, then they'd transferred him to a regular room. But since they'd brought me to him, he hadn't opened his eyes.

I was terrified of what was going to happen when he woke up.

Logically, I knew he wasn't in a coma. He was sleeping off the anesthesia from the surgery that had removed the bullet from his shoulder. He'd probably been given something for pain, which could make him sleep longer.

But logic wasn't holding much sway with me. Not after watching him get shot. Taking the bullet meant for me.

"Ivy?"

I turned at the quiet voice.

Eric looked around the curtain. "Can I come in?"

I kept hold of William's hand and nodded.

"You've been here all night, haven't you?" he asked.

"What time is it?"

"A little after eight," he said.

"In the morning?"

He nodded.

"Then yes, I have."

"You should get some rest," he said.

"Not until he wakes up."

He nodded again. "How is he?"

"Surgery went fine," I said. "What are you doing here? Did you hear about this already?"

"Yeah," he said. "Perks of the job. I talked to the police a little while ago. Have they talked to you yet?"

"At the scene," I said. "I told them what I could."

"I wanted to let you know there won't be any charges pressed," he said.

"Is that your doing, or because it was obviously self-defense?"

"A little of my influence, but mostly because of the circumstances," he said. "They're already finding all sorts of damning evidence against Blake. That was attempted first-degree murder, clearly premeditated. The gun was stolen. There's evidence he tried to hire someone to kill you, but it fell through. Might be why he took it upon himself. He was getting sloppy at the end."

"William thought he owed a lot of money to loan sharks," I said. "Gambling debts."

"He was right," Eric said. "Enough that Blake was probably afraid for his life. Justifiably so."

"What was killing me going to accomplish?" I asked.

"It would have put control of your accounts into Blake's department at Dorset Financial," he said. "At least temporarily. Long enough for him to attempt to embezzle some of your funds. There are other ways he could have stolen money, but I suspect at this point, it was personal."

"I can't believe this happened."

"It's a good thing William was with you," he said.

I nodded again.

"I'm glad to hear he'll be okay. Make sure you get some rest." Eric left, and the curtain swished closed behind him.

My body ached with fatigue, but I couldn't sleep until William woke up. I certainly wasn't going to leave him here alone.

The image of him collapsing to the ground was burned in my mind. Blood soaking his clothes. Blake's lifeless form on the street next to us. I was glad Blake was dead. Maybe I should have felt guilty about that, but I didn't. He'd tried to kill me, and he'd almost killed William. I was glad he was gone.

William's hand twitched beneath mine. I watched his face, anxiety making my heart pound. His eyes cracked open, then closed again. He took a deep breath, his chest rising, and opened them again. Looking around, he blinked a few times, his movements slow and halting.

"William?"

His eyes came to rest on me and his brow furrowed, like he was confused. He licked his lips and blinked again.

Please know me. Please know who I am. "Hey." I squeezed his hand. "Do you know where you are?"

He glanced around again, his eyelids heavy, and nodded. "Hospital."

I swallowed hard, afraid to ask for fear of the answer. "Do you know who I am?"

His piercing blue eyes returned to mine, focused and clear. "Of course. You're my Ivy." He paused. "Did I save you?"

Tears stung my eyes and I smiled. "Yes, baby. You did."

"Good." His face relaxed and his eyes drifted closed. He squeezed my hand and I held his in both of mine.

He had saved me. In more ways than I could ever have imagined. He'd saved my life—literally and dramatically. But he'd also saved my heart, well before I'd had a gun pointed at me.

I didn't know if I'd ever be able to explain the ivy-covered wall. How he'd seen it, before he'd even once heard my voice. Why it had shone so clearly in his mind that he'd been compelled to paint it, over and over. How it had not only been real, but the site of an attempt on my life. If we hadn't stopped to look at it, we might not have seen Blake coming. He could have shot us both on that deserted street and walked away before anyone saw.

But he hadn't. William had known. He'd known from the beginning that he would save me. And he'd been right.

Maybe he hadn't appeared on this planet out of nowhere, a man with no past, his mind filled with images of a woman named Ivy—the woman he'd been created to protect. He was just a man who'd grown up in Alaska. Who'd followed his instincts and left his hometown.

I suspected very few people would believe me if I told them the series of events that had brought us together. But I looked at him—at this man who had captured me, body and soul—and I knew it was meant to be. I didn't need to know how or why. I was his, and he was mine. He would forever be my protector, and I would forever be his love.

I leaned forward and laid my head on the edge of the bed. Exhaustion swept over me like a wave, leaching out every last bit of energy I had left. My eyes closed, and just before I fell asleep, I felt William's fingers sliding through my hair.

His voice, low and soft. "Sleep now, my sweet Ivy. I'll be here when you wake up. I'll always be here."

EPILOGUE: I REMEMBERED

WILLIAM

I knew my memories were coming back when I started dreaming of snow.

Thick drifts of white, muting sound. Covering the world in silence. My dreams were of trees and wood. A knife in my hand that I'd made myself, the handle smooth, the blade sharp. An ax sinking deep into a log. Air so cold it hurt to breathe in. Boards creaking beneath my feet.

During the day, they remained nothing but hints, flitting at the edges of my consciousness. They stayed in that place between sleep and waking. Where the first light of dawn makes the sky glow at the horizon, like watercolors bleeding into each other on a canvas. Purple, pink, and orange. I couldn't remember places or people. Nothing distinct. Just whispers. Fleeting thoughts that would pass through my mind for an instant before disappearing again.

I let it happen. I didn't chase them down, pursuing the glimmers of my past. If there were things I needed to remember, I would, when the time was right. I let the memories exist in the shadows, for my mind was always full of the present. Of the man I had become. And of her. My love. My Ivy.

She shifted in bed, stretching out one leg. Her eyes didn't open. It was still early, and I didn't expect her to wake for at least an hour. Her face was relaxed, her eyelashes brushing the tops of her cheeks, her full lips soft and pink. She took a deep breath and moved again. Her hand reached out, sliding across the crisp sheets, and touched my chest. Rested there, her fingers curling against my skin as she once again relaxed into deeper slumber. As if, even in sleep, she needed to feel me near her.

Smiling, I wrapped my hand around hers and held it close. Breathed in the scent of her.

I shifted a little and winced. My shoulder was still sore where I'd been shot. I didn't mind. It was a small price to pay to have her breathing softly next to me. I'd do it again in a heartbeat. Although as far as I knew, I wouldn't need to.

My mind had quieted since I'd come to after the surgery to remove the bullet. The visions of Ivy's past had already begun to fade as new memories took their place. But the brick wall that had loomed constantly at the forefront of my thoughts had become nothing but a glimmer. I remembered what it had looked like, both in my mind and in reality. But the colors weren't so vivid and blinding. It no longer crowded out other thoughts, demanding my attention.

I didn't know where it had come from, any more than Ivy did. It was the one thing we couldn't explain. And maybe we never would.

It wasn't something I worried about. Whatever it was, wherever it had come from, it had done its job.

Regardless of who I'd been in the past, I knew who I was now. I was William Cole and I'd been sent to save her. My visions of her life might not have been planted in my head. But I'd had them, just the same. I'd known her voice, remembered her name. I'd found her, and I'd saved her, just like I'd known I would.

I took her hand and brought her fingers to my lips for a kiss. She didn't stir as I slipped out of our bed.

Edgar looked up at me from his spot next to the fireplace, one eye still half closed.

"Hey, buddy," I said, my voice quiet. "Outside, or back to sleep?"

He settled his chin back on his front paws and closed his eyes.

I loved that dog. The first time I saw him with Ivy, I'd known he was special. He'd been protecting her long before I came along. Ivy wondered why Edgar had taken to me so quickly, when he generally didn't like people, but I knew. We understood each other. A man knows an ally when he sees one, and apparently a dog does too. A smart dog like Edgar does, anyway.

Leaving him to sleep a while longer, I went over to my easel. I turned on a lamp, so I had enough light, and prepared a few paints on my palette.

I didn't remember learning to paint. It was like speaking. I didn't remember learning to talk either, but I had mastery of the English language. Painting came naturally to me. Each picture I wanted to create existed in my mind. My hands were simply an extension of what I could already see. They knew what to do. When I thought about it too hard, the picture never came out right. But when I let my instincts take over, I was usually happy with the outcome.

But I was struggling with my latest piece.

I kept it under a canvas, so Ivy wouldn't see it. I was painting it for her, but I couldn't show her until it was perfect. It was too important. I had to get it right.

I pulled the canvas off and set it to the side. Studied the

painting so far. The colors were good. The lines right. It was close.

Holding the picture in my mind, I let my hands work. My hands and body held onto the memories my mind could no longer reach. I trusted them. Trusted the instincts that hadn't let me down.

I mixed colors. Changed brushes. Altered the tiniest details. With each stroke, it came to life. Just like the image in my mind. This wasn't a vision. It was a hope. A desire. A wish.

Ultimately, it was a question.

After painting for about an hour, I heard the muffled sound of a creaking floorboard, my cue that Ivy was getting up. Edgar cracked an eye open.

"It's either now, or you have to wait a little bit," I said. "I think this is finally ready for her to see and you can't interrupt us to go outside."

He stood, stretching his thick body. Shook out his white fur. I put my brush and palette aside and glanced down the hallway. Another small noise, the whine of a hinge. She was in the bathroom.

"Come on, Edgar." I went to the back door and opened it for him. "Do your thing, buddy. But hurry. You're going to want to see this."

I left the door open enough for him to come in when he was done. My phone vibrated, buzzing on the counter, so I checked my messages. I had a text from Peter. He was an early riser, like me.

Peter: Are we still on for tomorrow? Girls are going out.

Me: Yeah, sounds good. My place?

Peter: Sure. I'll pick up Thai. What do you want?

Me: Anything as long as it's spicy.

Peter: Got it.

Peter was a good guy—easy to get along with. He seemed

to understand me—or at least he wasn't put off by my memory issues. We hung out sometimes when Jessica and Ivy wanted to have a girls' night. It was nice to feel calmer about Ivy's safety—like I didn't have to follow her around everywhere. I trusted Jessica, so I knew I could relax while they had a good time.

Edgar came in, so I closed the door, then went back to my painting. A set of shelves held my supplies, and a few of my books. I pulled out a thick book from the bottom and opened it.

It wasn't really a book. I opened the cover to reveal a small keyhole. The key was hidden among my paints. I fished it out and opened the lock, breathing a sigh of relief. I knew it was still there—it had to be—but I was glad to see it just the same.

I pocketed the box and put the book back, then re-hid the key. I paused again, listening. Dresser drawers. She would come out any second.

An unexpected surge of nervousness hit me. That was odd. I had nothing to be nervous about. The painting was finished, and it was perfect. My plan wasn't elaborate, so there was little that could go wrong. And I certainly didn't have any doubts.

Maybe nervousness was a natural response. My lack of memories meant I didn't always know what was normal. I didn't have a long history of human relationships to draw upon like other men. It meant I didn't always react or behave the way people expected. I often said things that earned me funny looks, and I rarely understood why.

I'd asked James about it once. He'd said it was hard to explain, but there was something about me that made me different. That I seemed to have unusual ideas about things, and sometimes I talked like I came from another century.

Of course, James also said that the photos he took of me

were worth so much money because I looked simultaneously innocent and dangerous. I had no idea what he meant by that, so I took James's opinion with a grain of salt.

Ivy came down the hallway and my entire body lit up at the sight of her. Her blond hair a little wild in a messy bun on top of her head. The curves of her beautiful body dressed in a t-shirt and her favorite light gray pants. She still looked sleepy, rubbing her eyes as she walked.

God, I loved her.

I loved her so much she filled every bit of space inside me. She made my chest tight and my body ache to be near her. The only time I felt whole was when I held her in my arms. When our skin pressed together, and that overwhelming sense of tactile euphoria washed over me.

And when I made love to her. God, that was everything. When our bodies joined, and we lost ourselves—when I fucked her senseless until we were both gasping and spent—I was absolutely certain heaven existed. And I'd found it here, with Ivy.

"Morning," she said. "You're up early."

"Yeah." I patted my pocket, that strange sense of nervousness still making my stomach clench. "I was finishing something."

She tilted her head toward my canvas. "Do I finally get to see what you've been painting?"

"Yes. But close your eyes first."

She nibbled her bottom lip and covered her eyes.

I turned the easel around, so the painting faced her. Then I adjusted the lamp, illuminating the piece just right. "You can look now."

She moved her hands and opened her eyes. Her lips parted, her mouth rounding in the sweetest little O. I watched her take it in, waiting for her to notice the details. Willing her to see it, to solve the puzzle.

"Oh my god, William. I don't know what to say."

The painting was her. Ivy, looking over her shoulder. Her hair pulled back in a loose bun at the nape of her neck, a few soft tendrils falling around her face. Her lips turned in a hint of a smile. Her bright blue eyes, gleaming.

I'd painted her in a long white dress with little blue forget-me-nots in her hair. In her hands, she held a gathering of flowers. It was too loose and natural to be called a bouquet. It looked more like she'd picked up the ones she liked and held them.

She read the words I'd scripted across the bottom. *"We loved with a love that was more than love*. That's Edgar Allan Poe. Oh, I love that quote so much."

I nodded. *Keep going, Ivy. See the rest.*

Stepping closer, she studied it, her eyes moving across the canvas. I held still, waiting.

"This is me," she said, more to herself than anything. "I'm standing in front of the brick wall. But the ivy is all covered with snow."

I nodded again.

"That's the past touching the future, isn't it?" she asked. "The snow is your past—Alaska. And the wall is the vision you had of something in the future."

"Yes."

"The past and the future that brought us together," she said.

"I knew you would understand."

She kept looking, her eyes staying in one spot. Her lips twitched in a smile, and she glanced at me. "The language of flowers again. Forget-me-nots in my hair, because you remembered my voice. The red rose means love. The magenta flowers are Sweet William. And there's ivy. That's me."

"Ivy also means something else," I said. "And there's one more thing you haven't seen."

"Is it cheating if I look it up?" she asked. "The meaning of ivy?"

"Yes."

She pursed her lips in a playful scowl and went back to studying the painting.

I saw the instant she realized. She blinked, and her eyes widened, her eyebrows lifting. Her soft lips parted.

"I have a ring on my finger," she said. "Does ivy mean… marriage?"

I smiled, my heart swelling with pride and satisfaction. With my overwhelming love for her. I knew she would see it —understand every detail. She marveled at how well I knew her, but she knew me just as well. And she didn't have the benefit of months of unconscious listening.

Pulling the box out of my pocket, I walked toward her. Sank down on one knee and looked up at the most beautiful woman I'd ever seen.

"Ivy, my love for you is endless. I loved you before I ever laid eyes on you. I loved your voice, your words. I loved your heart, your soul. And I want nothing more in this world than to be with you." I paused to open the box and remove the ring, then met her eyes again. "Will you marry me?"

"Yes." Her shoulders trembled, and I couldn't tell if she was starting to laugh or cry. "Yes, William, I will marry you."

Her *yes* was the sweetest, most incredible word I'd ever heard. I slid the ring on her finger—a diamond in a white gold band made to look like delicate lace.

I stood and gathered her in my arms. Her warm body felt so good. I breathed in the lightly floral scent of her hair, enjoyed the bits of her skin that touched mine. She leaned back, and I kissed her mouth, slow and deep. Savoring her. Savoring this moment. I knew it was one I'd never forget.

My mind didn't remember being Will Green. But just like my hands still knew how to paint, my heart remembered who I'd been. I no longer wondered why there had been a hole in my chest. Why a deep sense of sadness had lurked just beyond the edge of my understanding. Will Green had suffered. He'd been lost and alone.

Just like Ivy.

She'd told me that I had saved her well before a gun was ever pointed at her chest. But she'd saved me too. She'd healed the wounds I hadn't been able to see. The wounds that had still ached, even though their cause had been lost to me.

Someday I'd recover all the pieces of myself. But even though I'd lost my memory, my mind hadn't failed me. It had held onto what was important. Kept the things I'd needed to know to find her. I was with her now—holding her and loving her—because when I'd forgotten everything else, I remembered her.

I remembered Ivy.

* * *

WANT MORE IVY AND WILLIAM? Turn the page for a romantic bonus epilogue.

BONUS EPILOGUE

IVY

*J*essica moved my beautifully curled hair aside and pulled the zipper up the back of my dress.

"There," she said, letting my hair fall down my back. "I think you're just about ready."

I turned and looked in the full-length mirror, running my hands down the sides of my waist. My strapless dress was simple, but elegant. The white fabric hugged my curves and shimmered in the light. I wore a necklace that had belonged to my mother and earrings Jessica had lent me. The hairdresser had spent almost an hour turning my long blond hair into a cascade of curls, and instead of a veil, I wore a circlet of blue forget-me-nots.

I'd never felt quite so beautiful.

"Oh my god, Ivy," Jessica said, dabbing at the corners of her eyes with a tissue. "You look stunning."

"Thanks," I said. "You look amazing, too."

Her pale blue dress looked beautiful against her dark skin, and her thick curly hair was pulled up in a twist.

The day had finally arrived. My wedding day. I was about to become Ivy Cole.

William and I had decided to get married at Salishan Cellars, a winery just on the other side of the mountains in central Washington. Nestled among the foothills, the setting was spectacular, and the winery itself was lovely—and dog friendly. It was the perfect place for our little wedding.

My stomach fluttered, and I took a sip of water. I'd picked up some kind of stomach bug recently and was hoping it wouldn't ruin my appetite for dinner. "Is everyone here?"

She clicked her tongue and rested her hand on her belly. She'd always had a motherly streak, and now she was going to make it official. Her baby boy was due in less than four months. "Stop worrying. All the important people are here."

"I know. I think I'm just a little nervous. Do you think Edgar is okay?"

"I'm sure he's fine," she said. "But would it make you feel better if I go check?"

"Yes," I said. "What if he needs to go out and William is busy getting ready and can't take him? I'm sorry, I know I'm being neurotic."

"It's your wedding day," she said with a smile. "You're entitled. I'll go make sure Edgar is fine."

"Thanks," I said.

Jessica left, and I peeked in the mirror to adjust my necklace. It felt good to wear something that had been my mother's. It also reminded me of my dad. He'd bought it for her when they'd gotten married.

I wondered how William was doing. He was getting ready with James and Peter. Was he nervous? He hadn't been nervous at all leading up to today. Nothing seemed to make him anxious, though. He was always so calm and collected.

His memories had started to return, although they seemed to be mainly glimmers and impressions. Once in a while he painted something that he thought might be a memory. A snow-covered forest.

Smoke curling from a chimney. Not long after he proposed, he'd been overtaken with inspiration and painted for days. The picture was a woman with dark hair. She was looking down and to the side, so only a little of her face was visible. But we were both sure it was William's mother.

After painting her, he'd decided to visit his hometown in Alaska. We'd spent two weeks there a few months ago. He'd said it felt familiar, although he hadn't been able to recall specific details. It was more instinct than memory. He'd been able to find his way around without knowing how or why, including how to get to his cabin.

We'd visited Jack, the man he'd worked for as a hunting guide. William said Jack and his family had seemed familiar to him as well. Even though he couldn't remember anything distinct, he'd been relieved that they hadn't felt like strangers. We'd spent hours with them, listening to stories from his past. It had been amazing to be with people who'd known him so well—who remembered him as Will Green.

From what I could tell, Will Green wasn't all that different from William Cole. His job was different now, of course. He wasn't leading people into the wilderness and tracking wild animals. But he'd always been protective, loyal, and a little bit of an outsider. He'd been artistic since childhood, and his love of painting had begun when he was still in school. Jack told us he'd learned by watching old Bob Ross episodes on YouTube.

The visit had been good for both of us. I'd been a little concerned he might want to stay in Alaska. Maybe even move back. But he didn't. He said he was glad his past no longer felt blank. He could sense there were memories there, and sometimes he recalled bits and pieces of his life before. But he wasn't Will Green anymore, and he was happy with our life now, together.

He wasn't Will Green legally, either. Once we'd discov-

CLAIRE KINGSLEY

ered who he'd been, he'd been able to get new ID. But instead of picking up his old identity, he'd changed his last name to Cole.

Just like I was about to do.

I turned at the soft knock on the door. Zoe Sutton, the winery's events manager, poked her head in. By my guess, she was about my age or a little younger. Her shiny brown hair was in a bun that managed to be both messy and stylish, and she wore a white blouse, fitted dark brown pants, and brown leather ankle boots. We'd been working with her for the last ten months to plan the wedding and I absolutely loved her.

"Hi there, beautiful," she said with a wide smile. "We're almost ready for you."

A sudden burst of nausea roiled through my stomach. I swallowed hard and nodded.

"Uh-oh." She stepped into the room and closed the door. "You look a little pale."

"Yeah, I feel a bit…"

My eyes widened, and I clamped my hand over my mouth. Oh god, no. Please don't let me throw up on my wedding dress.

Zoe was in front of me with an empty trash can in an instant. Seemingly out of nowhere, she'd produced a small towel and she quickly tucked the end into the neckline of my dress.

"Can you make it to the bathroom, sweetie?" she asked, her voice gentle.

I took a shuddering breath through my nose, my hand still covering my mouth, and nodded.

She gently rubbed my back and led me into the bathroom. My stomach held out until I reached the toilet, but Zoe was there to keep my hair back.

"You're okay," she said softly and helped me stand when I was finished. "Are you done, or should we wait?"

I glanced down at my dress. Miraculously, it was clean, as was the towel. My stomach still felt raw, but it was already starting to calm.

"I think I'm done," I said. "Oh my god, I'm so sorry. I don't know what's wrong with me."

Zoe took the towel and handed me a damp washcloth to wipe my face. "Don't worry about your makeup. I'll help you touch it up when you're sure that tummy of yours is finished being a bitch." She took the washcloth and gave me a small cup with mouthwash. "Here."

I rinsed my mouth and gave her a weak smile. "Thank you so much."

"It happens all the time," she said. "Okay, I'm going to get inappropriately personal, but there are four basic reasons I get puking brides right before a wedding. They're either hungover from an ill-timed but epic bachelorette party, marrying the wrong guy and afraid to go through with it, too nervous and excited for their own good, or pregnant. I'll be honest, I have a feeling I know which one it is for you."

"You do?" I asked.

"Yeah," she said. "You don't strike me as the partying type, so I don't think you're hungover. I've seen you and William together, and there's no way you're marrying the wrong guy. Your wedding is very intimate, so unless you're an anxious person in general, I doubt you're nervous to the point of puking. So that leaves…"

I looked down and pressed my hand against my stomach. Oh my god, could I be?

"I don't know," I said. "I don't think I'm pregnant."

"Do you want to find out now, or wait until later?" she asked.

"How could I find out now?" I asked. "The wedding is supposed to start soon."

Zoe opened the cupboard below the sink and pulled out a basket filled with supplies. I noticed tampons, maxi pads, bandages, tissues, a little sewing kit, nail polish, and a host of other odds and ends. She pulled out a box with a home pregnancy test.

"You keep those here?" I asked.

"This isn't the first time I've had a bride who needs one," she said. "Look, no pressure to take this. You're about to get married, and that's enough in and of itself. But if not knowing is going to be a big distraction, I'd suggest taking it. Then you'll be sure. Although, if you think the results either way will ruin your day, then I'd wait. Who knows, you could have just had something bad for dinner last night."

I held out a trembling hand and took the box from her.

"Do you want me to go find Jessica?" she asked.

I took a deep breath. This was really happening. "No, that's okay. I think… if I am pregnant, I want to be able to tell William first. And now that I'm wondering if I am, I have to know."

"Sweetie, this is your day. Whatever you need." She looked me up and down. "Let's get the dress off so it's easier to pee on that stick. And I'll let them know you just need a few more minutes to get ready. I don't want to add a panicked groom to my puking bride."

She unzipped my dress and helped me step out of it, then took it to the other room.

My stomach still felt a little shaky, but I took the pregnancy test. I was on birth control, so I shouldn't have been pregnant. But this wasn't the first time I'd thrown up in the last week. I'd figured it was just the stress of the upcoming wedding, or maybe I'd eaten something that hadn't agreed with me.

But birth control wasn't one hundred percent effective all the time, was it?

And to be honest, I wasn't stressed about the wedding. Not really. I was excited, and the anticipation had made it hard to sleep last night. But our wedding was small, and Zoe had everything under control. There wasn't anything to be stressed about. I had absolutely no doubts about marrying William. The only bit of sadness was that my dad wouldn't be here to walk me down the aisle. But that certainly wasn't worth vomiting over.

There was a soft knock on the door.

"How are you doing in there, sweetie?" Zoe asked.

"I'm okay." I opened the door and went into the dressing room. Zoe helped me back into my dress, then touched up my makeup.

"You look amazing," she said. "How's the tummy?"

I touched my stomach. "It's fine, now."

"I think that test is ready," she said. "Do you want me to leave you alone?"

I nodded. "Thank you so much."

"Of course," she said. "I'll be right outside. And if you need more time, just let me know. Remember, the bride can't be late. The wedding doesn't start until she's ready."

Zoe left, and I took another deep breath, then went to check the pregnancy test.

I'd left it sitting on the counter. For a second, I hesitated in the bathroom doorway, wondering what I hoped it would say. William and I did want children, but we hadn't planned on having one now. But the thought of creating a family together was so powerful, I knew instantly that I'd be disappointed if the test was negative.

Another deep breath, and I checked the test.

Pregnant.

Tears stung my eyes and I bit the inside of my lip so they

wouldn't fall. Oh my god, I was going to have a baby. William's baby.

And suddenly my wedding day was perfect.

Maybe most brides wouldn't wish for a positive pregnancy test just minutes before they walked down the aisle. But I couldn't imagine better news. I stared at that one, beautiful word—pregnant—and my heart felt like it was going to swell right out of my chest.

William and I were the only family each other had. With him, I no longer felt alone in the world. But this… this was the greatest gift I could have asked for.

I put the test in the box and tucked it in my bag. Jessica peeked her head through the door.

"You ready?" she asked, her eyes bright.

"Yes."

I went out into the hallway and Jessica handed me my bouquet—white roses surrounded by pale blue forget-me-nots and little sprigs of green ivy. Zoe caught my eye and winked while Jess fussed over my dress.

They led me down the hall. Peter and James stood outside a set of closed doors, dressed in dark gray suits. William was already inside, along with our small group of guests.

"Okay, peeps, let's do this," Zoe said. She got Jessica and James—my matron of honor and William's best man—situated in front of the door.

Peter offered his arm and I slipped my hand into the crook of his elbow. In a rare display of emotion, Peter had gotten misty-eyed when I'd asked him to walk me down the aisle. He adjusted his glasses, then pressed his hand over mine.

"Opening the doors," Zoe said.

A zing of excitement tingled my skin and I squeezed Peter's arm.

Zoe opened the doors, but I couldn't see past Jessica and

James. Soft music played inside, and they started walking forward.

William came into view and I hardly noticed Zoe fussing over my hair and dress. He looked incredible in his suit—so smooth and polished. His eyes locked onto mine and his face broke into the most adorable expression of awe and wonder I'd ever seen him wear. His lips parted, and he stared at me like he'd never seen me before.

"Ready?" Peter asked softly.

I nodded, and we started forward. I no longer heard the music or noticed our guests. I did see Edgar, sitting like the good boy he was right at William's feet, wearing a little black bow tie around his neck. And in the back of my mind I knew Jessica was there at the front, and James stood on William's other side. But it was as if no one else existed except for William.

He didn't break eye contact as I approached and dropped Peter's arm. William took my hand and drew me closer. For a second, I thought he was going to kiss me before the officiant could get started, but he blinked and seemed to remember we were about to have a wedding ceremony.

The wedding itself was brief, and I barely heard a word until it was time to exchange our vows. We'd written our own, and the officiant asked me to go first. I handed my bouquet to Jessica and William took both my hands in his.

"William, you came into my life like a summer rain," I said. "Unexpected, but sorely needed. From the moment we met, you captured me, body and soul. I am yours. I will be by your side through all the ups and downs that life sends our way. I will care for you, cherish you, and support you. And most of all, I will love you for the rest of our days."

He smiled down at me, those piercing blue eyes never leaving mine. The officiant prompted him to speak and he squeezed my hands.

"Ivy, you pierce my soul. I am half agony, half hope. I have loved none but you," he began, and I drew in a quick breath. He'd quoted Jane Austen. "I want nothing more than to be with you. For you to be the first thing I see each morning, and the last thing I see each night. To spend my days caring for you, protecting you, and loving you. You have my heart, and you always have. Whatever I can offer you, I'll give. Whatever you need, I'll provide. I will love you until I take my last breath, and even then, my love will not end."

Tears filled my eyes as we exchanged rings and before I knew it, I heard the words, "You may kiss the bride."

William pulled me close and gently touched my chin, tilting my face up to his. Slowly, tenderly, he pressed his mouth against mine. My eyes closed as his soft lips worked their magic, putting me under his spell. He teased my lips with his tongue, just enough to send sparks dancing across my sensitive skin.

He pulled away and the applause in the background finally registered. I smiled up at him, feeling like I could burst. He smiled back, his blue eyes vivid.

"I love you," he said, his nose still brushing against mine.

"I love you, too."

The officiant had more to say, but I could hardly hear it. He introduced us as husband and wife to more applause, and the next thing I knew we were walking down the little aisle and being ushered into the next room for the reception.

The photographer pulled us away for pictures. When we came back, we mingled with our guests as everyone sampled hors d'oeuvres and sipped wine. Edgar was calm, but Cooper Miles, one of the winery staff, came in with Zoe and offered to take him outside for us. Amazingly, Edgar went willingly. Cooper promised to bring him back after a good walk around the vineyard.

William kept his arm around my waist or my hand

clasped in his, as we wandered around the room and chatted with everyone. I wanted to tell him I was pregnant, but even with a small wedding, there seemed to be an endless stream of people to talk to.

So I kept the news to myself, a secret that was simultaneously tiny and so very, very big. It warmed me from the inside, making my eyes misty every time I looked at William.

The staff served dinner and I was grateful to my stomach for cooperating. The food was delicious. I declined the wine, but no one seemed to notice. Then we had cake, and Zoe let us know that Edgar was doing great with Cooper, whose parents owned the winery. Their house was nearby on the winery grounds, so Cooper was taking Edgar to go lie down.

After a while, the guests began leaving. Most were staying at one of the nearby hotels. I heard a few of my colleagues from work say they were going into town to sample more of the wine-tasting rooms. Jade, who often did William's hair for photo shoots, had snuggled up with a physics professor from Woodward, and I saw them leave together.

I picked at the last of my cake as we sat with Jessica and Peter, and James and his girlfriend Danielle. William rested his hand on the back of my chair, his fingers absently caressing my shoulder.

"Are you excited about the baby?" Danielle asked.

I stared at her for a beat before realizing she was talking to Jessica and Peter.

"We are," Jessica said, resting her hand on her belly. Her voice was a little dreamy. It always was when she talked about the baby. "We've been working on the nursery, and getting things ready."

"How about you?" James asked, looking at Peter. "Ready to be a father?"

Peter smiled at Jessica, and my heart melted a little. "As ready as I'll ever be."

"With you two as parents, he's going to be a genius," I said.

"Math genius," Peter said.

Jessica's eyebrow arched. "Not necessarily. Just because he's a boy doesn't mean he won't be artistic."

Peter shook his head. "Mark my words. Math or one of the sciences. Physics. Computer engineering maybe."

"Well, I'm getting him in art classes as soon as he's old enough to hold a paintbrush," Jessica said.

"Feel free," Peter said. "But you can't fight nature."

William glanced at me, a little smile playing on his lips. "Jess, I can teach him how to paint."

Jessica smiled. "Perfect."

"Traitor," Peter said.

The rest of us decided to go our separate ways. James and Danielle headed into town to sample the nightlife. Jessica and Peter decided to go back to their room at the hotel. Jessica was tired from the long day.

Zoe brought Edgar back to us and we took him next door to the hotel. We were in the honeymoon suite on the top floor, so we took the elevator up and went into our room. Edgar immediately went to his dog bed to go back to sleep. It seemed Cooper had done a great job wearing him out.

William laid his suit jacket over the back of a chair, then stood behind me to help me extricate the circlet of flowers from my heavily hair-sprayed curls.

"Well, we did it," I said as he set the flowers aside.

"Was our wedding everything you wanted it to be?" he asked.

"Yes," I said. "Everything and so much more."

"I don't think I can properly express how beautiful you look today," he said, sliding his arms across my bare shoulders.

I turned toward him, and he slipped his hands around my waist. "You look wonderful, too."

He leaned in and kissed me. His mouth was soft, but there was hunger in his kiss. He pulled me against him and slowly lowered the zipper on the back of my dress.

"William?" My heart beat faster as he trailed kisses down my neck.

"Yes, baby?" he asked. He ran his mouth up the side of my neck and kissed me again behind my ear.

"I have something to tell you."

He pulled away and touched my face, concern in his eyes. "Yes?"

I nibbled on my bottom lip, feeling a sudden burst of excitement and nervousness. "I'm pregnant."

His expression changed, from concern to surprise. His eyebrows lifted, and the corners of his mouth turned up in a smile.

"You're... we're... you mean a baby?"

I nodded. "A baby."

He pulled me close, wrapping his arms around me. We stood there, holding each other, just breathing. Living in the moment and feeling the tender rush of emotions at what this news meant.

"I love you," he said. He cupped my cheeks and kissed my lips, my nose, my forehead. "I love you so much."

"I love you, too."

"Are you feeling okay?" he asked. Kissed my forehead again. "Do you need anything?"

"I feel fine," I said. "I threw up earlier, but Zoe was there to help me get cleaned up afterward. But I'm okay now."

"Are you sure?" He smoothed my hair back and looked me up and down, as if he was certain he'd find something wrong with me.

"I'm sure," I said.

He placed his hand on my belly and leaned his forehead against mine. "I love you, Ivy Cole. And I'm going to love our baby just as much as I love you."

My eyes misted over with tears and I ran my hand up the back of his neck. "I know you will."

"Thank you," he said.

"For what?"

"For this," he said, rubbing my belly. "And for believing in me, and loving me. And becoming my wife."

"Thank you," I said, sniffing back more tears. "Thank you for finding me."

"It was always you, Ivy," he said. "It always will be."

His lips found mine and I melted into his kiss. Relaxed in the feel of his strong arms around me, his warm body pressed against mine.

He was my William. My love. My husband, and now the father of my baby.

He was everything.

AFTERWORD

Dear Reader,

This book was an interesting departure for me. I wrote it just after His Heart, which is another book that could be described as a departure. His Heart is an intense and emotional story (that I'm told requires at least one full box of tissues). It's beautifully heartbreaking, and I had no idea how I was ever going to top it.

So I didn't. I went in a different direction.

Like a lot of my best ideas, this one came from my husband, affectionately known to many of my readers as Mr. Arm Porn. Months and months before I started writing about William and Ivy, he had one of his random and brilliant ideas that seem to come to him out of nowhere.

The little kernel of an idea he had (a man in a coma hears a woman speaking to her dying father, then searches for her when he wakes) became this story.

This one was challenging for me in a number of ways. It's the first romance I've written that doesn't include the hero's point of view. Normally, I love writing the hero chapters. I love getting into his head and digging into who he is. But I knew early on that this story would best be told entirely from Ivy's perspective. The mystery of who William Cole really is would be that much more interesting if we didn't know what he was thinking.

That made outlining and plotting the book a challenge. I had to constantly keep in mind what William was thinking, even though I wasn't writing it. What would he do next? What was his plan? I had to make sure to spend time inside William's head, even though I wasn't writing those scenes.

But it was a welcome challenge, and I'm really happy with how this book turned out. And yes, it does leave you with that one open question—where did his vision of the ivy covered wall come from?

Life is full of little mysteries and unknowns. I like to believe there's still a little bit of magic in the world. And once in a while, we get a glimpse of it.

I hope you enjoyed Finding Ivy! Don't forget, you can get William and Ivy's extended epilogue for a little more from these characters.

Thanks for reading!

ACKNOWLEDGMENTS

Thank you to all my readers. Whether this is the first CK book you've read, you've been with me since the beginning, or somewhere in between, I love the crap out of you. You're the reason I do what I do.

To Nikki and Jodi, for your feedback and encouragement. Also, for gifs and memes. I don't know if I'd survive without them.

To Elayne for cleaning up the messy spots and leaving me comments that make me laugh.

To my husband for being endlessly supportive. And to my kids for being resilient and understanding when I'm a hot mess.

ALSO BY CLAIRE KINGSLEY

**For a full and up-to-date listing of Claire Kingsley books visit
www.clairekingsleybooks.com/books/**

**For comprehensive reading order, visit
www.clairekingsleybooks.com/reading-order/**

* * *

The Haven Brothers

Small-town romantic suspense with CK's signature endearing
characters and heartwarming happily ever afters. Can be read as
stand-alones.

Obsession Falls (Josiah and Audrey)

Storms and Secrets (Zachary and Marigold)

Temptation Trails (Garrett and Harper)

The rest of the Haven brothers will be getting their own happily
ever afters!

* * *

How the Grump Saved Christmas (Elias and Isabelle)

A stand-alone, small-town Christmas romance.

* * *

The Bailey Brothers

Steamy, small-town family series with a dash of suspense. Five unruly brothers. Epic pranks. A quirky, feuding town. Big HEAs. Best read in order.

Protecting You (Asher and Grace part 1)

Fighting for Us (Asher and Grace part 2)

Unraveling Him (Evan and Fiona)

Rushing In (Gavin and Skylar)

Chasing Her Fire (Logan and Cara)

Rewriting the Stars (Levi and Annika)

* * *

The Miles Family

Sexy, sweet, funny, and heartfelt family series with a dash of suspense. Messy family. Epic bromance. Super romantic. Best read in order.

Broken Miles (Roland and Zoe)

Forbidden Miles (Brynn and Chase)

Reckless Miles (Cooper and Amelia)

Hidden Miles (Leo and Hannah)

Gaining Miles: A Miles Family Novella (Ben and Shannon)

* * *

Dirty Martini Running Club

Sexy, fun, feel-good romantic comedies with huge… hearts. Can be read as stand-alones.

Everly Dalton's Dating Disasters (Prequel with Everly, Hazel, and Nora)

Faking Ms. Right (Everly and Shepherd)

Falling for My Enemy (Hazel and Corban)

Marrying Mr. Wrong (Sophie and Cox)

Flirting with Forever (Nora and Dex)

* * *

Bluewater Billionaires

Hot romantic comedies. Lady billionaire BFFs and the badass heroes who love them. Can be read as stand-alones.

The Mogul and the Muscle (Cameron and Jude)

The Price of Scandal, Wild Open Hearts, and Crazy for Loving You

More Bluewater Billionaire shared-world romantic comedies by Lucy Score, Kathryn Nolan, and Pippa Grant

* * *

Bootleg Springs

by Claire Kingsley and Lucy Score

Hot and hilarious small-town romcom series with a dash of mystery and suspense. Best read in order.

Whiskey Chaser (Scarlett and Devlin)

Sidecar Crush (Jameson and Leah Mae)

Moonshine Kiss (Bowie and Cassidy)

Bourbon Bliss (June and George)

Gin Fling (Jonah and Shelby)

Highball Rush (Gibson and I can't tell you)

* * *

Book Boyfriends

Hot romcoms that will make you laugh and make you swoon. Can be read as stand-alones.

Book Boyfriend (Alex and Mia)

Cocky Roommate (Weston and Kendra)

Hot Single Dad (Caleb and Linnea)

* * *

Finding Ivy (William and Ivy)

A unique contemporary romance with a hint of mystery. Stand-alone.

* * *

His Heart (Sebastian and Brooke)

A poignant and emotionally intense story about grief, loss, and the transcendent power of love. Stand-alone.

* * *

The Always Series

Smoking hot, dirty talking bad boys with some angsty intensity. Can be read as stand-alones.

Always Have (Braxton and Kylie)

Always Will (Selene and Ronan)

Always Ever After (Braxton and Kylie)

* * *

The Jetty Beach Series

Sexy small-town romance series with swoony heroes, romantic HEAs, and lots of big feels. Can be read as stand-alones.

Behind His Eyes (Ryan and Nicole)

One Crazy Week (Melissa and Jackson)

Messy Perfect Love (Cody and Clover)

Operation Get Her Back (Hunter and Emma)

ABOUT THE AUTHOR

Claire Kingsley is a #1 Amazon bestselling author of sexy, heartwarming contemporary romance, romantic comedies, and small-town romantic suspense. She writes sassy, quirky heroines, swoony heroes who love big, romantic happily ever afters, and all the big feels.

She can't imagine life without coffee, great books, and the characters who inhabit her imagination. She lives in the inland Pacific Northwest with her three kids.

www.clairekingsleybooks.com

Printed in Dunstable, United Kingdom